A. J. Ho

*Also by A. J. Holt*

Watch Me

# Unforgiven

## A. J. Holt

HEADLINE
FEATURE

First published in 1997
by HEADLINE BOOK PUBLISHING

First published in paperback in 1997
by HEADLINE BOOK PUBLISHING

A HEADLINE FEATURE paperback

10  9  8  7  6  5  4  3  2  1

ISBN 0 7472 4960 1

Typeset by CBS, Felixstowe, Suffolk

Printed and bound in Great Britain by
Mackays of Chatham PLC, Chatham, Kent

HEADLINE BOOK PUBLISHING
A division of Hodder Headline PLC
338 Euston Road
London NW1 3BH

With love, to my brother Tony,
the one who got me started down this road.

# PART ONE

## *Then*

---

# CHAPTER ONE

Even then, Renee Lucas knew that, more often than not, fate turned on the smallest hinge; a blink, a nod, a turn not taken, altering life for ever. A young intern's moment of distraction in the delivery room that led to her daughter Lauren's brain damage; the torn corner of a condom foil in David's pants pocket that took them spiraling inexorably to the end of their marriage. Beads on a string, links in a chain, the snapped threads of everyday existence. What her father referred to as 'the divine inexactitude of living'.

Wristwatches weren't allowed in Brockhurst, or any other psychiatric facility in the State of New York, so she could only guess at the number of hours she'd spent trying to identify the split-second circumstances that destroyed her life and banished her from the world for the better part of twenty years. A month of minutes, perhaps two or three, a billion ticks of an imaginary clock as she searched her memory for the image of that moment. And finding it, wondering for years afterward if there was anything she could have done to prevent the terrible things which followed.

Four thirty in the afternoon, according to the clock in the battered old Rambler American, twenty minutes west of Monticello on New York 17, heading for Binghamton, Syracuse and finally Buffalo. Wednesday, 18 September 1974. Indian Summer on the edge of the Catskills with the radio on and Terry Jacks singing 'Seasons in the Sun'. Again.

Renee leaned across the wheel and punched buttons on the unfamiliar dashboard of David's car. She'd heard the song at least a dozen times since leaving the city and it was driving her crazy. She wasn't having any joy, she wasn't having any fun and if she'd ever had a season in the sun, it was long gone. Between that and John Denver happily basking in the same sunshine, this time on his shoulders, it seemed as though everyone in the world except her was having a good time.

'Shit.' Out of the corner of her eye she saw the flicker of a Chevron sign as they sailed past a gas station. The gauge was dangerously close to the pin and she'd intended to fill up and give Lauren a chance to pee. She sat up and settled behind the wheel again, lighting up a Tareyton from the litter of packages in front of her. The radio had landed on Barbra Streisand crooning about 'The Way We Were', which wasn't a whole lot better than Terry Jacks. Beside her, Lauren was curled up on the front seat under her blanket, sound asleep. There was that to be thankful for at least. The sleeping five-year-old had the face of a dark-haired angel but awake she had

4

the attention span of a child half her age.

Taking a child like Lauren on the four hundred mile drive to her parents' house in Buffalo was tempting fate, but under the circumstances she didn't think there was any other choice. David wasn't about to let either one of them go without a fight and she'd chosen the path of least resistance. He was on double shift at the hospital, finishing off the last few weeks of his internship and he wouldn't notice that the car was gone until the following day.

She reached out a hand and let it rest for a moment on the small, hard mound of her daughter's hip. The child gave a small contented sigh and shifted slightly on the seat. It was always the same, the mixture of anger and guilt, fear and sadness. Knowing that Lauren would never talk, or read, or have friends home from school, or . . . anything.

Shortly after discovering the extent of the brain damage, Renee had been haunted by a recurring nightmare that Lauren had died, releasing them both from the private hells they occupied together. The dreams had led to long days of terrible, crabbing guilt and a dozen prescriptions from sympathetic doctors, including her husband.

The dreams and the guilt were gone now, along with the Miltowns and the Valium. Lauren and her condition were a fact of life that Renee had accepted, acknowledging that her daughter was going to be a child for the rest of her life, and that Renee would be mother to an infant until the day she died. Not what she'd expected, or planned for, but in its own way, still a mother's love.

Flipping the butt of the Tareyton out through the vent window, she glanced at the gas gauge again. Dead empty. Her first and last car, the clunker Ford she'd abandoned at Woodstock just before meeting David had been utterly predictable, going exactly twenty miles on empty before it shuddered and bucked to a stop, but the Rambler was David's and she didn't drive it often enough to know how far to push it. Running out of gas in the middle of nowhere with Lauren caterwauling beside her was a nightmare waiting to happen. A sign was coming up on her right.

## PROSPER

### Next Exit

There was a row of service club badges tacked to the bottom of the sign like an old soldier's medals. Lions, Knights of Columbus, Rotary, Four H and Junior Chamber of Commerce. The paint was faded on the sign and the Rotary badge had sagged, leaning drunkenly against the Knights of Columbus.

She smiled wistfully; it was all coming back. Sometimes they'd make a munchies run in the dune buggy from the commune to a store just on the outskirts of town. The wizened up old hick who ran the place always had some stupid comment to make under his breath, but he always took their money. Higgs? Riggs? Was that his name?

A ribbon of two lane blacktop curved off into the trees fifty yards past the sign. Almost without thinking she turned the wheel and left the highway, heading into the autumn-colored hills. Driving toward Prosper.

Three miles farther on, with the first real fear just beginning to gnaw, Renee spotted a large, log-cabin-style building with a pair of old-fashioned gas pumps in front of it. An ancient tow-truck roosted in a makeshift carport at the far end of the building and a bright red pick-up was parked at a sloppy angle beside the front door. A sign on the roof said: MIGGS, and nothing more.

*I remember now.*

Renee slid the Rambler off the blacktop and on to the gravel, small stones spitting up from under the wheels with a bony chatter. She pulled in front of the gas pumps and cut the engine, letting out a small sigh of relief.

'Made it.' She sat for a moment, listening to the hot ticking of the engine as it cooled. She glanced across the seat at her daughter, wondering if she could get away with leaving her in the car for a few minutes. Too late. Lauren's fawn-brown eyes were open, staring at her vacantly. 'Store,' Renee explained. 'Mommy has to get gas for the car.' She always explained her actions to Lauren, even though she doubted that the child understood much of what she was saying; the process of toilet training her had only ended in the last year and the simplest instructions usually required a pantomime demonstration to go along with the words.

Lauren answered her mother with a soft, snorting nod. She slid across the seat, the thumb of one hand hooking into a belt loop on Renee's jeans, the other thumb sliding wetly into her mouth. She made the snorting sound again and Renee nodded. 'All right. You can come inside with me, as long as you behave, okay?'

Miggs was a general store like the ones Renee remembered from summers spent at rented cottages in the Finger Lakes. Everything from dew worms to doughnuts. Aisles full of laundry detergent and breakfast cereal. Low ceilings, forty watt light bulbs, all of it smelling of the curling tendrils of fly paper that hung from the low rafters like old party decorations. Bare wood floors that creaked loudly when you walked across them.

Miggs himself hadn't changed much in the intervening years. Closer to sixty now than fifty, bald, reed thin, wearing a red checked shirt buttoned right up to his thin neck. He was sitting behind a low counter, one elbow propped on his cash register as he leafed through a newspaper. The *Prosper Advance*: 'FORD PARDONS NIXON'.

'Gas?' Miggs asked, looking up from the paper. Two looks; a short one for Renee, a longer, more curious glance at Lauren.

'Yes, please.'

'How much?'

'Fill her up,' said Renee. It was still a long way to Buffalo.

Miggs pulled the key out of the cash register lock, pocketed it, and came out from behind the counter. He gave Lauren another look, then went outside to fill up the Rambler. Renee caught a flicker of movement and, looking up, found herself staring into a large, round mirror, angled so that Miggs could see the rear of the store from where he sat at the counter. Reflected in the mirror, slightly distorted, Renee could see four teenagers, loitering around a magazine rack. Three boys and a girl.

As she stood there watching she saw one of the boys take a magazine and slip it under his jacket. The little shits were shoplifting. The tallest of the four, dark-haired and broad-shouldered, looked up and saw her staring at them. Renee looked away quickly, focusing on a display of candy bars by the cash register. At her side, Lauren made soft noises, sucking her thumb, staring at nothing. The floorboards creaked as the teenagers came up the aisle toward the front of the store.

'Nice ass.'

'I wouldn't kick her out of bed.'

'Bet she moans for the bone.'

'Screams for the cream.'

'Weeps for the meat.'

Stupid. Weep and meat didn't rhyme. She felt the anger rising, then the fear. She tried to push it down, like she had with David for so long, pretending it wasn't there. She felt Lauren huddle closer into her thigh. Renee risked a single flickering glance and saw in the mirror that the teens were standing at the end of the aisle, no more than ten feet away.

'The kid dim, or what?'

Renee glanced up again. The tall boy had taken a step forward. Renee turned, wishing Miggs would get back from filling up the Rambler.

She turned. 'I beg your pardon?'

'The kid,' repeated the tall boy. He was seventeen or eighteen, the face still soft with only a few vague patches of stubble on the upper lip and chin. He'd be handsome when his complexion cleared up and he lost the last of his baby fat. Hard-handsome, like David. 'Is the kid a retard?'

'Maybe you should mind your own business,' said Renee. Still no Miggs. The girl snickered. Shorter than her friends, slim, with shaggy hair the color of buckwheat honey. A hard little body, small-breasted and narrow-hipped. A generous mouth with full lips and large blue eyes.

The boys were dressed almost identically – button-down check shirts, tan corduroy jeans so tight she could see the packed bulges of their genitalia. White sweat socks and desert boots. The girl wore jean cut-offs, a plain white T-shirt and sandals. Her nipples were hard little buttons pressing against the T-shirt and her toenails were painted dark red. All four had on blue and green letter jackets, Woodrow Wilson High School, class of '74. Graduating seniors, although the girl didn't look more than fourteen or fifteen.

Suddenly the tall boy stamped his foot hard, lurched forward and bugged his eyes out, frightening

Lauren. The little girl began to cry, tugging hard at Renee's leg, making a mewling, panic-stricken sound high in her throat. The four teenagers were laughing.

'Maybe the retard will wet her little panties,' said the tall boy.

'Why don't you just take your stupid little comments and leave?' said Renee. 'Before I tell the owner you stole one of his magazines.'

*Oh shit! Why did I say that? It'll just make him angry.*

The tall boy frowned. He took another step toward Renee, backing her against the counter. He pushed out his lips into a simpering parody of fear.

'Mommy wouldn't tell on me, would she?' His breath smelled of alcohol and mint. Gum over vodka, or gin.

'Just leave us alone,' said Renee. 'Or I'll call the cops.' Another one of the boys laughed.

'That's rich,' the girl crowed, 'Mommy's going to call the cops.'

'I just want to pay for my gas and leave,' said Renee. 'So why don't you just go and steal another magazine or something, and I'll be gone before you know it.'

'What's the rush?' asked the tall boy, taking another step. He was less than a foot away from her now and Lauren's crying was working its way up the scale toward a full-scale screaming fit.

'Maybe she wants King Bone,' said the blond boy. His voice was excited and urgent with the moment. 'Slip her the snake, Robby, come on!'

'Yeah,' said one of the other boys. 'Let's take her and the retard for a ride.'

'Give her a red truck fuck.' This from the girl, enjoying the harsh weight of the four letter word.

Renee's heart jumped as she heard the slap of a screen door closing. She turned. It was Miggs.

'Eleven twenty,' he said. 'You must have been driving on fumes, lady.' He took in the scene and frowned. 'These kids bothering you?'

The tall boy stepped forward quickly, before she could respond. 'We weren't doing anything, Miggs. Just passing the time.' He paused, putting on a broad smile. 'You know us.'

'Yeah, I know you.' Miggs looked down at Lauren. Her crying had receded to a tearful hitch and sob. He turned his attention back to Renee. 'Are they bothering you?'

'Not any more.' She pulled a ten and two ones out of her jeans and dropped them on the counter. She put a protective arm around Lauren's shoulder and started guiding her toward the door.

The girl spoke. 'Bitch.' The word was whispered softly, but Renee heard it, even over the last of Lauren's crying. She pulled open the door and rushed out, dragging Lauren behind her, hearing the screen door slap shut. On the way back to the Rambler she paused and stared and bit her lip and then lifted up one foot and kicked in one of the red truck's rear taillights. Furious.

A few moments later she was back on the road again. Driving into Prosper.

Half a mile from Miggs' store the highway curved to the right and dropped down into an oblong valley between the autumn hills. Prosper lay on either side of the broad river that cut the town in half. She thumped over a set of railway tracks and followed the signs that would take her back to the main highway.

Behind the railway tracks and the red-brick business center there was a neighborhood of small frame houses ranged along a grid of treeless streets without sidewalks. Old cars rusted away on concrete blocks in front yards, and sheets flapped on clotheslines like white flags of surrender. An industrial cold storage plant – R.J. Frost since 1931. Reliable Warehouse, Prosper Millwork Company and Golden Valley Canning, Prosper Creek Farm Dairy, then another set of railway tracks and she was in the town itself, mostly brick, nothing more than five storys.

Still following the signs Renee turned right off West Street on to Pickman, only vaguely aware of her surroundings, one hand soothing Lauren who was curled up into a fetal ball on the seat beside her, still making those terrible animal sounds in the back of her throat. Renee lit another Tareyton, swallowing the taste of bile in the back of her throat, trying to blink away the hot tears forming in the corners of her eyes.

She spotted a White Tower restaurant on one corner but didn't even consider stopping, even though she was famished. She'd intended to buy groceries in Miggs' store, make her stop at the commune and have a little picnic for herself and Lauren but it was too late for anything like that now. All she wanted to do now was get the hell out of Prosper and back on the highway. She drove by the movie theater – the Roper. The last time she'd been in Prosper she'd seen *Butch Cassidy and the Sundance Kid* there, tripped on acid with half a dozen other kids from Morningstar. She caught the name on the marquee as she drove past – they were showing *The Exorcist*. She'd seen it with David the year before and that night she'd endured his angry, sexless thrusting yet again, thinking about the scene where the priest plunges down the staircase to his death.

She turned on to Peabody and crossed a narrow bridge over the river, leaving the business section behind her. The streets here, she noticed, had sidewalks, the cars in the driveways were late model, and the houses themselves were mostly large, split-level ranchers. The 'good' side of town from the looks of it.

As she climbed out of the valley the trees began closing in again, rich in a dozen shades of red, orange and brown and almost enough for Renee to forget her anger at the way she and Lauren had been treated by the four teenagers at Miggs' store. Almost.

The older one; Robby? So much like David. Arrogant, full of some terrible power that had no source except the dark anger of his misunderstood manhood. Who'd taught him that? Father, mother, older brother? Or was it born with him? And the girl, too pretty to be so cold. What could be driving her to join with a roving pack of animals like that?

She almost missed the small sign nestled in the trees by the side of the road.

LEAVING PROSPER

'Thank God for that,' she whispered.

# CHAPTER TWO

It caught up with her a mile or so after leaving town and she pulled over on to the gravel shoulder as the familiar symptoms began to build. Renee knew that within the next ten minutes the migraine would make it virtually impossible for her to move, let alone drive a car. Thankfully, Lauren had crawled into the back seat and burrowed under her blanket, fleeing into sleep.

It always began the same way; a gentle, firm hand across her brow, and the sense that someone had drawn a shade down to the level of her eyes. No pain at first, just simple pressure, the firm hand becoming firmer until it was a tight band around her head, the shade dropping lower, becoming leaden, forcing her eyes to squint, and finally to close, the faintest ray of light a potential death ray that could stab into her brain with searing force.

Renee knew that the taunting children at Miggs' store weren't really responsible for the steadily increasing pain in her head, they'd only tipped the scales. The truth of it was that she'd brought the migraine on herself, repressing the terrors of her decision to leave David, refusing to even consider the consequences of what she was doing, knowing that if she hesitated, or even paused long enough to evaluate her actions she would be doomed. And the other thing, the real reason she'd taken this road rather than sticking to the Interstate, knowing right from the start that coming here was part of it.

*My first born.*

*Still born.*

Eyes half closed she kept two wheels on the gravel and let the car drive itself at a crawl. It couldn't be very far, she was sure of that. Anytime now she'd see the old lightning-split pine that marked the turn. A hundred yards then, two hundred.

*If Lauren wakes up and sees me like this she'll go hysterical.*

*There it is.*

The gray remains of the tree was like a gnarled, skeletal hand pointing the way. She managed to turn the wheel on to the narrow track leading deep into the woods, branches slapping at the windows, with the deep ruts doing the driving for her as the pain increased. Half a mile and she'd be home again. She'd get someone like Rainbow to help her down to the magic pool at Rivendell and then she'd slip into the cool black water, letting it rise up around her neck, soothing away the headache, the only thing that had ever really worked.

Her ears became filled with a cicada whine and the memories began to fill her head, vivid as hallucinations, bright as an acid dream, a two-edged sword, the memories real as life itself, but a bad sign because it meant the migraine was about to take her into its deep, blinding well of infinite pain.

The storm the night before had left everything crisp and clear, the sun rising through the trees throwing enormous, elongated shadows as she walked naked to Crystal Pool on the western edge of Max Yasgur's farm. Somewhere far behind her she could hear Jimi doing his crazy version of 'The Star Spangled Banner', ripping it through the air like a blinding knife.

She stepped into the pool and for the first time she saw that she wasn't alone, even though it was awfully early. He was standing facing her, the water coming to his hips, half covering his genitalia. He was tall and brown, with long dark hair like an Indian that hung around his shoulders in thick wet strands. The hair on his chest was thick, slicked down over his hard flat belly, down to his groin. Even half hidden by the water she could see that he was hung like a bull and already half erect.

At first she thought he was a vision from the dope Paul had set her up with before they all left Morningstar to come down to the festival. Primo acid that had turned the world upside down. She'd dropped it on Friday when Richie Havens started his jam, and it was still ringing inside her head like a big brass bell.

Lifting her arms she dove into the water, then rose and blinked the water out of her eyes. He was still there, closer now, his arms outstretched to her, a smile on his face. She shivered, feeling the skin of her breasts tighten as he stepped forward, shivered again and held out her arms as well until their fingers touched and her heart stood still. A minute later, or perhaps it was an hour, she lay beneath him under the trees, opened herself and felt him slide into her enormously and without any difficulty at all. His orgasm erupted inside her so powerfully she knew beyond any doubt that he'd made her pregnant in that single instant, giving her what she wanted more than anything else in the world.

*Lauren.*

Renee blinked, hearing the grinding of the underbrush against the side of the car, going so slowly now she was sure the engine was going to stall. She tried to blink away the pain but it only made things worse. She felt bile in her throat. What she'd taken for overwhelming passion had turned out to be nothing more than premature ejaculation, and her fantasy of a child to replace the one she'd lost had become the reality of mental retardation. Dreams always came to an end; only nightmares went on for ever.

She came to the end of the road and out into the clearing. She'd come home at last. To Morningstar, the only place in the world she'd ever really felt safe, or wanted or important.

And Morningstar was gone.

The commune had once occupied a ten-acre sloping clearing in the forest with Paul's hexagonal, split log 'Alamo' as its focal point with almost a dozen other buildings scattered around it in a rough circle. Some of the buildings had been fragile as tipis, others were geodesic domes, or reasonable facsimiles created from used plywood and sheet metal from old cars. Abandoned windows with dropsheet plastic instead of glass filled the empty panes.

All gone. The tipis had vanished completely and there were only vague ruins where the domes had been. The old Chicken Coop close to the road that had once been the single men's quarters was a sway-backed ruin overgrown with sawgrass, and the only thing remaining from the Alamo was a charred roof beam and the round river rocks they'd dragged up from Stoney Creek for the foundations. Someone had burned Paul Goodman's dream to the ground.

*Townie bastards. Had to be.*

*Can't think about that now.*

Renee switched off the engine, fumbled for the flashlight David always kept in the glove compartment and climbed out of the car. The silence rushed over her like a shroud and the cicada sound in her brain was like a buzzsaw now. She managed to lock the door, ensuring that Lauren wouldn't wander off, then staggered to the foot of the clearing. There was still enough dusk light to make her way and she quickly found the path that led through the trees to the pond. Rivendell, named for the hidden valley at the edge of the Wild in Tolkien's *The Hobbit*. That and *The Lord of the Rings* were Paul's favorite books and half the places around Morningstar were named from the complex, seemingly never-ending tales that he read to them around the big hearth in the Alamo every night.

The dark water of the pond was like a black hole in the forest floor, a few fallen branches trailing in the water on the far side, bark fuzzed with heavy moss. She dropped the flashlight, stripped off her clothes and sank into freezing oblivion without a second thought, relief coming almost instantly as she dropped deeper into the numbing cold. Sinking, she thought of drowning, wondering, just for a moment, if there would be lights and angels and the face of Christ shining before her as her mother and father had promised so long ago when she was a child asking a child's questions about death and dying.

She knew better now. She emptied her lungs slowly, eyes wide, watching the huge silver bubbles of her breath rise in front of her. She tilted her head back, looking up, seeing the last ghosts of light from the dying day and felt the claw grip of the headache recede. Deep beneath the water she smiled and shook her head, feeling the long silk tendrils of her hair brush against her cheeks, wishing she could stay down for ever, suspend time beneath the water and be one with it, waiting here like some Catskill Lady of the Lake, ready to give Excalibur to some other once and future king.

Her feet touched the slime of the bottom ooze and the grisly feeling of it shocked her back into the present. She kicked and rose, lungs bursting for air and then she exploded up to the surface, gasping, falling back, swallowing water, coughing and coming to the surface again, then calming herself as she floated gently, letting the water cradle her, the headache falling back, and back and back until it was nothing more than a distant howl somewhere deep within her brain. Rolling over, she took three quick strokes to reach the bank and climbed out into the night air, almost balmy compared to the frigid, healing water of the pond.

She bent, picked up the flashlight and her clothes, then, naked, found the path that led around the pond and deeper into the woods. She could feel the air drying her and knew that if she stayed too long she'd catch a chill.

*Your death of cold.*

That's what her mother always said.

*Catching death.*

She found the hidden dell to the west, behind the pond, screened by the trees, a place she'd always found especially magical. Even in the full daylight it was always dark here, the saucer-shaped depression in the forest floor a hundred feet across, its mosses and ferns and sweeping beds of trillium and purple gentian never seeing more than a dappled sun. Once someone had wanted to build a dome here but Paul had forbidden it. According to him the place really was magic and not to be disturbed under any circumstances. She swung the beam of the flashlight across the dell, picking up a pattern in the ground as though some forest god had pushed his fingers lightly into the earth and then she saw the special place, just where she remembered. The wood marker they'd left, etched with Tolkien runes, had rotted into the soil now, joining the remains a few feet below.

*This is where we buried Matthew.*

Stillborn from the womb, sliding dead into the light and into Rainbow's hands. Some punishment for something, somewhere, sometime that she couldn't fathom either then or now. Any more than she could fathom Lauren or even David. She sank down to the ground and put both hands flat on to the soil. A lightning rod for unhappiness, like something out of a sad Ray Bradbury story. She could feel tears tracking down her cheeks, but she felt nothing more than emptiness. How could you mourn for someone who'd never been any more than a name, the name never spoken, or written down, or used to call him home?

She stood, dressed, then swept the flashlight once more around the dell, fixing the place in her mind, knowing that she'd never be coming back here in this life, and then she turned away, went through the trees and took the long way back to the car. The headache was still there, but she knew she could control it now, at least until she reached her parents' house in Buffalo. Just before she reached the edge of the main clearing she thought she could hear laughter.

*Who?*

She saw a truck parked fifty feet or so from the Rambler, engine running headlights on. From where she stood she could see the back of the truck and the taillights. One of them broken. Where she'd kicked it.

*Oh God.*

They were standing at the rear of the Rambler, features blurred in the darkness, but easily identified by the blue and green high-school jackets. The three boys were standing together, watching the girl, who was crouched down by the rear quarter panel of the car. A sudden flare of orange light lit up her grinning face and in a single, horrifying instant Renee saw what the young woman was doing.

The Rambler's chrome gas cap lay at her feet and a length of rag drooped down from the open tank. There was a gleaming silver lighter in the girl's hand, the sputtering flame turning her eyes into bright, flickering stones as she leaned forward and put the lighter to the rag. The girl came out of her crouch and began to run as blue fire climbed the rag then vanished into the tank.

'NO!'

Renee ran forward, screaming Lauren's name, stumbling through the darkness toward the car, arms outstretched. For a small, frozen moment she thought she saw her daughter's face in the rear window and then the gas tank ignited, the force of the explosion so powerful that the back wheels of the car lifted almost six feet into the air. The trunk lid blew off and spun upward into the night sky, trailing a ragged, comet-tail of fire, and then the entire vehicle disappeared in a white hot ball of flame expanding outward with a guttering roar like the furious blossoming of some terrible dragon flower.

The force of it threw Renee to her knees and by

the time she'd regained her feet the blackening skeleton of the Rambler was the tortured base of a column of fire that rose almost fifty feet into the air, great twisting sails of red and yellow spitting out charred embers that tossed up and out in drunken arcs, tripping on the hot wind and threatening to ignite the surrounding trees.

She stumbled forward, but the heat of the fire was like a slapping hand, burning into the skin of her face and arms and singing her hair. Suddenly, she felt a terrible blow strike the back of her head and she began to fall, staggering forward another step and then half turning. In the last moment before she struck the hard packed ground she thought she saw a face looming over her, and then there was only blackness.

When Renee came to her senses she found herself on the rutted side road that led back to the highway. Somewhere in the distance she could faintly hear the sound of approaching sirens, but at first she made no coherent connection between the sound and her present circumstances. Her mind was numb, completely focused on the single thought that she had to get help for Lauren. If she could find someone to help, everything would be all right.

She reached the highway just as the first of several police cars came to a wailing stop at the entrance to the side road. Within seconds she was surrounded by half a dozen uniformed policemen and the world became a confusing whirl of bright flashing lights and harsh voices calling back and forth to each other.

She felt strong fingers grip her wrists, forcing her arms behind her back, and then the metal bite of handcuffs. Someone else pushed down on the back of her head, ducking her down into the rear of one of the police cars and then the door beside her slammed. She lurched back against the seat as the driver accelerated, tires squealing as he whipped the cruiser into a racing turn and, siren wailing, headed back into Prosper.

'They killed my little girl,' she whispered, the vision of the rising flames dancing in front of her eyes. 'They murdered Lauren.' But the sound of the siren was too loud and no one was listening to her anyway.

# CHAPTER THREE

The Prosper Police Department was located at the rear of the large, red-brick Municipal Building on Courthouse Square with offices on the main floor and half a dozen cells and a windowless interrogation room in the basement. The morgue and the Medical Examiner's Office was also in the basement as well as the Records Division of both the County and Municipal courts located upstairs.

Renee had been seated on a plain wooden chair in the interrogation room for more than two hours, handcuffed wrists resting on the edge of an equally plain wooden table in the center of the room. The only other piece of furniture was a second chair on the far side of the table. The walls were made from concrete blocks painted an institutional green and the floor was cement. The low ceiling of the ten foot by ten foot room was fitted with a single tube fluorescent fixture and a small ventilator with a squeaky fan.

So far Renee had told her story to a uniformed sergeant named Trepper and a plainclothes detective named Luteki. She had also been examined by a doctor in a white lab coat named Alberoni who cleaned the blood off her face and neck, then applied a dressing to a deep gash on her right temple. He'd also given her some kind of shot that was making her feel weak and woozy. For the last thirty minutes she'd been left alone with her thoughts, the only sound in the room coming from the squeaking fan.

The door opened and a second uniformed man appeared. He was tall, square-jawed and handsome, with graying hair cut very short. He appeared to be in his mid-fifties. The khaki uniform looked tailored and fitted the man perfectly. Instead of chevrons on the upper arm of his shirt like Sergeant Trepper, this man had a gold badge pinned to his breast pocket and a thick, yellow, twisted silk lanyard that ran from the pocket to the epaulette on his right shoulder. He was wearing highly polished, lace-up riding boots and he carried a peaked officer's cap under his left arm. He had a clipboard in his right hand. He stood in the doorway for a moment, then stepped into the room, closing the door behind him. He sat down across from Renee, placing the cap on the table directly in front of him and the clipboard to one side of it.

'My name is Skelton. I'm the Chief of Police in Prosper.' The man paused, staring at her closely. She noticed that his small eyes were a surprisingly vivid shade of green and his eyelashes were almost transparent. In his younger days the man's hair had probably been carrot red. He glanced at the clipboard, then back at Renee. 'Your full name is Renee Gabrielle Lucas?'

'Yes.'

'That sounds French.'

'My mother is French. A war bride.'

'You live in New York City?'

'I don't live anywhere. My husband and I are separated. I was on my way to my parents' place.'

'That would be in Buffalo?'

'Yes.'

'They were aware that you were coming?'

'No.'

'With your daughter?'

'Yes.'

'Was your husband aware of this?'

'No.'

'You removed your daughter without his consent?'

'I wasn't aware that I needed it.'

'How old was your daughter?'

It was the first time Renee had heard Lauren referred to in the past tense and she felt something tear, deep within her heart.

'Lauren was . . . five.'

'You told Sergeant Trepper and Detective Luteki that you locked the car when you went to take a swim in the pond.'

'That's right.'

'Why?'

'Lauren is . . . was retarded. I didn't want her wandering off.'

'I see.' The Police Chief paused and consulted the clipboard again. 'What were you doing up there anyway? The hippies are all gone now.' He paused.

'Funny time to take a swim, don't you think?'

'No. I was desperate.'

'Desperate to have a swim in the middle of the night?'

'I get migraine headaches. Cold water is the only thing that seems to help.'

'You could have stopped at a motel, had a cold shower.'

'I just wanted to get out. After what happened at the store I wasn't in any mood to spend any time here.'

'The store. That would be Miggs' place?'

'Yes.'

'You say that several teenagers harassed you?'

'Yes. The same ones who . . .' She felt bile rise into the back of her throat and she swallowed hard. 'The same ones who set fire to the car. Who murdered Lauren.'

'You seem pretty sure of yourself. How could you tell? It was dark.'

'I had a flashlight. And the truck.'

He looked at his clipboard. 'A pick-up?'

'It was red.'

'There are lots of red pick-up trucks around here.'

'At the store. I kicked in one of the taillights. The same taillight was broken on the truck at the commune.'

'You kicked in a taillight on a truck because some kids teased you?' He smiled calmly. 'You sound like a pretty angry lady.'

'I was.'

The Police Chief sat forward in his chair. 'Angry enough to set fire to your own car?'

Renee recoiled. 'What?!'

'Angry enough to murder your own daughter after you locked her in?'

'This is insane! You know who did it! I told you! Three boys and a girl. Teenagers. The one with the truck! I even know his name! Robby! His name is Robby! They must have followed me from the store!' She shook her head back and forth and slammed her handcuffed wrists down on the table. 'They were teasing Lauren about being retarded, making dirty comments about me, so I kicked in the taillight on the way out. Ask the man who owns the store!'

'We did,' said the Police Chief, shaking his head. 'Miggs says there wasn't anyone else in the store except you. He says you asked him to fill up the tank, that's all. There were no kids. Just the one who saw the fire. Coming back from his friend's place. Came right here and reported the incident. Didn't know anything about a little girl locked up in the car.' He paused. 'We found that out for ourselves.' He shook his head. 'Looks like you stopped your car up there, locked it, then torched it. Walked away and had your little swim.'

Renee stared across the table, stunned. 'No,' she whispered. 'It wasn't like that. It wasn't like that at all.' She could feel the tears welling up, then tracking down her cheeks. 'Why would I do something like that?' she sobbed. 'Why would I kill my little girl?'

'I don't know the answer to that,' said Chief

Skelton. 'What I do know is that you need a lawyer before this goes any farther.' Behind Skelton, Renee was vaguely aware of the doctor coming into the room. A moment later she felt the sting of another shot in her arm.

Then everything went dark. When she woke again she could barely think. Her mouth felt like old metal and every breath was torture. There was a plastic cup of water on the table in front of her. She drank it down and sat there, waiting, not knowing if it was day or night.

The lawyer turned out to be a young man named Winston Tucker. He was in his early twenties, thirty pounds overweight and appeared in the interrogation room wearing a lumberjack shirt, a loden-green corduroy jacket with leather elbow patches, faded, wheat-colored corduroy jeans and a battered pair of desert boots. His hair was a tousled mess of sandy curls and he stared at her owlishly through a pair of tortoiseshell glasses. When he smiled his round cheeks dimpled like the kids on the Campbell's Soup label and a single gold molar gleamed in the back of his mouth. He looked as though he'd been dragged out of bed only a few minutes before. He sat down in the chair across from her, introduced himself and yawned.

'You don't look old enough to be a lawyer,' said Renee.

'Twenty-four,' he answered, yawning again. 'Sixty-second out of a class of a hundred and thirty-four at Columbia, called to the New York Bar last year.'

'I can't pay you anything,' she said.

'You don't have to.' He smiled, showing off his gold tooth and his dimples. 'There's no PD in town, so I get most of the work.'

'PD?'

'Public Defender. Supreme Court says you have to have a lawyer, even if the state is the one who provides it.'

'They're saying I murdered my daughter?'

'Did you?'

'No.'

'Too bad,' he answered, shaking his head. 'A guilty plea would have been easy. I could have done some plea-bargaining. Not Guilty is going to be tough under the circumstances.'

'What circumstances?'

'Were you Mirandized?' asked Tucker, ignoring her question.

'Mirandized?'

'Informed of your rights. Miranda v. US Supreme Court, 1966. They read you your rights when they arrest you.'

'I haven't been arrested.'

'And they handcuffed you?'

'Yes.'

'Not cool,' said the lawyer, shaking his head again.

'You said, "under the circumstances",' Renee insisted.

'Yeah.' Tucker frowned. 'Pretty tough.'

'What is?'

'You talked about a red truck, a kid named Robby?'

'Yes.' She nodded. 'And his three friends.'

'I don't know about the friends, but the only Robby in this town who owns a red truck like the one you described is Robin Skelton, the Police Chief's son.' Tucker sighed, staring at her through the round lens of his spectacles. 'I'm no fortune-teller, Mrs Lucas, but I think you are swimming around in some very deep water here.' He shook his head again. 'In fact, I'd say you're pretty much screwed.'

'I didn't do what they said.'

'Foster wants you to have a psychiatric evaluation.'

'Who's Foster?'

'Doug Foster. The District Attorney.'

'I'm not crazy.'

'You're calling the Police Chief's son a liar and a murderer. In Prosper that's a pretty crazy thing to say.' He paused. 'It may be a good idea.'

'I don't understand.'

'It's a way to go. Insanity plea.'

'I'm not crazy. It was those four kids. The guy at the store, Miggs, is lying, and so is the Chief's son. Robby.'

'Will you go along with a psychiatric evaluation? Prove that you're not crazy?'

'If I don't?'

'It would just make things worse.'

'Then I guess I'll do it.'

Tucker disappeared a few minutes later and a skinny, hard-faced matron in a blue uniform came and took her to a small cell across from the kitchen area. A big, round IBM clock on the kitchen wall

clanked methodically. It said five thirty. When Renee
woke again the clock said seven twenty-five and the
kitchen was up and running with several men and
women dishing up plastic plates of scrambled eggs
and sausage and huge piles of white bread toast. She
passed on breakfast and at ten ten by the clock on
the wall, the matron appeared again with a little
paper cup filled with pills and another paper cup of
water.

'What are these?'

'Doctor's orders,' said the matron. She stood over
Renee, one hand on her wide leather belt. Renee took
the pills. When she'd swallowed them the matron
took her by the arm and escorted her down the hall,
guided her through the aisles of filing cabinets in
the records room and put her into a small office next
to the boiler room and fans. More concrete blocks,
these ones painted off-white, another table and chair
set, two chairs on one side of the table, one chair on
the other side. Renee sat down and waited. The pills
she'd taken were making her woozy again and she
was beginning to regret not eating breakfast.

It seemed like a long time before the door opened
again, but Renee couldn't be sure how much time
had passed because of the pills. Dr Alberoni came in,
carrying a briefcase. He wasn't wearing his long white
coat and in his business suit and tie she almost didn't
recognize him. A balding version of the fat guy in
*Deliverance*.

'You're the doctor who gave me the shots.'

Her tongue didn't seem to be working. Everything

was dry as alum and she couldn't keep a single line of thought in her head.

'That's right. My name is Alberoni.'

'You look like the guy in the movies.'

'Ned Beatty.' Alberoni nodded. 'I've been told that.'

'*Deliverance*. The one who gets . . . raped.'

'He was on the stage before he went into film.' Alberoni sounded almost defensive. Renee's head was reeling.

'What kind . . .' She lost it and had to start again, swallowing, looking for any kind of moisture in her mouth. 'What kind of pills did you give me?'

'Something to calm your nerves.'

'Stoned.'

'I beg your pardon?'

'I feel really stoned.'

'You use drugs then?'

'Not any more.'

'But you did.'

'Yes.'

*Drugs David brought back home from the hospital and before that . . .*

'Can you tell me your name?'

'Renee.' She blinked. 'Why are you asking me these questions again?'

'I'm here to do your psychiatric evaluation.'

'You're not a psychiatrist.'

'I'm a doctor. By law that's all that is required. The evaluation is a standard form.' He lifted the bound test paper that seemed to have appeared magically in his hands. Renee found herself laughing.

'Eithel Ivrin.'

'I beg your pardon?'

'The pools of Ivrin were beautiful, their water pure.'

'I'm afraid I don't understand.'

*Jesus, what kind of pills have I been given?*

'What were you doing at the old commune?'

'The pool.'

'You went swimming?'

'Yes.'

'Because of your headache?'

'Yes.'

'No other reason?'

'Matthew.'

'Who is Matthew?'

'Son.'

'Your son?'

'Yes?'

'I thought you had a daughter. Lauren.'

'Before.'

'Matthew was before?'

'At Morningstar.'

'You were at Morningstar?'

'Time ago.'

'A long time ago?'

'Yes.'

'And you went back?'

'For Matthew.'

'What about Matthew?'

'He died.'

'When?'

'When he was born.'

'I don't understand.'

She laughed weakly, the drug taking her far, far away. 'Me neither.'

'Matthew was stillborn?'

'Yes.'

'You went to visit his grave?'

'Yes.'

'At Morningstar?'

'Yes.'

'You found it?'

'Yes. Saw the place, all the little flowers.'

Alberoni stared at her silently. Sweat had broken out in little glistening pearls along his upper lip. 'Dear God,' he whispered.

Renee smiled. She had it now.

*Magic.*

'"Seek for the spells."'

'Spells?' asked Alberoni. He was jotting things down furiously.

'I can't . . .' she began, and then she was sobbing uncontrollably. Alberoni left the room and came back a few moments later with the matron. He gave her another shot. The world began to fade away, taking reality with it.

*Why are they doing this to me?*

It was the last coherent thought she had for the better part of twenty years.

# PART TWO

## *Now*

# CHAPTER FOUR

The Victorian tower office jutting up from the seventh floor of the old Van Helder Block at State and Madison was Winston Tucker's favorite perk as senior legal counsel to the Prosper Chamber of Commerce. His partnership office at Scales, Bowles, Pixley & Tucker was pleasant enough, but this was his 'tower of power', all honey-colored wood paneling, soft, deep green leather and an antique partner's desk the size of a grand piano. The Van Helder Block was still the tallest building in town with the exception of the Courthouse Dome and, from his window, Tucker could see everything worth seeing.

Not much had changed in downtown Prosper since his arrival a little more than twenty years before, it had just expanded, much like his own waistline. There were cheese shops, wine stores and galleries along Water Street, instead of the old lumber warehouses, but the White Tower Restaurant was still open at State and Roper and the Grand Theater across the street still had five hit horror marathons for the kids on Saturday even though the concession now sold cappuccino and Evian as well as popcorn and Pepsi. Quentin Woo continued to operate his take-out joint two blocks down on the far side of Snelling Street, even though no one called it 'Chink's' any more, and Horace Bing still went about his somber business at the Glades Funeral Parlor on Kenikill Street, nestled in behind Eddie Castro's Chevron and Prosper Chev-Olds.

There were a few new buildings scattered around – the hard-edged, glass and brick wedge of the County Services Building on Church Street, the featureless cube of the Prosper Holiday Inn, built on the ashes of the old Prosper House Hotel, burnt down in '82, and the slab-sided bus terminal on Carteret Street, three blocks down from Courthouse Square.

Tucker smiled at that. He could remember when the only public transportation in or out of Prosper was the Tuesday, Thursday and Saturday milk run from Newburgh to Elmira that made a fifteen minute pee stop at the White Tower. Now there were half a dozen express buses a day and, during the ski season, 'Specials' from New York were parked on the side streets from Horace Bing's place all the way down to the courthouse.

Glancing out of his window, Winston Tucker watched as a big Greyhound thumped over State Street Bridge, then turned on to Water Street, avoiding the heavy traffic. The lawyer watched as the bus swung down Church street, cruised past County Services, then turned again on Snelling. It stopped there for a few minutes, dropping off passengers booked into the Holiday Inn, then crossed

44

State Street, rumbling past the Chink's and then into the bus station parking lot. A year ago the Chamber of Commerce had hired a fancy consultant group from New York that figured out the average length of time each visitor stayed and how much each one spent. According to their figures, a Greyhound full of tourists was worth about six thousand dollars. Smiling happily, Tucker turned away from the panoramic view and went back to work.

The woman who now called herself Rachel Kane climbed down from the Greyhound and waited for the driver to unload the luggage from the belly of the rib-sided aluminum beast. She pulled her small, black canvas suitcase from the growing pile, picked it up and went into the bus station. She bought a package of Tareytons at the smoke shop, lit one, then left the station, going through the swinging doors that led out on to Snelling Street.

*Christ, what am I doing here?*

*Taking back your life. Finding the four people who killed your daughter and stole twenty years from you.*

*Getting even.*

There were two small, red-brick buildings directly across from the bus station, one with a neon Genessee beer sign in the window. The bar was tempting and in another incarnation she might have given into it, but this Rachel Kane was dry.

The building beside the bar had a swinging sign over its door that said: TAXI. There was one car out front, a bright yellow stationwagon that had seen better days. There was no company name on the door, just the word 'Taxi' again, in thick black letters, with a phone number beneath it. She crossed Snelling Street and headed for the taxi stand.

The driver of the stationwagon was asleep, head leaning on the door post, cushioned by a balled-up windbreaker. He was thickset and balding with dark, slicked-down hair. There was a copy of the *Prosper Advance* folded on the dashboard in front of him. Rachel climbed into the back seat of the taxi, but the man continued to sleep. According to the plastic laminated license hanging over the headrest his name was Carl O'Neill and he was forty years old. In 1974 he would have been eighteen. A football player at Woodrow Wilson High? A friend of Robby Skelton's perhaps? She nodded to herself, filing away the man's name in Rachel's memory banks. Carl might be useful.

She reached out and tapped him lightly on the shoulder. He stirred, yawned, then glanced in the rear-view mirror. His eyes were small and his cheeks were sprinkled with old acne scars, but when he smiled into the mirror his face seemed to open up as though he had an entirely different personality in sleep.

'Power napping,' he grinned. 'You just come in on the bus?'

'Uh-huh.'

'Name's Carl. Where can I take you?'

'I'm looking for a place to stay.'

'Holiday Inn's only a few blocks away.'

'More like a rooming house. Not too expensive.'

'Madame Tussaud's.' The driver nodded.

'Excuse me?'

'Eileen Wax. Everyone calls her Madame Tussaud. She calls it a bed and breakfast, but it's really just a rooming house.'

'Nice place?'

'Nice enough.' Carl shrugged. 'Supposed to be quite the gourmet chef.' He yawned again, turned on the ignition and dragged down the shift lever on the steering column. 'What do you say?'

'Worth a look.'

Carl nodded, then put his foot down on the gas.

Madame Tussaud's was on South Kennikill Street, just barely managing to be classified as 'downtown' rather than 'Mechanicsville'. According to Carl the taxi driver there were differing opinions about what the qualifiers were; some people said it was the railway cut that ran east and west from Golden Valley Canning and the Brook Hill Dairy siding, while others insisted it was the Baseline Road, which followed the original southern town line.

The house turned out to be a turn-of-the-century, rambling, three-story monstrosity sprawled on a weedy corner lot and surrounded by a gap-toothed picket fence. Over the years the house had been added on to a number of times and any architectural integrity had long since vanished among an assortment of opposing rooflines, dormers, porches and rickety wooden fire escapes. The only thing binding the building together was its dull green paint trimmed in an uncomplimentary chocolate brown. Masses of flowers had been planted around the house in a jarring blaze of color, and huge purple lilac trees crowded around the porch by the front door.

The taxi pulled up at the curb beside the front gate. There was a plank sign dangling on chains from a metal post. The sign looked as though it had been made with a child's wood-burning set. It said 'House of Wax'. There was a second, smaller sign hanging underneath that said: 'Vacancy'.

'Everybody gets the joke except her,' said Carl as he stopped the car. 'I don't think old Lady Wax has ever set foot inside of a movie theater.' He nodded toward the house. 'It's just about the only place in town that isn't hooked up to QC.'

'QC?'

'Quinn Cable. Old Eileen won't allow it.'

'Isn't the District Attorney here named Quinn?' Rachel asked. Six months ago the Prosper DA had made the Buffalo papers by winning a long-running postal fraud case and there'd been one or two sidebars about her potential as an upcoming gubernatorial candidate for the Republicans.

Calf half-turned in his seat. 'That's right. D'Arcy Quinn. She won the election last year when old man Foster punched his ticket. What the Parkers don't own in Prosper, she does. I used to go to school with her as a matter of fact.' The taxi driver frowned. 'I thought you said you were new in town? How come you know about D'Arcy Quinn?'

'Saw her name in the papers.'

'Yeah,' Carl nodded. 'She's a comer all right. You want some help with your bag?'

'No thanks.' She shifted toward the door. 'What do I owe you?'

'Three bucks,' said Carl. 'Flat rate in town.'

Rachel handed him a five dollar bill and waved off the change. 'Maybe I'll see you again,' she said, opening the door.

'Count on it.' Carl laughed. 'Prosper's not a very big place.'

She climbed out of the car and watched as the yellow station-wagon did a U-turn and headed back up the tree-lined street. Rachel pushed open the squeaking gate in the picket fence and walked up the paving stone walk to the front porch of the house. The front entrance was a wide single door with decorative panels of etched glass on either side. In the middle of the door there was an old-fashioned twist bell. She dropped the heavy shoulder bag, turned the bell handle twice and waited, breathing in the rich, sweet scent of the lilacs. This was the first step in the process – stepping out of her world and into theirs, wolf in sheep's clothing, shrike in sparrow's plumage.

Cocking the gun.

The door opened.

'Yes?' The woman at the door was thin as a coathanger with a narrow, small-featured face, pale as the ash on the tip of the cigarette in her bony hand. Long gray hair spilled out of an untidy bun perched on the top of her skull. She was wearing a shapeless, faded flowerprint dress that hung from her shoulders like a shroud. There was a pair of glasses on a piece of string around her neck.

'My name is Rachel Kane. I'm looking for a room.' She looked over her shoulder. 'I saw your vacancy sign.'

'Always there,' said the woman. 'Always a vacancy.'

'Do you think I could see it?'

'One twenty-five a week. You get a toast and coffee breakfast, and supper. Supper's at six thirty. Miss it, you eat elsewhere.' She took a puff on her cigarette and put her glasses on, eyeing Rachel carefully. 'Rachel, that's a Jewish name, right?'

'I guess it can be.'

'Are you?'

'No, as a matter of fact.'

'Not that I have anything against them.' She puffed on the cigarette. 'Jews, that is.'

'No, of course not.'

'Only two rules here. No fooling around between the guests and I don't take people with that AIDS thing.' She took another puff on the cigarette. 'You don't have it do you? That AIDS thing?'

'No.'

'Well, you won't get it here. I run a clean kitchen.'

'I'd like to see the room.'

'Sure.' The woman pulled the door open wider and stepped aside. 'I'm Mrs Wax. I own the place.' Rachel stepped into the house.

Eileen Wax's 'bed and breakfast' was a patchwork maze of rooms and halls laid out more to suit the needs of wandering laboratory rats than human beings. By the time she reached the second floor of the house, Rachel Kane had counted nine different colors of paint, of which six were shades of green, and five different wallpaper patterns, all of them floral. The carpet runners down the narrow halls were worn Axminsters and the artwork on the walls of the dining room looked as though it had come from K-Mart. The air inside the house was stale, a bitter combination of old cigarettes and pot-pourri from a spray can. Underlying everything was the musty perfume of age, invisible spoor from the fragments of a hundred lifetimes lived within each room.

According to Eileen Wax there were fourteen bedrooms in the house, twelve of which were presently occupied. She rattled off an assortment of names, none of which meant anything to Rachel. Several of the tenants were retirees but most were working men and women. Only one, Marjory White, was a student. One of the empty rooms was on the third floor, facing an overgrown vegetable garden, a ramshackle carriage house and a back alley. The other room was on the second floor, adjoining one occupied by a man named Bob Wren. According to Eileen Wax, Wren was a detective on the Prosper Police Force. The room on the second floor looked out on to the street. Both of the vacant rooms were furnished almost identically with a single bed, a chest of drawers and a small writing desk, but the room beside the cop had a narrow bay window and came with a worn upholstered chair and an oval rope rug.

'I'll take this one,' said Rachel, dropping her bag on the chenille bedspread. 'I can give you references if you'd like.'

'No point,' answered Eileen. 'Two weeks in advance is the best reference you could give me, dear.'

'No problem.' Rachel paid her, in cash.

'Good,' said Eileen, going to the door. 'I've got enough problems of my own.' She paused, one hand on the old-fashioned, cut-glass doorknob. 'I suppose you'll be looking for a job?' She glanced at the folded wad of bills in her hand.

'Yes.'

'Savings don't last for ever, do they? Secretarial?'

'Maybe. Law office, library, something like that. Why?'

'Bulletin board at City Hall. Usually a few things tacked up.'

'Thanks for the tip.'

'Pleasure. Welcome to Prosper.' She turned, pulled open the door and left the room.

# CHAPTER FIVE

The following morning, Rachel came down to breakfast late. The only thing left on the dining-room table was a pile of cold toast on a butter plate and a big plastic Thermos of coffee. Through the archway Rachel could see Eileen Wax seated at the kitchen table reading the *Prosper Advance* and drinking from a huge yellow mug dotted with fat red cherries. A cigarette fumed in a tin ashtray beside her. Rachel found a clean cup on the buffet and then sat down across from the only other person at the table, also reading the paper. As she sat he lowered it and smiled. He was wearing a tweed sports jacket, pale blue shirt and a simple striped tie. He was in his mid to late fifties, obviously in shape, with rough good looks that reminded her of James Garner.

*Now what ever happened to him I wonder?*

She couldn't resist it. 'You look like James Garner.'

'I hated *The Rockford Files*,' the man answered. 'But I liked him in *Murphy's Romance*.' The smile broadened. 'Mind you, that might have been Sally Field. I've had a thing for her since *Gidget*.'

*What the hell is he talking about? What does the*

*flying nun have to do with this?*

He held a hand out across the table and she took it. Dry and firm and he didn't hang on for too long. He looked a little surprised at the strength of her own grip.

*That's what you get for pumping iron in the loony bin.*

'My name's Bob Wren.'

'The cop.' She smiled back. 'You've got the room beside mine.'

'That's right. And it's detective actually.' The smile stayed switched on. 'You like movies?'

*Play it safe, you've been on a trip for twenty years, going nowhere, madly.*

'Old ones.' She nodded. 'My name's Rachel. Rachel Kane.'

'Dramatic. You're not an actress are you?'

*Only when I have to be.*

'Journalist.'

'Looking for a job?'

'Got one.'

'With who?'

Rachel leaned forward and looked through into the kitchen. Eileen was still lost in her newspaper. She spoke softly to Wren. '*Life*'s doing a special issue on small-town America. But that's supposed to be a secret if you don't mind. People know you're from *Life*, it kind of skews how they react and respond. I'm trying to keep a low profile.' It was a cover story she'd had in mind for weeks.

Wren smiled. 'I won't tell a soul.' He zipped a finger

across his lips. 'Anything I can do to help?'

'I'm looking for a car.'

'Stolen?'

She laughed. 'Used. I want to sort of blend in with the locals.'

'Barney should have something for you.'

'Barney?'

'Friend of mine.' He turned the smile on ever higher. 'I can drive you down there if you like. It's on my way to work.'

'Great.'

He drove a cop's car, a big dark green Caprice with a shape like a pregnant walrus and a rock-hard suspension meant for high speed chases. It was one of the first things she'd noticed when they released her from Brockhurst and assigned her to the halfway house in Schenectady – the cars had all become middle-aged, wide-hipped and bulging at the rear, just like the people who owned them. Wren drove the car casually, one arm looped out the window, the other draped across the wheel. He didn't seem to be in any kind of a hurry.

'Why Prosper? Your choice or the magazine's?' he asked, glancing across the broad bench seat.

It was an obvious question and she'd been expecting it. 'Mine. I spent some time here when I was younger. I was looking to get away for a while anyway . . .' She let it dangle.

'Divorce?' asked Wren, filling in the blank.

*Something like that.*

'Yes.'

'Kids?'

'No.'

'I always wanted to have kids.'

'Divorced too?'

'No. My wife died.' A short look of pain crossed his face. 'Cancer.'

'I'm sorry.'

'It was a while ago.' They drove a few more blocks in silence.

'Couldn't be much work for a detective in a town this size,' Rachel said finally.

'You'd be surprised. When the college is going there's usually something – someone stealing computers, or some kind of sexual harassment thing. Burglaries, lots of cottage B and Es in the fall after things close up. We get our fair share of missing persons as well.' He shrugged again. 'Better than the Bureau.'

'You were with the FBI?'

'For a while. I got tired of moving around all the time, playing Lew Erskine.'

'I remember him. Efram Zimbalist Jr. He had great hair.'

Wren grimaced. 'He looked more like an FBI agent than I did.'

'Why did you choose Prosper?'

'My wife was born here. She wanted to come home.' Rachel caught the tone and meaning and left it alone. Wren turned on to State Street and headed into the downtown core. 'After she died I decided to stick around. Got hired by the Prosper PD.'

'You're happy here?'

'Who's happy?' He pulled the Caprice across the street and into a lot full of cars surrounded by waving plastic flags and banners. There was a rickety-looking cottage-style prefab at the back of the lot with a huge blow-up plastic Kraft teddy bear bobbing on the roof. A strip of plastic had been glued over the Kraft logo changing it to BARNEY'S A BEAR. Next door was the lot for Prosper Chev-Olds. No plastic bear but lots of flags and brand-new cars.

'Barney's a bear?'

'My wife's older brother. His nickname was the Bear when he coached high-school football.'

*At Woodrow Wilson?*

'And now he sells cars?'

'His team was lowest in the district five years in a row. He figured it was time for a change.' Wren smiled. 'Tell him I sent you,' he said. 'He'll give you a deal.'

She took the hint. 'Thanks.' She popped the door and turned to him. 'Maybe we'll meet at breakfast again.'

'I hope so.' He threw her another smile and she returned it, then climbed out of the car and closed the door. He wheeled around neatly and headed back on to the street. She watched him go, then headed for the car lot office and Barney the Bear, who might have been Robby Skelton's football coach.

A man came out of the office who had to be Barney – big, broad-shouldered and wearing a brown suit. She introduced herself, gave him a price range and he started pitching, taking her from one car to the next, fondling fenders and patting roofs as though each vehicle was a precious possession. In the end she settled on a low mileage late-eighties Volkswagen Golf that was the same color as Barney's suit. It was plain and boxy, but at least it didn't look like the smooth-sided new cars on the lot next door.

Barney patted the roof of the chocolate-colored car. 'Great choice, great choice,' he nodded, which is precisely what he would have said no matter which one she'd chosen. She didn't offer her hand but he took it anyway. 'Barney Benechuk. Why don't we go back to the office and figure out how we're going to finance this baby.'

'I'm paying cash,' Rachel answered. Barney's eyes widened a little.

'Even better,' he chortled. The big man put a large, protective hand against her back and gently ushered her forward and up the steps to the prefab. While Barney put together the paperwork and phoned to set up the insurance, Rachel wandered around the room inspecting the walls, all of which were covered in trophies large and small as well as literally dozens of plainly framed team photographs. Boys. Standing and kneeling, all in variants of the same uniform, teenagers bulked out by heavy padding and big helmets with entwined Ws on the sides. Enough testosterone to fight a war. She peered at the pictures, one by one, and finally found the 1974 team. She went over the faces but she couldn't see him. She turned to Barney.

'Bob said you coached football?' Calling the policeman by his first name felt odd.

'That's right.'

'Ever coach a kid named Skelton?'

'Robin Skelton?' His face darkened.

'That's him.'

'Why?' asked Barney.

'No particular reason,' Rachel answered, lifting her shoulders, trying to keep it light. 'Just a name from the past.'

'He was basketball,' said Barney. 'He tried out for the team but . . .'

'But?'

'I didn't like his attitude.'

'So you kept him off the team.'

'Team is the operative word,' said Barney. 'And he didn't know the meaning of it. A showboater all the way. Grandstand plays. Me, me, me. You know the type.' He shook his head. 'Drove Morini right out of his mind.'

'Morini?'

'Math teacher. Subbed as the basketball coach.'

Rachel nodded. 'Any idea what became of Skelton?'

Barney tapped the ownership papers and the rest of the forms into a neat little pile on the desk in front of him. 'Sure,' he said, his voice sour. 'The arrogant little prick is Chief of Police, if you'll pardon my French. Just like his daddy before him.'

She paid Barney with a check drawn on her account in Buffalo and used her freshly minted Visa card as identification.

*Even crazy people can get credit if they've got enough cash.*

She offered to pay for a call to the bank but Barney declined and made a joke about having Wren arrest her if the check turned out to be rubber. Rachel asked him for directions to the Prosper Library and she found out that it was only a few blocks away. They went out to the car, Barney pasted on a new set of tags and she drove off, barely able to keep her hands from shaking. She turned off State Street on to Kennikill, went past Coban's Grocetria and pulled over to the curb. She switched off the engine and fell back against the seat, closing her eyes, hands gripping the wheel.

*Chief of Police. Dear God.*

For all those years she'd played the game of Robby growing up in a thousand different scenarios. Robby getting drafted and dying a dozen grisly deaths. Robby in Attica or on Death Row in some godforsaken state where they still hanged people. Robby with a loving wife and children, then having it all wiped out by some drunk on the interstate, broken glass and blood all across the pavement. Dread diseases eating flesh and muscle down to bone.

Not this. Chief of Police? It was the old nightmare all over again. She'd stepped into a time-warp and gone back to where she'd been.

*Isn't that exactly what you want?*

The tiny part of her she'd kept from all the shrinks and evaluation committees wanted nothing short of Skelton's blood for Lauren's. A painful death by her

60

own hand if Fate hadn't already done the job for her.
But that was only the crazy part of her, the part built
up over more than twenty years in madhouse
bedlams like Brockhurst and all the others, where
clocks ticked as slow as death and one scream echoed
endlessly into the next down long gray hallways
leading nowhere.

She opened her eyes, sat forward and took a long,
shuddering breath. She cranked down the window
and glanced across the street. Neat, Victorian houses
in dark greens and browns, white trim around the
windows. Shutters and box planters. The swish of
sprinklers and a young girl in shorts and T-shirt
learning how to in-line skate while her father
watched from the narrow laneway where he was
washing his car. The rustle and rush of a summer
breeze in the line of maples on both sides of the street.
A patch in the asphalt exactly the same shape as
Australia.

*Normal.*

'It's okay,' she said to herself, softly.

Except it wasn't. Somewhere nearby, probably
within a mile or so of where she was parked, Robin
Skelton was sitting, or standing, or walking, or
driving, dressed in the same crisp uniform and high
boots his father had worn that night.

*I wonder what happened to the truck?*

*'Maybe she wants King Bone. Slip her the snake,
Robby, come on!'*

*'Let's take her and the retard for a ride.'*

*'Give her a red truck fuck.'*

61

Clear as glass, as though it had been only a few minutes ago. She looked at the kid on the in-line skates, listened to the hiss of the hose in her father's hand. Watched the foaming water make white snaking paths through the dust down to the sidewalk and the gutter.

*Normal.*

*Hold on tight. It'll pass. It always does.*

It did. She rummaged around in her purse, pulled out her Tareytons and lit one, dragging the smoke deeply into her lungs, willing herself not to see the image of those four faces, bright in the blazing light of the fire that was consuming her child alive. She wanted to scream. Instead she started the car again and followed the directions she'd been given by Barney the bear.

The Prosper Public Library was located on the corner of Church Street and Snelling, five blocks north of the bus terminal. Beside the library was a glass and steel cube with a sign outside announcing that it was the Prosper Community Services Building, and behind it was the looming wood and gingerbread mansion housing the Prosper Heritage Society.

The library itself was a classic red-brick and white-columned building dating back to the Carnegie era and came complete with two crouching lions at the top of a broad spread of granite steps leading to the front entrance. The structure had a faintly sinister look, like the building of an old black and white horror movie. There was even a compass weather vane on the peak of the roof, topped by a crowing cock and a corkscrewed lightning rod.

The interior of the library fulfilled the exterior's promise. Worn hardwood floors creaked softly underfoot, floor to ceiling bookcases of darkly varnished oak ran in gloomy aisles from front to rear on two floors connected by a squeaking, wrought-iron spiral staircase and half a dozen long, formica-topped study tables were set out within plain sight of the checkout desk and the photocopier to the left of the front doors. To the right of the doors there was a short row of four, hand-operated microfilm readers. The air was still and smelled faintly of ancient plaster, dust and thick, pale binding paste, clotted on stiff, black bristle brushes.

Rachel went to the main desk, asked a weary looking woman if she could see microfilm copies of the *Prosper Advance* for 1974, not specifying any particular month. She told the librarian that she was researching an article about Courthouse Square and, five minutes later, the woman returned with a box of film spools. It didn't take long to find the ones she was looking for. September and October of 1974, the parentheses surrounding the nightmare between her arrest and final incarceration. The period she'd come to think of as The Time of Her Trial. Sometimes she could smile at the words – the title of the private soap opera of her life. But the smiles were rare.

The story was easy enough to follow. She had been arrested on 21 September, a Saturday, and the first report of the incident appeared in the Monday edition of the paper. It was brief, only three paragraphs and was printed without a by-line. 'Suspect Arrested in Mysterious Death on Stoney Creek Road.'

It gave her name, Renee spelled incorrectly with only one e, and laid out the bare facts of the event as related by the reporter's 'high ranking source' at the Prosper Police Department. Oddly, the story made no mention of the old Morningstar commune, simply referring to the location as being located on the Stoney Creek Road. Beyond that the only thing of interest was the name of the man who was to perform the autopsy on the victim – Dr Amos Alberoni of the Prosper Medical Center, who did double duty as the County Coroner. Although there was no mention of it in the news story, Rachel knew that Alberoni practised as a family physician and, like a lot of rural coroners, was not qualified as an actual Medical Examiner and had no specialized interest or training in pathology. The first weak link in a fractured chain of incompetence and deceit. Her first step along the dark, winding path of retribution she had chosen for herself.

*Justice, not revenge, remember?*

*Fuck you.*

The rest of the stories followed her meanderings through the Prosper judicial system, from Winston Tucker signing off on a preliminary hearing, Alberoni's judgment about her mental fitness and, finally, Tucker's plea-bargain that sent her off to an indefinite stay at Brockhurst. Most of which she barely remembered, thanks to Alberoni's medications.

All of this had been done under the auspices of the Honorable, Judge J. Randall Quinn of the Prosper County District Court. Presumably Judge Quinn was some relation to the present District Attorney. Rachel had a sneaking suspicion that she hadn't even brushed the surface when it came to the connecting fibers that bound Prosper together.

*I need an ally.*

Rachel Kane rewound the spool, watching time spin backward on the screen. She smiled, wondering what the shrinks would do if she told them she talked to herself inside her head.

She packed up the spools and brought them back to the tired looking woman at the front desk. Rachel asked if they had a city directory and the librarian swivelled around and handed her a thick brown volume from a shelf behind her. Rachel took it to a table close to the microfilm viewers and started going through it. She found what she was looking for almost immediately: Dr Paul Goodman, Oneida College, and a telephone number with an extension.

*Doctor?*

There was a home address and phone number as well. She jotted down both numbers, returned the directory to the librarian and followed the signs to a pay phone by the main doors. She dialed the number for Goodman at the College.

A woman's voice answered, bored, almost a sigh, 'Department of Psychology.'

Rachel hung up. Paul was a shrink? She vaguely remembered him talking about having a degree from

Columbia and that both his mother and father had been in the medical profession right here in Prosper. The father a doctor, the mother a nurse? Something like that. When they died he'd inherited the tract of land that eventually became Morningstar. Maybe after the end of the commune he'd gone back for another degree.

Rachel went back to the librarian one last time.

'How do I get to the Oneida College?'

'State Street west to the town limit; you'll see Pinecrest Cemetery and the old folk's home on your left. Turn right on County 5 and you'll run right into it.'

'Thanks.'

She left the library, climbed back into the Golf and headed back toward State Street. Twenty minutes later she was driving through the ornamental gateway at the edge of the Oneida College campus. She pulled up to an information kiosk just inside the gates, got out of the car and consulted a large color-coded plastic map bolted to the side of the booth. According to the diagram the campus was bisected east to west by College Way and north to south by the road she was now on – Chancellor Boulevard. The west side of the campus appeared to be given over to technical studies like Veterinary Science and a Dentistry School, while the east side was mostly Arts and Humanities. The Psychology Department was on the far east side of the campus. From the number of buildings and faculties charted on the map Oneida College was getting close to university size.

Rachel got back into the car and continued along Chancellor Boulevard until she reached a large, brutal-looking piece of modern, poured-concrete architecture with a cast aluminum sign out front identifying it as the Student Union Building. A smaller sign, this one scrawled with felt marker on cardboard announced that the SUB pub would be closed until September. Of the dozen or so buildings Rachel had seen so far, none of them appeared to be more than ten or fifteen years old. She went by a glass cube called the J. Randall Quinn Library and a thinly landscaped red-brick residence called simply Quinn House. As it turned out, the Psychology Department was housed in a long, low, cedar and glass Frank Lloyd Wright knock-off named Parker Anncx. Rachel pulled into a space in the row of slots in front of the building and climbed out of the car. What had Carl the taxi driver said? Whatever the Parkers didn't own in Prosper, the Quinns did? At the far end of the row of cars in front of the building she spotted a battered, open Jeep, windscreen folded forward, painted gray, with a black line of runic symbols running along the door. The WWII army surplus vehicle had been old when Paul had driven it in the sixties; now it was truly ancient. According to Paul the Jeep had been used in Guadalcanal and once upon a time he'd kept a huge Malay machete in a hidden sheath under the passenger's side seat and made jokes about using it when the straights and hippies finally went to war with each other.

*Back when we thought there was really going to be a revolution.*

The Vorpal Blade he'd called it, from 'The Hunting of the Snark' by Lewis Carroll. Smiling at the memory, she went into the building. On the directory board just inside the swinging glass doors he was called Dr Paul Goodman Phd, Psychology 220. She found his office but it was closed and locked. The building seemed empty but she wandered around and finally found him in the cafeteria, seated at a heavily varnished picnic table. The back wall of the low-ceilinged room was all glass and looked out over a narrow creek-gully that ran behind the psychology building, but Dr Goodman wasn't looking at the view. He was listening to a girl in her late teens or perhaps her early twenties, long-haired and blonde. She had a pile of books in front of her, almost like a shield.

*Some things never change.*

Rachel watched him. In 1969 Paul Goodman had been in his late twenties or early thirties, hard-muscled enough to spend most of his time without a shirt on, jet black hair sweeping down over his powerful shoulders, even then touched with a distinctive scattering of white. Most of the time he dressed in a pair of silk-soft doeskin jeans that Rainbow had made for him, the leather soft and supple enough to cling to him like a second skin, tauntingly erotic.

Everything about him had been tinged with drama, from the hard-roped thighs to the single curving scar that arced across his back. She'd slept with him once, almost publically in the Alamo at one of the weekly 'gatherings', almost a rite of passage and acceptance for a woman at Morningstar, but he'd never called her to his bed again until she came back from Woodstock with David in tow.

That night she'd slept with both of them together in his private loft above the Alamo's huge hearth, and the experience had been overwhelmingly powerful, a totalness of being she'd never felt before or since. But it had been touched with something else as well, as though David had been the younger wolf in the pack acquiescing to his leader, offering her up like some sexual token of his fealty.

All these years later and little had changed. He had to be in his fifties now but there was still a startlingly powerful electricity around him. The hair was still long, still jet black except for slashes of white at the temples, and now he wore a full beard, black, shot with gray. He was dressed in a dark blue T-shirt under a perfectly fitted suede jacket and tight, black denim jeans with matching black leather moccasins. She walked across the room and stood at the end of the table. He looked up, smiled, and in that instant she knew that, incredibly, he'd recognized her.

'Earendel,' she said, smiling, using the Tolkienesque name that Goodman had given himself, and which, according to him, was Teutonic for Venus, the Morning Star.

'Luthien,' he answered, without the slightest hesitation, using the name he'd given her more than twenty-five years before. 'Daughter of Thingol, the most beautiful of the Children of Iluvatar.'

The blonde girl stared at both of them. 'Cool,' she said, smiling, wide-eyed.

Goodman gave her a short look. 'I'll talk to you later, Beth.' It was a dismissal and the young girl knew it. Beth the blonde gathered up her armload of books and scurried off. Rachel took her place on the bench and stared at her old friend.

'Been a long time,' she said.

He nodded. 'Couple of lifetimes.' He paused. 'For both of us.'

It was true; she felt as far from Morningstar and those young days as she did from Mars. Hearing him call her Luthien had brought it all back in a rush, but it also hammered home the childishness of it all. So much energy and all of it had come to nothing. Wasted time as everyone grew up to be their parents.

'I never imagined you as a professor.'

'Me neither,' he said. He shrugged. 'Just happened.'

'We grew up.'

'I guess that's it.'

'Or gave up,' she said, realizing that it sounded almost like an accusation.

'You've changed,' said Goodman.

'Like you said, a couple of lifetimes.'

'You're not as . . . soft as you used to be.'

'That's true enough.' She knew how bitter she sounded. 'Where I've been, soft doesn't get you very far.'

She took out her cigarettes but then she saw that there were no ashtrays on any of the tables in the cafeteria.

'Smoke-free environment,' said Goodman. 'School policy.'

'Like bans on micro-minis and long hair.' She smiled.

'Sort of.' He smiled back.

'I'm just teasing,' she said softly.

He reached out and offered his hand to her palm up. She put her own into it, felt the hot burst in her chest as she touched him. 'I know.'

They sat like that for a long moment. With an effort, she withdrew her hand. 'What happened to Morningstar?' she asked. 'I came back here in '74 and everything was gone. It looked like someone set fire to the place.'

He lifted his shoulders. 'Kids. I was already gone by then. Back to California. Graduate school.' He looked at her closely. 'I heard about what happened . . . When you came back. I'm sorry.' There was real concern in his voice and she felt herself melting into the intimacy of it.

'What did you hear?'

Goodman looked uncomfortable. He ran both hands back through his hair, reaching for a ponytail that wasn't there any more, an old habit she remembered well. 'I heard you ran away from David with your daughter. You came back here. To Morningstar.'

'Looking for you and all the others.'

'There was a fire. Your car. Your daughter was trapped, locked inside.'

'She was murdered.'

'They said you did it. That you were insane.'

'Do you believe that?'

He shrugged again. 'I teach deviant psychology here,' he said. 'I know what can happen in an unhappy mind.'

'I didn't do it. There were four kids standing at the car when I came back from the pool that night. One of them was an adolescent boy named Robin Skelton.'

Goodman nodded. 'His father was Chief of Police back then.'

'And *he's* Chief of Police now.' She made a snorting sound. 'It's like that old Joni Mitchell song, remember? "The Circle Game." It just goes "round and round."'

'Is that why you've come back now?' asked Goodman. The concern was still in his voice, but there was something else there as well. A distance. Fear?

'I'm not sure why I came back.'

'How long have you been . . . out?' More hesitance. She suddenly realized that he *was* frightened, something she'd never seen in the old Paul Goodman, ever.

'Year and a half,' she said, smiling. 'The first six months I spent on day passes in a halfway house. I've been clearing up my parents' estate since then.'

'You never said much about your mother and father when . . . we knew each other.' There it was again, the hesitancy. More distance. Sadly, she knew that this was no ally, this was just someone she'd known a long, long time ago.

'I didn't know my dad had died until three or four years after the fact. They don't let crazy people go to funerals. My mother died when I was living in the halfway house. Cancer.'

'I'm sorry.'

'Don't worry about it.'

Goodman cleared his throat nervously. 'Are you staying long in Prosper?'

She reached out and patted his hand. 'Don't worry, Paul, I'm not going to make a pest of myself, or a scene. I guess you could say I came back here to lay the old ghosts to rest.'

He smiled at that. 'And I'm one of them?'

She smiled back. 'I guess so.' She glanced around the cafeteria, nodded toward the view. 'Almost as pretty as Morningstar.' She paused. 'You've done okay for yourself, Paul.' She paused. 'What about family?'

He made a face. 'Not my thing, you know that.'

'No wife and kids and house with a picket fence?'

'You're teasing me again.'

She stood up. 'Yeah, I suppose I am,' she said quietly. He stood across from her.

'It was nice to see you again, Renee.'

'You remembered my old name.'

'Old?'

'It's Rachel now. Rachel Kane.' She raised an eyebrow. 'You're the deviant psych doctor, Paul, you know why people like me change names. What do the textbooks call it, "the pathology of abuse"?'

He frowned, confused. 'Abuse?'

'What else do you call spending half a lifetime in a madhouse for something you didn't do?'

He blinked, smiled awkwardly and reached into the back pocket of his jeans. He took out a slim wallet, plucked a business card from it and handed it to Rachel. 'It's got my office number on it, but if I'm not there I usually have my calls forwarded to my cell phone.'

'Cell phone?' asked Rachel. 'Pretty hi-tech for an old back-to-the-lander, don't you think?'

'Times change.' He shrugged lightly. 'So do people.'

'I guess you're right,' said Rachel.

She gave him a last smile, then turned and walked away. She blinked back tears and bit her lip. A word she hadn't thought of since the sixties popped into her head.

*Cop-out.*

There'd be no help, or aid, or even sympathy from him. Whatever it was that she *had* come back to do, she'd be doing on her own. There was no Narnia, no Middle-Earth, no Revolution Number Nine. There was only passed time, dimming snake-pit memories of a cold, empty place in her heart that she could see no way to fill or warm.

That night, in her narrow bed in Eileen Wax's rooming house she listened to the small muffled sounds of Bob Wren moving around in the room beside hers and thought about all the things she'd lost and could never hope to have again. Love, sex, her child's voice, loud with laughter. How were you supposed to live when your life ended at the age of twenty-two and started up again when you turned forty-five?

She slept finally, but had no dreams.

# CHAPTER SIX

Prosper County had long ago outgrown the cramped, brick and stone confines of Courthouse Square and most of the district's day-to-day operations were carried out in the modern, eight-story, step-sided building across the street. The glass and steel structure rose above a three-level underground mall and parking garage and was officially called the County Administration Block, but most people in town used its nickname – Stairway to Heaven. The eighth floor, last step before heaven itself, was fully occupied by the Prosper County District Attorney, with D'Arcy Quinn's own suite of offices overlooking Madison Street and Courthouse Square.

At thirty-eight, D'Arcy Alexandra Quinn was the youngest District Attorney in the county's history, and the first woman ever elected to that office. In Prosper, the name Quinn was as ubiquitous as Coca-Cola. Her father, Judge Randall Quinn, had been Mayor of Prosper from the mid fifties to the late seventies, owned a dozen business in the county and ran the County Court on the other side of the street like a personal fiefdom. Her mother, Jessica Parker

Quinn, sat on the Board of Regents at Oneida College and her uncle, Hamilton Parker, owned the Farmers' Union Bank on State Street. Surrounded by power and influence, D'Arcy Quinn had consciously chosen not to exercise it to fulfil her professional ambitions; at a relatively early age she'd decided that who she *became* would not simply be a result of who she *was*.

Graduating from high school at the top of her class in 1976, she took a pre-law degree at the University of Western Washington, then spent two years with the Peace Corps under the federal ACTION program, working as a paralegal in the Ozarks. After being offered a Langdell Scholarship in 1981, she spent the next four years at Harvard Law School, once again graduating at the top of her class.

Courted by a score of major law firms from around the country, all of them hard-pressed to fulfil their equal opportunities quotas, the young lawyer decided instead to accept a junior position in the Dade County District Attorney's Office, once again keeping at arm's length her own connections in Prosper. Following her five years in Florida she joined the US Attorney's Office in Washington and added a degree in Criminology from Georgetown University to her already impressive *curriculum vitae*. Finally, in 1993, she returned to Prosper as Deputy DA.

Six months later, longtime District Attorney Doug Foster stepped down for health reasons, naming Quinn as his appointed and anointed heir. Six months later he was dead. During the election that followed, D'Arcy Quinn was swept into office virtually unopposed. Courthouse scuttlebutt had her marked for a fast-track trip to Albany, but the same scuttlebutt also pondered the question of why, at almost forty, a prospective Governor of New York still lived alone and was still unmarried, with no likely suitors on the horizon.

Seated at her sprawling, reproduction partner's desk, her back to the window, D'Arcy Quinn sighed, idly pulling back her long, toffee-colored hair and snapping a rubber band around it to create a makeshift ponytail. Of the forty or so buff file folders stacked everywhere on the desk only three or four were even mildly interesting. By both training and inclination she preferred criminal cases, but the District Attorney's job also required that she act as the county's chief legal counsel in non-criminal matters.

While Prosper was one of the smallest counties in the State of New York it had become both wealthy and densely populated over the past decade or so and the vast majority of D'Arcy Quinn's work involved civil actions and legal liaison with the City of Prosper, Albany and various Federal Government offices, institutions, and organizations. She employed half a dozen Deputy DAs, twice that many assistants and a score of clerks and support staff to handle the muddy, ever-rising tide of bureaucratic banality, but in the end she had to give each and every case at least some cursory attention as well as her signature.

There were criminal matters to deal with, of course, but even those were often muddled by complicated, generally frustrating jurisdictional questions. Most crimes in the county were committed in the City of Prosper, and were therefore handled by the City of Prosper Police Department. However, if a burglary took place in Prosper and the burglar was apprehended on a county road it became a matter for the Prosper County Sheriff's Office. On the other hand, if, after committing a burglary in the city, the burglar then used a county road to reach a State Highway, it came under the jurisdiction of the New York State Highway Patrol. God help everyone if the burglar had an underage accomplice and made it across the Pennsylvania State line, thus invoking the Mann Act, which would bring the FBI on to the scene.

The recently adopted Uniform Act of Fresh Pursuit made this kind of thing a little less problematical, but it also required even more paperwork to bring the captured criminal before a local magistrate and then institute extradition proceedings.

A year before, Quinn had dealt with a purse snatching in a Safeway parking lot that had taken more than three months to unravel and involved seven different tiers of the judicial system in three states. When the little shit who'd committed the crime was finally brought into Magistrates' Court for arraignment and assignment to a District Court it was discovered that the main piece of evidence – the purse – had been lost somewhere along the way and the case was dismissed.

Sighing again, D'Arcy reached into the pocket of her rust-colored Anne Klein suit, took out a package of Kents and lit one with her battered Harvard Law Zippo. She reached out and pulled a file folder from the top of the nearest pile. 'In Re: Bay Ridge Lodge and Golf Resort.' Her cousin, Michael Parker, looking for a zoning easement. A ski resort, three marinas, a string of fitness clubs and now they wanted to get into golf. She made a small snorting sound and blew smoke across the file; what they were really looking for was yet another liquor license.

She looked up as Ted Harmon, her personal assistant, stepped into the room. At twenty-six the recent Columbia graduate had all the charm and charisma he was ever going to get, which wasn't much. He had carroty, curly hair, no visible eyebrows and a moon face splashed with freckles. Harmon was barely five feet tall and suffered from a severe case of 'short man syndrome' complete with aggressiveness, abrasiveness and a suspicious nature that stopped just short of clinical paranoia. He also had the markings of an extremely good lawyer. She knew perfectly well that he wanted her job, and knew just as well that the people of Prosper County would never give it to him.

'Sorry to barge in on you.' From the expression on his face he wasn't sorry at all.

'What is it?'

'Dr Amos Alberoni.'

'What about him?' D'Arcy asked. The old man had been her doctor when she was a kid and she vaguely recalled that he'd also been the acting Medical Examiner for the county at one time in the distant past. At the age of twelve, after being poked and prodded in places she didn't want to be poked or prodded, she insisted that her mother find her another doctor, preferably a woman. That was the last direct contact she'd ever had with the man.

'He's dead,' said Harmon.

The District Attorney shrugged. 'So what?' she said. 'He was old.' He'd been in his fifties when she was a kid, which would put him in his late seventies or early eighties now.

'He was murdered.'

Now *that* was interesting. Murders in Prosper were rare and almost invariably domestic. As far as she recalled, Alberoni had been a confirmed bachelor. 'Who says?'

'Prine.'

George Prine was the chief and only pathologist at the Prosper Medical Center and also acted as Medical Examiner for the county when necessary. 'What exactly does Dr Prine say?'

'Dr Prine says that Dr Alberoni was standing in the examination room of his home office when somebody stuck him with a knife.'

The District Attorney frowned. Somehow it seemed like an unlikely way for an old man like Alberoni to die. 'He was stabbed?'

'Under the ribs and up through the heart.' Her assistant made an upward thrusting gesture with one hand. 'Once.'

D'Arcy's frown deepened. She'd worked dozens of stabbing murders in Florida and they were almost always multiple wounds, like the O.J. Simpson case. A single, killing wound was unheard of. 'Does the good doctor have any idea how long he's been dead?'

Harmon shrugged his narrow shoulders. 'Says he won't know for sure until he gets the body back to the Medical Center.'

'Any guesses?'

'According to him there's fixed lividity in the body and the corneas are cloudy. At least twelve hours, more like eighteen.'

D'Arcy did the math. 'Yesterday afternoon or evening.'

'Probably.'

'I guess we'd better go take a look.' D'Arcy stood, gathering up her purse and keys. 'Who's on it?'

'Wren.'

Kenny Spearing, Wren's junior partner, was waiting for him on the porch of Alberoni's turreted Victorian house on Princeton Street, an enclave of turn-of-the-century wooden mansions that all seemed to carry a faintly holier-than-thou attitude around their fretwork eaves and the fancy curving ballisters of their front porches. Spearing was rake-thin, smooth-faced and spent most of his salary on clothes like the dark brown leather bomber jacket he was wearing. He regularly gave Wren fashion tips, all of which the older detective ignored. Unlike Wren, Spearing was Prospect born and bred and had come up through the ranks, spending his first year on the Prosper Police Force walking a parking ticket beat on State

Street, and the next two in a squad car. This was his
first real 'crime' and as Wren walked up the neatly
tended walk he could see that Spearing was almost
beside himself with excitement.

Wren saw that there were four cars crammed into
Alberoni's driveway – a bronze, late model Mercedes
Benz, that undoubtedly belonged to the late doctor,
a Prosper PD cruiser with its cherry bar still
blinking, Kenny Spearing's beloved jet black
TransAm, and a silver stationwagon with tinted
windows – the pick-up car from the Glades Funeral
Home that did double duty as the Medical
Examiner's meat wagon. Two young men in black
suits were waiting patiently in the front seat.
Blocking all of them was Jerry Weems' fire-engine-
red Jeep Cherokee. Weems ran the local Lens and
Shutter Camera Shop and made extra money
freelancing for the *Prosper Advance* and doing crime
scene photography every once in a while.

'Everybody still inside?' asked Wren, climbing the
porch.

Spearing nodded. 'I told Dr Prine to wait for you
before he removes the body.'

'Thanks.'

Wren pulled open the screen door and stepped into
the house, Spearing on his heels. He found himself
in a wide foyer. To the left he could see into an
antique-filled living room. Directly ahead a long,
carpeted hallway with a stairway on one side ran
down to an old-fashioned country kitchen. On his
right Wren caught the sudden burst of a photo-

grapher's flash coming through the crack between two sliding doors.

He pulled open the doors and found himself in Dr Alberoni's waiting room. Once upon a time it had probably been a parlor. There was a bay window facing out on to the street and a fireplace against the far wall. Half a dozen wooden armchairs were ranged around the room and there was a plain coffee table loaded down with magazines. The photoflash had come from another room leading off the first.

Wren stepped forward and stood in the doorway of what was obviously Alberoni's examination room. There were five people in the room if you counted Alberoni, who was sprawled across the floor on his back, making movement difficult for the live bodies milling around him – Prine, who was using a big liver needle to take the corpse's temperature, two uniformed Prosper cops who weren't doing much except gawking at what was probably their first real homicide victim, and the pudgy, thirty-something figure of Jerry Weems, two-stepping in all directions, snapping flash pictures with his big motor-drive Nikon, hands clutching the camera above the heads of the onlookers like some macabre paparazzo for the dead.

Wren snapped his fingers to get everyone's attention, then jerked his thumb over his shoulder. 'Out,' he said to the two uniforms. 'Secure the outside and make sure nobody touches the Mercedes.' The uniforms nodded and edged around him. Wren glanced at the photographer. 'Jerry?'

'Just about done.' He took a few more shots then left the room as well.

Wren moved into the room and squatted down beside Prine. Spearing waited in the doorway. Alberoni had been polite enough to fall on his back and die quickly, so the only blood was the plate-sized brownish stain centered on the middle chest of his white lab coat. On the way down to the linoleum floor his gold-rimmed eyeglasses had come unhooked from one ear and were now skewed across his face along with his stethoscope. The odor in the room was a mildly nauseating mixture of emptied bowel and bladder, the copper tang of spilled blood and cherry-flavored pipe tobacco. The pipe in question was half out of the top pocket of the lab coat. Alberoni's eyes were wide open, the clouded corneas and the waxy color of the bald man's head giving him a faintly artificial look, like a well made store mannequin or a figure at Madame Tussaud's.

Wren glanced at Prine. 'You worked in the city before you came out here, right?'

The curly-haired pathologist nodded, checking the figure on the liver thermometer and making a note on his pad. 'Morningside Heights. Bellevue before that.'

'So you've seen stab wounds before.'

Prine lifted one eyebrow. 'A few . . . thousand.'

'So, what's wrong with this picture?'

'There's only one,' the pathologist answered promptly. 'They usually come in half dozens.' He shook his head. 'This was almost surgical. Right up under the good ol' Xiphoid Process, slice through the pulmonary artery and on into the heart.'

'Very neat.' Wren stood, groaning slightly, his right knee popping loudly.

Prine frowned. 'Clicking-knee syndrome. You should get someone to look at that.'

Wren grimaced. 'Just middle-aged turning into old.' He stared down at the body, then looked back toward the examination table. It was the old-fashioned kind – beaded black leather with an adjustable headpiece and stainless steel stirrups that telescoped into the frame. There was a roll of white paper at the head end of the table but it had been torn off cleanly. Wren peeked into the waste basket. A wadded-up receipt from the local courier company to the lab at the Medical Center. There were half a dozen more of them spiked on the doctor's desk. Irrelevant.

'He was examining someone. Whoever was on the table drove the knife into him. He fell back and died.'

'Something like that,' Prine nodded. He stood up himself, snapping his bag shut. 'I'd say the blade was about four inches long. Nothing you couldn't buy in a half-decent sporting goods store. I'll know more when I open him up.' He sighed. 'You mind if I call in Boris and Igor?'

Presumably he meant the two men in the meat wagon. Wren nodded. 'Go ahead.' The doctor stepped over Alberoni's body and left the room. Wren followed and found Kenny Spearing waiting for him. 'Who called it in?'

The young detective pulled a small notebook out of his bomber jacket and flipped it open. 'A patient. Connie Cudmore.' Spearing cleared his throat. 'Connie Cudmore is . . .'

'I know who he is,' Wren interrupted. Constant Cudmore was the octogenarian owner of Cudmore's Department Store at State and Roper. The detective had been living in Prosper for the last six years but Spearing treated him as though he'd arrived the day before yesterday. Unless you were Prosper born and bred you'd always be an outsider. 'What time did Mr Cudmore make the call?'

Spearing frowned and looked down at his notepad again. 'Dispatch has it logged as 9:07.'

Wren checked his watch. An hour and a half. When his beeper went off he'd been halfway to the State Police Office in Kingston, tracking down a suspected car-stripping operation. 'Mr Cudmore had an appointment with the doctor?'

'For 9:00.'

'You talked to him?'

Spearing nodded. 'He arrived on time and saw that the door was open. He went inside, found the body and called it in.'

'Where is he?'

'He said he wasn't feeling too well. I, uh, sent him home.' He looked worried. 'That's okay, isn't it?'

Wren sighed. 'I suppose. Did you take his prints?'

Spearing looked shocked. 'You don't think Connie Cudmore is a suspect, do you?'

'No, but I'd like to have his prints so we can count

him out once we get this place dusted.'

'Dusted? Who's going to do that?' asked Spearing.

Wren sighed again. 'You are, Kenny. The kit is in the trunk of my car.' He dug into his pocket and tossed Spearing the keys. 'As soon as Dr Prine gets the body out you can go to work. Start in the examination room and work your way out.'

'Will do.' Spearing headed out of the waiting room, almost at a run. Wren went back into the examination room for a last look at the body before it was taken away from the scene. For Wren, that was when the clock began to tick. The more time that passed after the corpse had been removed, the less 'real' the murder became, like an old photograph fading after too much time in the sun. The vaguer things got, the less likely you were to solve the murder.

Wren made a little snorting sound. What the hell did he know about it? He'd handled at least twenty or thirty murders in his time with the Bureau, but there was rarely any mystery involved – mob shootings, a psycho who liked to slash hookers' breasts off with a carving knife, a McDonald's franchise owner facing hard times who killed his wife for no good reason, then stuck her in the trunk of his car and tried to bury her in the next state. None of them were what you might call brain teasers. In Prosper, the five wrongful deaths he'd investigated had all been domestic or suicide and had all involved handguns. Run-of-the-mill, bread and butter and ho-hum in the day-to-day life of a cop.

This was different. Wren wandered out into the

hall, stepping out of the way as the two blank-faced boys from the Glades came in carrying a long wicker coffin between them that looked for all the world like a gigantic picnic basket; the politically correct version of a body bag. They disappeared through the waiting-room doors and Wren meandered into the living room on the other side of the hallway.

A single stab wound to the chest, precisely aimed, wasn't the mark of someone who grabs up the nearest weapon in a fit of rage or passion; nor was it the sweeping Jack-the-Ripper throat slash of a madman. It was the mark of a killer, one who liked to get up close and personal; this was no mob hit, one shot to the head with a low velocity :22, but it was close. An execution.

Boris and Igor reappeared, weighed down by the basket, now heavy with Alberoni's corpse. Boris switched hands and pulled open the door with practised ease, pushed open the screen door as well and then they were gone. With Kenny and the other two outside Wren finally had the house to himself. He looked around the living room, trying to get some sense of who Alberoni had been and why someone would want to kill him.

There were several big rugs in the living room, Persian or Chinese, or both, and the furniture was mostly Arts and Crafts – Stickley chairs and tables, with lots of plain, black-lacquered bookcases stuffed with big artsy looking volumes. His choice of artwork and knick-knacks ran to eighteenth-century architectural drawings in ornate frames and equally ornate wooden and plaster architectural models, a lot of them of Gothic-style churches and an equal number of model staircases. There was also a collection of Victorian birdcages ranged along the tops of the bookcases.

Weird.

*Gay?*

Not a chance. Not in Prosper, at least not overtly. Even a whiff of it and Kenny Spearing would have appended it to any description of the doctor – 'Dr Alberoni? You mean the fag on Princeton Street?' Kenny could be numbingly provincial and naive, but he was also a litmus test for the local population. The younger man's father had been the local pharmacist in Prosper for half a century and Kenny had made bicycle deliveries for him throughout his childhood and adolescence. If Kenny didn't know you, you weren't worth knowing.

Wren left the living room and went down the hallway to the kitchen. Nothing there except what you'd expect. The back door was locked and showed no signs of having been tampered with. Frowning, Wren went back to the front of the house.

Murder, Wren knew well enough, required three things – motive, means and opportunity. Means and opportunity were clear enough – someone comes in, probably at the end of the day, gets ready for an examination, and knifes Alberoni as he leans over the patient/killer. But what about motive? Why do you shank an elderly, semi-retired small-town doctor? A ludicrous image leapt into his mind – Dr Alberoni examining his secret, geriatric, drag-queen lover who suddenly sinks a knife into his chest in senile rage. Wren snorted. Why not turn the drag queen into old Monsignor Gadsby from the Catholic Services Bureau and really shake the town up?

He went back into the waiting room. Nothing had changed, but something was bothering him. Waiting room, examination room, but where the hell was Alberoni's office? Even if he didn't have a receptionist or a nurse, he had to have files on his patients somewhere, some kind of record keeping. He stepped into the examination room and immediately saw what he'd missed before; on his left was a louvered door he'd initially mistaken for a supply closet.

Wren pulled open the door and found himself in the doctor's private office. It was small, not much bigger than the examination room, furnished with a plain Berber rug, a desk, two armchairs and a computer workstation built into the wall-to-wall, floor-to-ceiling bookcases. The workstation looked ultramodern and up to date but Wren didn't know very much about it. There was a plastic bottle of glass cleaner and a roll of paper towels on the desk. Either Alberoni had just cleaned his computer screen and keyboard, or the killer was very methodical about cleaning up after himself. Wren could see the possibility of getting any useful prints winging out the window. There was another door leading out into the hall so patients could leave without going back through the waiting room. He let out a long breath, tried not to think about how long it had been since he'd last had a cigarette and then went outside to fetch his partner.

A few moments later he had Spearing seated at Alberoni's desk. 'I can't find any filing cabinets. He must keep all his records on computer.'

Spearing nodded. He reached out and touched a rack of plastic-boxed diskettes, then ran his hand over Alberoni's equipment. 'He's got a dream set-up here. Brand-new Pentium with a quad spin CD-ROM, NEC monitor, Lumina 2000 scanner-fax, all the goodies.'

'None of that means jack-shit to me,' said Wren. 'Can you operate it?'

'But of course, mon General,' grinned Spearing. 'Nothing here I haven't handled. He's running Windows so it should be a snap.' He switched on the computer, tapped WIN at the C-prompt and waited for the familiar Microsoft flying window logo to appear. A few seconds later the big screen filled with a score of smaller boxes.

'What's all of that?' Wren asked, peering over his young partner's shoulder.

'The software he was running.'

'Is there one that keeps files?'

'Computers keep files,' said Spearing, looking back over his shoulder at Wren. 'That's the whole point. You have to be specific.'

'Appointments?'

'Sure.' Spearing clicked on one of the little boxes and the screen went black for a moment, then resolved itself into something that looked like a cartoon Rolodex.

'Can you bring up yesterday's appointments?'

'Easy.' Another keystroke and an eyeblink change in the screen. 'It starts at 8:30 a.m.'

'I thought he was retired?'

'I guess he had a lot of friends.'

'Go to the last appointment.'

Spearing worked his way through the entry times until he reached the last card. 'Shit,' he said.

'What's the matter?'

'7:00 p.m. The last person he saw was Allan Sloane.'

'Never heard of him.'

'He's a vet, Cambodia or Laos, or somewhere,' said Spearing. 'I think he was Special Forces, Green Beret or something like that. My brother Dan went to high school with him. He lives in the woods outside of town. Everybody says he's crazy.'

'Crazy enough to stick a knife into Alberoni?'

Spearing nodded. 'At least that crazy.'

There was a knock. Wren turned. One of the uniforms was standing in the doorway.

'Thought you'd like to know. Ms Quinn just pulled up.'

'Showtime,' Wren sighed.

# CHAPTER SEVEN

Rachel pulled the Golf off the highway and on to the shoulder. Miggs' store had vanished. In the middle of the gravel lot in front of the wall of trees there was an old truck up on blocks with a rickety-looking wood and glass box fitted behind the cab. A neatly painted sign tacked on to the side of the box said WALLYBURGER, with the 'W' in Wally done in bright yellow like upside down McDonald's arches. In front of the truck there was a raw island of concrete stubbed with rusted metal fittings – all that was left of Miggs' gas pumps. On either side of the truck there was a scattering of picnic tables and a few fifty-gallon-drum trash barrels. At the far edge of the clearing, close to the road, was a telephone booth.

Someone, presumably Wally, was working inside the truck. He was big and fat, wearing a white apron and a Manhattan-style deli cap. Rachel pulled up beside the truck and switched off the engine. The smell of hot peanut oil rolled over her like a cloud. She'd only just finished breakfast at the House of Wax, but the familiar odor set her mouth watering. French-fry wagon fries. Suddenly she was a thousand years in the past, in high school, in Buffalo on a summer evening, ordering fries and onion rings from a place just like this, wondering if Toby Berkowitz was going to try to get his hand under her bra this time when they went to Bryant Park to neck.

'Oil's not hot yet. Another hour or so.' She was standing in front of the truck and the big man inside was bent over, talking to her through the open pass-through.

'Sorry,' said Rachel. 'The smell just took me back.'

'Makes me a little nauseous myself,' said the man. 'But like I said, I won't have any fries for at least another hour.'

'I didn't come for fries,' she answered, looking up at the man.

He looked surprised. 'You actually want a burger this time of the morning?'

'No.'

'Coffee?' he suggested. 'I got coffee.'

'Sure. I've got a couple of questions too if you don't mind.' She put two quarters down on the little serving shelf in front of the pass-through. The man's big, hairy-backed hand scooped it up.

'Naw. I don't mind.' The man poured two Styrofoam cups of coffee, handed one through the pass-through, then took the other one and came out through the rear of the stand and down on to the gravel. 'Hate being cooped up in there,' he said. He walked with Rachel over to one of the picnic tables and sat down heavily. He plunged under his apron, came up with a package of cigarettes and lit up. Rachel joined him.

'What kind of questions?' he said. His breath came in little short bursts and there was a line of sweat beads at his temples and above his upper lip. The cheeks were rosy, but not from good health. The man looked one step away from a heart attack. He took another drag on his cigarette and chased it with a slug of black coffee from his cup.

'I'm doing a magazine story on small-town life. Sort of a then and now thing.'

'Oh yeah?'

'There used to be a store here, a long time ago, isn't that right?' She nodded towards the remains of the gas pumps.

'Yeah.'

'Miggs, wasn't that his name?'

'Yeah.'

'What happened to him?'

'He got old. Me and Ronny, we put him into the old folks place.' He was like something out of *The Simpsons*, come to life.

'You're related?'

'Yeah, sort of. Son-in-law. Ronny's his daughter. My name's Kapelka.'

'Wally.'

'You got it.'

'You took over the store?'

'Naw. Gas company wasn't making enough dough so they shut down. I was in the army. Me and Ronny got back from Georgia, wasn't a fuck of a lot . . . Sorry, wasn't very much of the place left, and the old man was already going see-nile. Anzhemers or whatever you call it, the thing Reagan got.'

'Alzheimer's,' Rachel supplied.

'Yeah, like that,' Wally nodded.

'So you tore the place down?'

'It was going to fall down anyway. Kept the property. I was a cook in the army. Opened up this place. Does good in the summers, like now. Kids, tourists sometimes. Cottage people going to the lakes. Winters me and Ronny stay in Key West. Got a camper van, you know?'

*Burgers and fries pays for all of that?*

'You going to expand?' asked Rachel. 'Turn Wallyburger into a real restaurant.' She glanced around. 'Lots of room.'

Wally took another swig of coffee, dragged on his cigarette, then flicked the butt away. 'Naw. Too much work.'

'So which old folk's home did you put your father-in-law into?'

Wally Kapelka frowned. 'How come you're asking so many questions about Chester?'

'I told you, it's for an article. A then and now story.'

'Yeah.' He nodded, remembering. 'You said.'

'Which old folk's home?'

'There's not but one. Beechwood. The old taberkellar place by the cemetery.'

'Thanks,' said Rachel she stood up.

'Didn't drink your coffee.'

'Wasn't thirsty.'

'Shouldn't litter,' he grumbled.

'I won't,' said Rachel. She picked up her cup, took

it over to one of the trash barrels and tossed it in.

'Like I said, fries'll be ready in about an hour.'

'Maybe I'll come back,' said Rachel.

*And maybe not.*

She climbed into the Golf and drove away.

Rachel drove on for a quarter mile, stopped to pick a bouquet of wildflowers from beside the road, then made her way back along the route she'd followed to Oneida College the day before. At the cemetery she turned left instead of right and half a mile later she reached Beechwood, a gigantic, turreted, gone-to-seed Victorian pile that looked like a cross between the Addams Family mansion and a clapboard Versailles. The grounds seemed well kept, with nicely manicured lawns and a lot of colorful flowerbeds. A dozen or so residents were arrayed, blanket-tucked into wheelchairs, on the wide front porch while an ancient, almost bald woman with a walker stood by the front doors, eyeing Rachel as she came up the stairs, flowers in hand.

Rachel smiled as she walked by and the woman's blue eyes flared for an instant.

'I only *look* old,' she whispered fiercely. Then she stumped away along the porch to join her wheelchair-bound companions.

Inside the main doors there was a circular information desk that looked completely out of place in the old-fashioned foyer. Rachel approached the receptionist, who was wearing a white, starched nurse's cap and uniform.

'Yes?'

'I'd like to see Chester Miggs.'

The woman banged a few keys on the computer in front of her, then looked up at Rachel suspiciously.

'Relative?'

'Yes.'

'Name?'

'Kapelka,' Rachel answered. The woman checked the computer again, nodded, and then passed Rachel a clipboard.

'Sigh here.' Rachel did as she was told and the receptionist gave Rachel a room number on the second floor. She thanked the woman and went up the broad, double staircase. Both sides of it were fitted with stair escalator platforms big enough for a wheelchair and on a table on the landing there was a large, cheerful bouquet of flowers arranged in a glass vase. Brockhurst had smelled of cleaning solvent, piss and vomit. Beechwood smelled of freshly waxed floors and roses.

*Expensive.*

She thought about Wally and his French-fry truck again.

No way. Unless Chester Miggs had his own rich uncle stashed away somewhere, there was definitely something out of whack. She found the right room and knocked. There was no answer, so she knocked again, then turned the handle. She stepped into the room, her eyes slowly adjusting to the dim light.

The room was on the small side, furnished with an adjustable bed, bedside table with a telephone, dresser and a straight chair by the bed as well as an upholstered chair set by the window. A roller blind had been pulled down, but the window itself was open, letting in a pleasant breeze, the plastic ring from the blind tapping lightly on the windowsill as the soft wind moved the shade back and forth.

The bed was crisply made with military corners, and Chester Miggs was in it, his shrivelled face like a mummy's head against the white linen of the pillowcase. Rachel put the bouquet down on the bedside table and sat down in the straight chair. There was a line of drool coming out of the corner of Chester Miggs' mouth. From the looks of it, he didn't have any teeth. Rachel leaned forward and pulled the drawer of the bedside table. There was a package of tissues inside. She took one, then wiped away the drool. Chester Miggs showed no response at all. His eyes were closed and the only sign that he was alive was the faint movement of his chest beneath the blanket.

'So why did you lie?' she said quietly, looking down at the empty, human shell. Miggs had been mostly bald when she'd had her run in with him all those years ago, and now his skull was completely smooth except for a scattering of pale, shapeless liver spots. The skin on his face was drawn over the bones of his skull like oiled parchment and there was only the faintest trace of whitish stubble on his narrow chin. Even though the room was being refreshed by the breeze from the window there was a sour smell around the bed that nothing could remove. Not the smell of death, but the pale odors of slow dying. She'd come here on the faint chance that Miggs would have something to say, perhaps even recognize her, but that was obviously out of the question. She was dialing, but Chester Miggs wasn't home to answer the phone.

She glanced at the telephone on the bedside table. It was like an old-fashioned hotel phone, with a rotary dial, a message light and a sliding number tray on the bottom. Rachel pulled out the tray and checked to see what numbers had been written on it. There were two. She managed to get an outside line and dialed the first. It rang six times and then a tired woman's voice answered.

'Yes?'

Rachel hung up. She was willing to bet that the voice belonged to Ronny Kapelka, née Miggs, Chester's daughter. She dialed the second number. It was picked up on the first ring.

'Farmers' Union. Trust Office. Andy Clark.'

*A bank?*

Rachel hesitated for a second time, then decided to go with it.

*Make her bright-eyed, bouncy, blonde and brainless. About nineteen.*

'Hi? This is Shelley Willenbrink at Beechwood?'

'Yes.'

'Uh, I'm in accounts and I've got a problem with one of our patients? Regarding billing for extra services?'

'Which patient?'

102

'Uh, Chester Miggs?'

There was a pause. 'We handle his affairs, yes.' Another pause. 'Exactly what seems to be the problem?'

'Whoops!' said Rachel. 'Little computer screw-up. Solved it myself! Sorry to bother you!' She hung up a second time. Miggs was drooling again, but this time Rachel let him. What the hell was Chester Miggs doing having his affairs managed by a bank trust?

Miggs' daughter, Ronny, really did live on the wrong side of the tracks, in this case the defunct B&O rails that led to the old Prosper Creek Dairy siding, in what was known locally as Mechanicsville. Rachel had a vague memory of driving through the area after leaving Miggs' store all those years ago – a wasteland of weedy front yards, cars up on concrete blocks and tiny houses that were only one step up from the Tom Joad tarpaper shacks of *The Grapes of Wrath*.

Stopping at a phone booth on the way back into town from Beechwood, Rachel had looked up Kapelka's name and number in the Prosper telephone directory. She tried to call first, but after a dozen rings she was informed by a mechanical voice that the number she was dialing was not in service. It sounded like Wally and Ronny weren't too hot at paying their bills on time. Rachel scribbled down the address and drove there, using the 'official' Barney's a Bear streetmap of Prosper that had come with the car, courtesy of Barney himself.

The house was like all the others around it, a

cream-colored clapboard box with a tarred roof and two windows looking out on to a front yard that looked like a dozen oil pans had been flushed out on to the hard-packed earth. There were no sidewalks – just a ditch on either side of the potholed street. No one had ever bothered to bring cable TV out in this direction and every house except the Kapelkas' had a big, old-fashioned rake-style antenna. Instead they had a huge, tilted satellite dish. The reasonably late model RV parked to the right of the Kapelkas' front door was half the size of the house itself and looked as out of place as the TV dish in a tired looking community that tended more toward twenty-year-old pick-up trucks than it did Winnebagos.

Rachel parked the Golf and walked across the oily yard to the front door. The woman who answered was the ectomorphic version of her outsized husband. She could easily have been Eileen Wax's scrawny daughter, complete with ropy neck, skinny arms and an invisible body wrapped up in a stained housecoat with an applique clown face on its big patch pocket. Answering the door, she had a cigarette in one hand and a can of Coke in the other. Her dark hair was tied up in what appeared to be a kitchen J-cloth. Over the woman's shoulder Rachel could see into the gloomy living room. There was a leather couch, two Barcaloungers and a big-screen TV showing *Jeopardy*.

'Yeah?'

'Mrs Kapelka?'

'Yeah?' There was a siren sound from the

television. Ronny Kapelka glanced over her shoulder, then back at Rachel, annoyed that she was missing 'Final Jeopardy'.

'My name is Smith,' said Rachel. 'From Farmers' Union Bank?' She smiled. 'Apparently your telephone is out of order.'

'Yeah.'

'I'm Andy Clark's assistant.'

'The trust guy.'

'That's right.'

'So? There's some problem or something?'

'No problem. Just some pesky paperwork.'

*Pesky? Jesus!*

'Oh yeah? Like what?'

'We'd like to check the original trust documents if that would be possible.'

'Don't you got copies?'

'Just on computer, we need the actual trust filing date. You know, the rubber stamp they put on it in Albany?' Rachel had no idea what she was talking about, but she doubted that Ronny Kapelka did either.

'Oh yeah?'

'Yes.'

*Big smile now.*

'So, you want to see them?'

'If that would be convenient.'

'Yeah, I guess. Come on in. I'll get the stuff.' She moved aside and Rachel stepped over the sill. The carpet on the floor was thin and gray. The walls were painted the same color as the outside of the house and there wasn't a single piece of artwork to be seen and no books anywhere. There wasn't even a magazine or a newspaper on the coffee table between the two Barcaloungers. Instead, there was a large plastic bowl half-filled with what looked like a mixture of caramel popcorn and pretzels. She could see that the far chair had a huge dip in the seat, crushed to one side; Wally's throne no doubt. 'You want a Coke or something?' asked Ronny. She was standing in the middle of the room, one eye on Rachel, the other on the television. Alex Trebeck was signing off. Rachel blinked, aware again of the hole in her life – the last time she'd seen Alex Trebeck he was hosting a Canadian kids' quiz show that you could get in Buffalo if you had a big enough antenna on your roof.

'No thanks,' said Rachel.

'It's no trouble,' Ronny insisted.

Rachel wondered if Ronny got very many visitors. Or any at all.

'No, really.'

'Whatever.'

Ronny vanished and Rachel stood on the edge of the living room, watching as the credits rolled up on the big-screen TV. Out of the gloom Rachel could now make out a large entertainment center to one side of the TV: stereo, VCR, cassette deck and multi-disc CD player.

The woman came back carrying a legal-sized manila envelope. She handed it to Rachel. The Farmers' Union name and logo was printed, dark green, in one corner. A pseudo wood engraving of a farmer in silhouette tying up a sheaf of wheat. There were two entwined letters on the sheaf of wheat: F-U. Rachel wondered if anyone had ever picked up on it. Every kid at Woodrow Wilson High since time began, no doubt.

Rachel slid the documents half out of the envelope then looked up at Ronny Kapelka.

'Maybe it would be easier if I just took these back to the bank with me and had them photocopied. I could have them back to you by tomorrow.' Rachel put on a small frown and pout of worry. 'Unless you think your husband would mind.'

'Screw him,' said Ronny Kapelka. 'The trust was set up for my father, not him.' She jerked her chin toward the envelope. 'Be my guest.'

'Thank you,' said Rachel. She held out her hand. Ronny Kapelka shook it.

'No sweat.' Rachel could feel the bones in the woman's fingers. The hand was dry and lifeless.

'I'll be sure to put them in the mail first thing tomorrow,' Rachel promised.

'Whatever,' said Ronny. Rachel heard the theme music for *Gilligan's Island* and both she and Ronny turned toward the screen. Suddenly Rachel found herself staring at Bob Denver, who was staring back, framed by a life preserver from the SS *Minnow*.

'He's wearing a red sweater,' said Rachel, stunned.

'Yeah? So?'

'I never knew it was red,' she answered, realizing her mistake. She'd watched it as a child and it had never occurred to her that the show had been shot in color.

'I guess you don't watch much TV,' said Ronny Kapelka.

'No,' said Rachel. She put on her best smile again and held up the envelope. 'Thanks for your cooperation.'

'Sure,' said Ronny. She settled down into her Barcalounger, eyes on the big screen, one hand reaching blindly for the snack bowl beside her. Rachel opened the door and left the woman with the castaways and the caramel popcorn. Ten minutes later she was back at her rooming house, checking through the trust documents from the Farmers' Union bank. It took her a little while to sort through the cross-indexed numbers and the legalese, but she eventually put together a reasonably accurate chronology of events.

In 1974, not quite a month after the murder of Rachel's daughter, a trust agreement had been drawn up between Chester Andrew Miggs and the Farmers' Union Bank, the bank itself acting on behalf of an unnamed trustee while the law firm of Scales, Bowles, Pixley & Ross was acting for two others. The trust agreement provided that the mortgage on a property described within the trust documents, and which, from the description, was referring to Miggs' store, was to be paid in full by the Farmers' Union Bank and that a further $1,000 dollars per month was to be deposited in an account of Chester Miggs' choice for the duration of his life. From the looks of things

Chester Miggs hadn't done much with the money and, eighteen years later, in 1992, compound interest had turned the monthly stipend into a healthy wad of cash. In the middle of that year it appeared that the trust account had been taken over by one Veronica Miggs Kapelka, daughter and only surviving relative of Chester Miggs, and Ms Kapelka's spouse, Walter Lance Kapelka. From that point on large amounts had been taken out of the trust account, including a regular, monthly automatic withdrawal to Beechwood Home Adult Care Corporation, a 'proprietary facility' duly registered with and licensed by the New York State Bureau of Long Term Care Facilities in Albany. The chief administrator of the Beechwood Home was none other than Dr Amos W. Alberoni.

In other words, Chester Miggs had been bought off by one or more people, and bought off handsomely. Rachel knew that the trust might have been set up for some other reason, but the conjunction of the dates was too much to be a coincidence as was the fact that Miggs eventually wound up in an old folk's home operated by Alberoni, almost certainly one of the original people involved in the cover-up. Even after all this time there was no doubt in her mind that Alberoni had kept her drugged until she reached Brockhurst, obviously on the orders of the other people involved. But why?

Rachel looked up from the trust documents, lit a cigarette and went over to the window seat overlooking the street below. It was a question that had haunted her through all the shadow years she spent being out of her mind in the corridors and cells of Brockhurst and all the other places she'd come to know. Why?

George Skelton, the Chief of Police and Robby Skelton's father, had an obvious reason for covering up – his own son's involvement. But how had Robby's father put his conspiracy together so quickly and so completely? How did he convince Alberoni to drug her? Who were the members of the trust that was still paying for Miggs' silence, even though his brain had clearly dissolved into the barely sentient Swiss cheese of a late-stage Alzheimer's sufferer?

Within hours of Lauren's murder by Robby Skelton and his three anonymous companions the lid had been slammed down and locked tight. More than two decades tight, which was a miracle as far as conspiracies went; Nixon's Watergate cover-up hadn't even lasted a year. It was also clear from the documents that someone at the bank knew what was going on, or they wouldn't have acted for their unnamed trustee, and it stood to reason that at least one of the lawyers mentioned in the trust also knew the score. Would so many people be so willing to condone wilful murder, even if it involved their own children?

Rachel stubbed out her cigarette. There was only one way to find out.

*Keep digging.*

# CHAPTER EIGHT

The days were gone when a county DA or a local town cop could reach out and arrest someone quickly on the slim and entirely circumstantial evidence Wren had on the Vietnam veteran, Allan Sloane. Except for the fact that he had been Alberoni's last patient on the eve of the doctor's death there was nothing in particular to connect him to the murder.

After a long conversation with D'Arcy Quinn at the crime scene it was decided not to go forward with an actual arrest, since at this stage of the game there was the strong possibility that it would be returned No True Bill if presented to a Grand Jury for indictment. Instead, the District Attorney suggested getting a search warrant for Sloane's premises in the hope that some new evidence connecting him to the case would be discovered. The bureaucracy relating to getting such a warrant took the rest of the morning and it wasn't until early afternoon that Wren and Kenny Spearing drove out to Sloane's cabin in the woods.

'I don't think I've ever been up this way,' said Wren, glancing at his young partner, seated at the wheel of the cruiser. They'd turned off the main highway a mile out of Prosper and were now heading north into the mountains.

'Old Highway 3,' Spearing answered, keeping his eyes on the narrow strip of asphalt. 'Used to get you to Spencerville if you knew what you were doing.'

'Why does Sloane live out here?'

Kenny Spearing shrugged his shoulders. 'I think his dad had some land up here. Good fishing in Vly Creek and the Big Red Kill. I think he tied his own flies or something like that.'

'Sloane?'

'His old man. He was a dentist.' Spearing turned to Wren and flashed his front teeth. 'Screwed braces into my face when I was twelve and unscrewed them two years later. Made me the great lover I am today.'

'Spare me,' Wren snorted. 'Anything else up here?'

'Just the old commune. I was too young to hang around up there in the sixties but my older brother Dwayne did.'

'I didn't know you had an older brother.'

'I don't.'

'And I don't get it.'

'He died in 'Nam. Gia Lai. Seventy-five miles north of Da Nang. 101st Airborne.' It was a rote-learned litany, a mantra he knew by heart.

'I'm sorry.'

Spearing shrugged. 'Long, long time ago.'

'Did your brother know Sloane?'

'Yeah, I think so,' Spearing nodded. 'They were on the same basketball team or something.' The younger man turned the cruiser down a barely visible notch between the trees that resolved itself into a narrow gravel road. Small stones rattled against the wheel wells and brown, sun-dried cedar boughs smacked and whispered against the cruiser's flanks. Wren could hear the high-pitched heat-drawn drum of a cicada. Spearing heard it too. 'I used to think there was something wrong with my ears when I heard one of those,' he grinned.

Wren smiled. 'Some things are universal. My dad used to tell me it was the sound telephone wires made when they got hot in the summer.' He shook his head at the memory. It suddenly occurred to him that his father had made up the story about the overheated wires because he really hadn't known what caused the sound. He lit a cigarette and glanced out into the dense bush. He hadn't thought about his father in years and for some reason that bothered him.

The brush ended abruptly and they found themselves driving into a large clearing that sloped down to a curving, rock-strewn creek a hundred or so yards away. Sloane's cabin was perched with its back door in the trees and its front deck overlooking the creek. The cabin was a simple A-frame that looked as though it had been cobbled together from the remnants of a dozen other houses. It was obviously well built though, and tidily put together.

'I was expecting something different,' said Wren.

'Yeah,' Spearing nodded, pulling the cruiser to a stop. 'Like man-traps and foxholes and a perimeter strung with razor wire.'

Wren nodded. 'Something like that.' He climbed out of the car and stood with the open door between him and the cabin.

'Nobody home,' said Spearing, slamming the driver's side door shut.

'How can you tell?'

'He drives an old beat-up Bronco. Seen it in town often enough. Painted with orange rustproofing paint. Can't miss it and it's not here.' He pointed to a sloping piece of green corrugated fiberglass attached to one side of the A-frame to create a makeshift carport. The area under the plastic canopy was empty. Wren and Spearing began walking across the clearing to the house.

'What does he do?' asked Wren.

'What do you mean?' said his partner.

'For a living.'

'Nothing as far as I know. Disability pension maybe.'

They climbed up on to the deck. Wren went to the tall windows beside the door but the slats of the Venetian blinds were angled too far down for him to make out anything inside the cabin. Spearing went to the door and tried the knob. It turned under his hand.

'Not locked,' he said, turning to Wren. 'What do we do?'

'We've got a warrant,' said Wren. 'We go inside.'

Spearing stood aside and let his older partner go into the cabin first. Wren stepped across the doorsill, one hand on the 9mm handgun holstered on his hip.

The whole place was filled with the smell of cedar and the sweet, rich odors of linseed oil and turpentine. Wren went to the front windows, turned the wand on the Venetian blinds and let in the sun. He looked around.

There were two main rooms on the first floor, separated by a free-standing filed-stone fireplace and a galley kitchen. The front room was large, airy and without furniture except for a pair of wooden armchairs beside the fireplace and a massive Victorian sideboard against one wall that looked completely out of place. On the left a rickety looking wrought-iron spiral staircase led up to a second-floor sleeping loft. Wren walked around the fireplace and bypassed the kitchen area. The back room was an artist's studio, complete with easel, a wheeled taboret loaded down with brushes upended in tin cans, an industrial-looking flat storage cabinet that appeared to have been designed for architectural blueprints, and shelves loaded down with more brushes, paints and other artist's materials. This room was the origin of the linseed oil and turpentine smells. Wren went back to the main room. Spearing was checking out the framed artwork on the walls.

'Weird,' he said. Wren joined him and moved slowly along the gallery of foot-square watercolors and pen and ink drawings. The watercolors, dozens of them, were all botanicals, each one titled neatly in pencil and signed 'a.S.' and dated: 'Cramp Bark', 'Black Haw', 'Sweet Violet', 'Queen's Delight'.

'He's very good,' said Wren, impressed. He moved

on toward the pen and inks and saw immediately that they were updated versions of William Blake's illustrations for *The Divine Comedy* done in a sixties, psychedelic style: 'The Primeval Giants Sunk in the Soil', 'The Punishment of the Thieves', 'The Wood of the Self-Murderers'. There were at least fifty of the drawings hung around the room.

'Is this guy nuts or what?' asked Spearing. He was standing in front of Sloane's drawing of 'Satan, Sin and Death'. Flames writhing behind a naked Satan brandishing a spear and carrying a shield, Sin as a woman with twisting serpents instead of lower limbs and Death, hair on fire, a ghostly, dark figure, crowned and brandishing a spear like Satan's. The work was disturbing, certainly, but it was also brilliantly executed. Wren wondered if the insanity of the image was Blake's from almost two hundreds years ago, or Sloane's own madness. Either way, Sloane was a talented individual. With a talent for murder?

'Hey, look at these,' said Spearing. He was pointing to a quartet of framed eight-by-ten photographs hanging on the wall beside the fireplace. Once again, each of the four pictures were neatly titled: 'Raymond Chrysler – Firebase Cherokee': a bleak-looking man of nineteen or twenty, seated beside a rudely made camp stove with the truncated hands and legs of three or four other people behind him. 'Jack – Roung-Roung Valley': a skinny, bespectacled boy out of focus in a T-shirt and fatigues, standing alone in a barren, muddy landscape holding something that looked like a dead snake. 'FDC Bunker – Firebase Hopalong': a rectangular pile of sandbags on the edge of a razor-wire perimeter. 'Hopalong – 19 July': the same bunker, but this time with seven M1 carbines, bayonets jammed into the hard-packed earth, each carbine capped by a helmet, a pair of combat boots below.

'How old is Sloane?' asked Wren, frowning.

'Sloane is forty-one,' said a voice behind him. Wren turned. 'And just who the fuck are you and what are you doing in my house?' The voice belonged to a tallish man with sun-whitened strawberry blond hair tied back in a long ponytail. He wore wire-framed glasses, a pale-green army T-shirt and fatigue pants. He was carrying an armload of groceries.

'My name's Detective Sergeant Wren. Prosper Police Department.' He nodded toward Spearing. 'This is my partner, Detective Spearing.'

'That answers half my question,' Sloane nodded. He walked past Wren and dumped the bag of groceries on the counter of the kitchen pass-through. He turned. 'So answer the other half. Why are you here?'

'You went to see Dr Alberoni last night.' It was a statement, not a question.

'That's a crime?'

'If you stuck a knife into his chest it is,' said Wren. 'Did you stick a knife into Dr Alberoni for some reason, Mr Sloane?'

'No.' Sloane's face had gone hard. No emotion, no expression, no anxiety, no surprise. Nothing.

'You were his last patient.'

117

'So?'

'What time did you leave his office?'

'I have no idea.'

'Roughly.'

'I have no idea.'

'Was it still light?'

'Yes.'

'Which would make it before about eight thirty or so.'

'If you say so.'

'Why did you go to Dr Alberoni in the first place? You sick?'

'That's none of your business.'

'The doctor was murdered, Mr Sloane. You were his last patient. How come you won't help us out here?'

'What do I get out of the deal?'

'You get to keep your ass out of jail,' said Spearing, stepping forward.

Sloane turned to the younger man, his face still expressionless. 'You're going to arrest me?'

'Not necessarily,' said Wren quickly. 'We'd like to ask you some questions, that's all. To pin things down.'

'What things?'

'Time of death for one,' said Wren. 'If you could tell us when you left his office that would give us a better understanding of when he . . . died.'

'I had an appointment at seven o'clock.'

Wren nodded. That fit with the computer appointment schedule. 'Why so late?'

'It was the only one he had open.'

'Why did you want to see him?'

'I told you, it's none of your business.'

'Okay, we'll pass on that for a minute.'

'Good.'

'Was there anyone else in his office when you were there? The waiting room?'

'No. I told you, I was his last patient.'

'How about when you came in? Did you see anyone leaving?'

'Not that I can remember.'

'So no one saw you go in, and no one saw you go out?'

'I guess not.'

Spearing broke in again. 'So you can't prove what time you left the office, right? No alibi?'

Sloane turned to the younger man again. He nodded. 'That's right.'

*He doesn't seem to care.*

'You were in Vietnam?' Wren asked.

'That's right.'

'When?'

'That's none of your business either.'

'I could call the Veterans' Administration and find out.'

'So do it.'

'Why are you being so hostile?'

'Because I value my privacy. You've invaded it.' Sloane put out his wrists, touching them together. 'So either arrest me, or get the fuck off my property.'

'We're going,' said Wren. He nodded to Spearing.

His partner gave Sloane a long, cold look, then brushed past Sloane and went out through the door. He gestured to the watercolors and pen and inks on the wall. 'I like your work,' Wren said, meaning it.

'What does a small-town cop know about art?' said Sloane.

Wren shrugged his big shoulders and smiled. 'I studied Blake in school.'

Finally a twitch of emotion. Curiosity. 'What school is that?'

'The Pratt Institute in Seattle. I took a couple of night courses.' Wren let his smile widen. 'We'll be back,' he said, and stepped out on to the deck, closing the door behind him.

Spearing was standing at the bottom of the steps, smoking a cigarette and looking angry. 'So?' the young detective said.

'I don't think he's our killer,' said Wren.

'He's an asshole,' said Spearing.

'True,' Wren nodded. 'But I still don't think he killed Alberoni.'

They walked back to the car. This time Wren got behind the wheel. Turning the car around he caught a glimpse of Sloane, standing in the doorway, watching them.

Woodrow Wilson High was a classic thirties' institution from the 'glue factory' school of design. It was a massive, three-story yellow-brick rectangle facing out on to Brock Street in the east end of Prosper, squatting at the edge of a two-block-square campus that was entirely taken up by sports facilities including a baseball diamond, four asphalt-surfaced basketball courts, a six-lane oval cinder track and a full-sized football field complete with end-zone bleachers. There were shade maples along the Brock Street side, but the rest of the grounds were baking in the hot sun. Rachel parked the Golf on the street, directly in front of the main entrance to the school. There were some pre-teen kids whacking a softball around the baseball diamond, but other than that the playing fields of Woodrow Wilson High were empty.

Locking up the car, Rachel went up the concrete walkway and climbed four worn granite steps to the wood and glass arched main entrance to the school. She pulled open one of the doors and stepped inside, spinning instantly back in time. It was the smell more than anything; something pine-scented over a mixture of mildewed clothes, sweaty gym clothes and abandoned brown bag lunches in rows of ancient lockers. Over that, the faint waft of male and female sex and anxiety sweat, all of it combining into something that was indefinably 'high school'.

Directly in front of Rachel, across a wide, low-ceilinged hallway was a long, glass-fronted case full of framed sports pictures and trophies in assorted sizes ranging from half-pint cups to massive multi-tiered Everests of gleaming silver plate. A little farther along the case were more pictures and framed plaques, these flanked by matched US flags and a sign made out of tinfoil-covered letters: LEST WE FORGET. The tinfoil looked old. The plaques came in three versions, World War II, Korea and Vietnam. From the rows of names and the sizes of the plaques it looked as though the alumni of Woodrow Wilson had done more than their fair share for God and Country; from the dust it also seemed that, while perhaps not forgotten, they had at least been overlooked.

The school library was next door to the row of glass cases. The front wall was glass, just like the trophy cabinets. It wasn't very big and Rachel wondered if it was a made-over classroom. There were only seven or eight rows of books and a few more in cases around the walls. A small, neatly dressed man wearing a white shirt and a bow-tie was standing behind the librarian's desk. He wore glasses, had a small tight mouth as neat as his bow-tie, and his short back and sides hair was going gray at the temples. Rachel went into the library and approached the librarian. There was a nameplate on the desk: Mr Halloran. No first name, no initial.

*Uptight.*

'Can I help you?' he asked, looking up. The voice was tired; not enough laughter and too many sighs. The eyes behind the glasses were worn out. Mr Halloran looked as though he'd lost something a long time ago, and still hadn't found it. Even from that distance she could smell his sour breath, like the taste of a freshly drilled tooth in your mouth. She took a step backward.

'I was wondering if you had a collection of yearbooks.'

'You're not on staff.'

'No. I'm a magazine writer.'

'This isn't a public library; it's for school use only.'

'I understand that. Part of the story I'm writing involves a group of students from Woodrow Wilson High School.'

*No word of a lie, Mr H.*

The narrow-shouldered man looked at her carefully, his small lips pursing, making his small mouth even smaller. 'Perhaps you should clear this with Mrs Campion.'

'Mrs Campion?'

'The Principal.'

'Can you tell me how to get to her office?'

'It's just across the hall.' Rachel turned to go. The librarian spoke again. 'It won't do any good. She's on holiday. Crete.'

'Knossos?' asked Rachel.

The librarian's eyes widened behind the lenses of his spectacles, surprised at her use of the place name and its correct pronunciation with a hard 'K'. 'You're interested in archaeology?' he asked. There was a faint movement at the corners of his mouth; what passed for a smile.

'Mary Renault used to be a favorite of mine,' said Rachel. Which was true enough. She'd read everything the woman had written by the time she was thirteen. It had never occurred to her up until then that Alexander the Great had been gay, and it certainly hadn't been part of any school curriculum she'd ever come in contact with. It had been her first lesson in how easily the past could be rewritten to suit the present.

'I teach *The Bull From the Sea* to my freshman English class,' said Halloran. 'They seem to enjoy it.' He frowned. 'God knows, it's probably the first and last time they'll ever learn anything about classical history.'

Rachel gave him her widest smile. 'Let alone good popular literature.'

'Quite,' Halloran nodded.

'What do I do about the absent Mrs Campion?' Rachel asked.

Halloran thought about it for a moment. Rachel watched as the man's hands moved across the piles of books layered up on his desk. They were very small, the fingers perfectly manicured. A musician's hands.

'What magazine are you writing your article for?' asked Halloran.

'*Life*,' Rachel responded. 'But that's a bit hush-hush.'

'I understand perfectly,' Halloran nodded, keeping his voice low. He glanced around as though spies were going to scream out warnings from the belltowers that there was a *Life Magazine* writer in town. 'What years would you like?'

'1974,' Rachel answered.

'Any particular reason for choosing that year?'

Rachel shrugged. 'Just about the end of the Vietnam War. Watergate was winding down with the Nixon pardon. It just seemed like a good place to start.'

Halloran nodded, then gestured toward one of four reading tables close to the door. 'Why don't you sit down, Miss . . .?'

'Kane. Rachel Kane.'

'John Halloran.' His lips twitched again. 'I'll fetch you the yearbook.'

He disappeared for a moment, and Rachel sat down, taking a spiral-bound steno notebook and a felt pen out of her bag. Halloran returned carrying a volume bound in burgundy-colored fake leather. There was a silver-embossed decoration on the front that looked like a starburst, and the word 'WILSONIAN' embossed in silver as well. Halloran put the yearbook down in front of Rachel. 'I'll just be over here if you need me,' he said, nodding towards his desk a few yards away.

Rachel nodded and gave him another smile. 'Thanks.' Halloran looked as though he was going to speak again, then thought better of it. He turned away and Rachel opened the yearbook. The first two pages were given over to messages from the Principal and the Vice Principal. The Principal in 1974, a man named Katz spent a paragraph talking about 'Youth and Maturity' while VP, O. Froggett, meandered on for three paragraphs about 'Consideration' in the 'fast-moving, ever-growing world of today', taking his text from the school's Latin motto: '*Omnibus Consulamus*'. Katz looked like a chipmunk and Froggett had giant ears and big lips. She could almost hear the students back then calling them 'Kitty' Katz and 'The Frog'. The next few pages were filled with mug shots of department heads and faculty, then a picture of the Head Boy and the Head Girl, and then an editorial from the yearbook editor, a senior named Steve Gregg. She jotted his name down – yearbook editors were the type who liked to arrange information; if Gregg was still in Prosper he might turn out to be useful.

The graduating seniors came next, each with a small photograph and a brief quote or message. They were arranged by their home-room class designations and it took her a while to find Skelton. Then she spotted him, a one-inch-square picture:

R. Skelton:
'Do tomorrow what you don't feel like doing today.'
Robby's ambition is to lose himself somewhere up north, get into the Marines before the war is over, join the French Foreign Legion or become a plumber. His activities are his truck, ROTC and a girl named Sue.

Rachel stared down at the picture, feeling the hot, sour bile rising in the back of her throat. She swallowed hard and felt a flush of heat rise up across her chest and throat, then up into her face. Years peeled like shedding skin and the face was two feet away, the hard male smell of him.

*'Maybe she wants King Bone. Slip her the snake, Robby, come on!'*

*'Yeah. Let's take her and the retard for a ride.'*

*'Give her a red truck fuck.'*

Then she blinked it all away, feeling her back teeth clamping together and the pain in her jaw as she fought to keep herself from screaming. She focused on the words. A girl named Sue? The girl standing beside the truck in the darkness with the lighter in her hand? Rachel scanned the other pictures and names of the grads.

'Sue Hughes: Ambition, to marry a large bank account. She likes Pete (the guy with the large bank account!)'

Not her.

'Sue Shorkey: Ambition, to get her license and to buy a sharp car.'

But not good looking enough for Robby, not by a long shot.

Sue Brazeau's ambition was to graduate and get a job. Glasses. Not a chance.

Sue LaFrance wanted to pass her bookkeeping course with a C, but she liked someone named Bryan.

Rachel ran out of Sues.

There was a blank spot with a silhouette of a girl in a mortarboard and the name S. Marsden. She decided to take a chance. She made a small throat-clearing sound in Halloran's direction. He looked up.

'Yes?'

'Were you teaching here in 1974?'

'Yes.'

'Do you remember a girl named Sue Marsden?'

Halloran thought for a moment, then nodded. 'Yes, as a matter of fact.' His chair scraped back and he stood, his knuckles tapping thoughtfully on the wooden desktop. 'I think she was in the band that year.'

He came around the desk. Rachel flipped through the yearbook. Concert band: thirty kids on three raised rows of chairs, all wearing dark, military-style uniform jackets with gold piping at the cuffs and lapels. Mr Halloran, baton in hand, standing off to one side. His face was a tired blur behind his glasses. He hadn't changed very much except in the photograph his hair looked darker. Rachel checked the names below the picture. Susan Marsden was in the front row. Even seated she was clearly quite tall with dark, short, shaggy hair and a pretty, knowing face, turned slightly towards the camera, but not playing to it. Robby's type certainly, but definitely not the girl she'd seen that day in Miggs' store. Rachel looked again and saw Robby Skelton in the same row at the other end. He had a trumpet in his hand, resting on his thigh. Too close to his crotch. A private joke for a few of his friends that everyone else missed.

*King Bone.*

A hand came into Rachel's line of sight and a finger jabbed at the picture. Halloran was standing behind her, looking over her shoulder. Too close. She could smell the faintly sour body odor. He'd been wearing the same suit for too long.

'There she is,' said the librarian unnecessarily.

Rachel shifted slightly in her chair. Halloran got the hint. He moved away and sat down at the end of the table. 'You were the bandleader.'

Halloran nodded, his lip-twitch smile appearing again. 'Yes. Music was my first love.' He glanced around the room. 'The school didn't have a librarian, so I volunteered. That was thirty years ago.'

Rachel made a show of looking down at the picture again, then back up at Halloran. 'I see the name Robin Skelton here. Any relation to the Police Chief?'

Halloran's lips twitched downward. 'One and the same, believe it or not.' His brow furrowed. 'He and Sue Marsden were an item back then, now that you mention it.'

Rachel smiled. 'You sound as though you don't approve of the Skelton boy. Which is it, then, or now?'

'Both,' Halloran answered. 'The boy was a bully. And a show-off. He thought he could get away with anything just because his father was the Chief.'

Rachel feigned ignorance. 'His father was Chief of Police as well?'

Down went the lips again. Halloran nodded crisply. 'Perhaps he thinks he's starting some sort of dynasty.'

Rachel looked down at the picture. 'They make a good couple. Susan Marsden was very pretty.'

'Still is,' Halloran nodded.

'She still lives in Prosper?' A potential gold mine of information about Skelton and his friends.

'No. Her sister does. Anne McConnel. Susan comes to visit from time to time. I saw her at her twenty-year reunion a while back. Three children if I remember correctly.'

Rachel smiled. 'You've got a good memory.'

'Sometimes I think that memory is all there is,'

Halloran answered, a strange, lonely expression crossing his face. He stood up, tapped his knuckles twice on the table, and went back to his desk. Rachel jotted down Sue Marsden's name and the name of her sister, then went back to the yearbook.

Robin Skelton was everywhere except the Honor Society and the Student Council: Senior Stage and Lighting Crew, Senior Volleyball, Senior Hockey, Senior Basketball. A candid shot of Skelton with Sue Marsden backed halfway into a locker, Skelton leering into the camera. Robby and Sue necking beside a light-colored VW bug. Rachel saw that most of the candid photographs in the yearbook were credited to a 'J. Weems'. She found him in the group photo for the camera club. Pudgy, smiling and wearing a cardigan. Mr O'Shea, the teacher was wearing a white lab coat. She jotted his name down, then flipped back to the grad pages. There were seventy or eighty photos and names; too many to transcribe. She picked up the yearbook and went over to Halloran's desk.

'Is there any way I could photocopy a few pages of the yearbook?' she asked. Halloran looked up and studied her. The lips twitched down.

'I suppose that would be all right,' he said finally. He stood up and held out his hand for the book. Rachel gave it to him.

'Any pages in particular?'

'The graduating class.'

'Why?' Halloran asked.

'I'd like to get in touch with some of the ones who

are still here, get a feel for what Prosper was like back then. Background for the story.'

'I see,' Halloran nodded. He put the yearbook down. 'We don't need this,' he said. 'Follow me.' He turned his back and, taking a quick breath, Rachel slid the yearbook under her jacket, gripping it with the side of one arm pressed against her side.

Halloran led Rachel out of the library and across the hall to the main administration office. It was empty except for a secretary working away at a word processor. Halloran ignored her and went through a gate in the counter. Rachel followed as Halloran threaded his way around several secretarial desks and headed down a narrow hallway to a small office. He opened the door and stood aside to let Rachel in first.

The office barely rated the name; it was more like a large, well-lit closet. There were a dozen dark green filing cabinets, built-in cubbyholes stacked with various school publications and a large photocopier. Halloran stood in front of the cubby-holes, looking back and forth. Finally he reached up and pulled a newsletter out of a stack in one of the upper shelves. It was pale blue and obviously computer-generated: *Alumni Newsletter*. It was six stapled leaves and the headline on the front page announced: '20th Approaches for Class of '74'. It was dated several years previously.

'That should give you what you're looking for,' said Halloran. Rachel flipped through it quickly – name after name, updating activities and whereabouts.

131

'Thanks.'

'Tell me something?' Halloran asked.

'Shoot.'

'Exactly what kind of article are you writing for *Life Magazine*?'

Rachel had prepared herself for this one, and done the appropriate research in the library back in Buffalo after her release. 'In 1967 the magazine did a special on small-town America. Prosper was one of the towns that was looked at.'

'I remember the issue,' Halloran nodded. 'It was my first year as a teacher. My first year here as a matter of fact.'

'Well, the magazine has decided to do it again,' said Rachel. 'Writers have been sent out to all the towns that were done in 1967 to see how things have changed. The photographers are going to come later and match the shots that were used then to the same locations today as well as the same people.'

'I see,' Halloran nodded. 'I neglected to ask you for credentials.' His grudging cooperation seemed to be fading fast.

'Magazine writers don't have credentials. The best I can do is a driver's license.'

'You have nothing to prove that you're writing an article for *Life*?'

'I've got a letter back at the bed and breakfast authorizing my trip expenses.' She frowned. 'You want me to go and get it for you?'

'No. I suppose not.'

'You seem a bit suspicious.'

'It's my nature,' Halloran answered.

'Well it's not mine,' said Rachel. 'Maybe you should take this back if you're not comfortable with giving it to me.' She pushed the newsletter into Halloran's hands. She couldn't afford to have someone like him spreading his suspicions around town. He gave her a long look, then handed the newsletter back.

'I don't suppose it can do any harm.'

'I don't have to mention your name in the article,' Rachel said. 'You can be as anonymous as you like.'

'Yes, I think I'd prefer that.'

'Then you've got it.' Rachel paused. 'If you'd like to show me the way out of here, I'll be out of your hair for good.'

'Certainly,' Halloran said, bobbing his head. Three minutes later, Rachel was back in the Golf and on her way back to Eileen Wax's rooming house, smiling to herself and breathing a sigh of relief, the stolen yearbook on the seat beside her.

# CHAPTER NINE

'I suppose I shouldn't be telling you all of this,' said Wren. The detective and his rooming-house neighbor were sitting in identical wicker chairs on the front porch of Eileen Wax's, watching the sun go down and sipping after-dinner mugs of coffee. Storm clouds were gathering in big, dark thunderheads against the mountains. 'I don't think the Chamber of Commerce would take too kindly to me discussing a murder investigation with a magazine writer.'

'I work for *Life*,' Rachel grinned. 'Not *True Detective* or *The Inquirer*.' She reached over and patted his hand lightly. 'I know how to keep secrets, believe me.' She withdrew her hand and lit a cigarette. 'You're sure it's not this Vietnam vet you told me about?'

Wren shook his head. 'There's nothing in the evidence that points to him. And he paints William Blake knock-offs and watercolor botanical studies.' Wren shook his head firmly. 'He doesn't fit the profile.'

'Profile?' Rachel asked, confused.

'Pattern,' Wren explained, looking at her oddly. Hadn't she ever heard the phrase, 'fit the profile'?

'Like Hannibal Lecter in *The Silence of the Lambs*.'

'Yeah, right,' nodded Rachel. Wren put on a smile. She'd never heard of Hannibal Lecter either.

*Where the hell has she been living, Mars?*

No, that wasn't right. Men were from Mars, women were from Venus, and the woman sitting beside him was definitely a woman. Wren let his eyes wander slightly. She was wearing black tights, a mini-skirt and a dark blue T-shirt on top. Her biceps were full and sculpted and the muscles of her neck were strongly developed as well. From where he was sitting her belly looked flat as a board. She was the first woman in a long time who'd had him this interested.

'A crime of passion?' Rachel asked. 'Some kind of jealousy thing?'

'Possible, but I doubt it. Alberoni was an old man and the death wound wasn't made in hot blood, I guarantee it. It was a killing stroke. More like an assassination.'

'Which brings you back to your Vietnam vet,' said Rachel. 'Presumably he had the training.'

'But what's the motive?'

'Who knows? Maybe you'll have to dig around and find one.'

*And I want to hear about it when you do.*

Wren changed the subject. 'What about your day?'

Rachel lifted her shoulders. 'Did a little more digging. Checked out the high school for sources.'

'Find anything?'

'Not really. I guess yearbooks are the same wherever you go.'

Wren smiled. 'Nerdy guys with bad haircuts and the prom queen is always a blonde.'

'Pretty much.' She took another drag on her cigarette and glanced at the man on the chair beside her. 'I found out that your boss wasn't terribly well loved at his *alma mater*.'

'Doesn't surprise me,' Wren answered. 'He's not very well loved down on Courthouse Square either.'

'Does it bother you working for someone so much younger than you?'

'Thanks a lot.' Wren grinned, throwing her a look. 'And the answer is no. I don't really work for Skelton. He's the Chief, I'm a detective. He does what Chiefs do, I do what a detective does.'

'The librarian at the school said that his father was the Chief too, once upon a time.'

Wren nodded, sipping his coffee. He put the mug down on the arm of the chair, keeping his forefinger hooked in the handle. 'That's right.'

'Isn't that a little strange?'

'Not really.' Wren paused. 'Do you know anything about how they select Police Chiefs in a place like Prosper?'

'Not a thing.'

'The town council, or the mayor's office, or the county DA puts an ad in a bunch of newspapers soliciting applicants. Most of the people who call or write are nutcases, a few of them are lieutenants or captains from big police forces looking for a place to semi-retire. You don't really get a lot of people who really *want* to be Chief – they've all got their own

137

personal agendas. Skelton was perfect. He was a local, he knew everyone in town, he knew the job, and he had the qualifications.'

'He was a cop?' asked Rachel. It was the first she'd heard of it.

'No.' Wren shook his head. 'He was an MP.'

'Military Police?'

Wren nodded. 'That's right. He did a couple of years at the Presidio in San Francisco and another two at Fort Benning. Came back here and set up a private security service for some of the new companies that opened up. When his father passed away he applied for the job. A shoo-in.'

'Even though nobody liked him.'

'I wouldn't say nobody,' Wren answered.

'Your friend Barney the Bear thought he was a bully, wouldn't let him play on the football team. Halloran, the school librarian called him a bully and a show-off. Said he thought he could get away with anything because his father was Chief of Police.'

*Thought he could get away with murder, and he did.*

'I guess that just about sums it up,' Wren smiled again. 'He gets the uniforms specially tailored in Albany and he had the force re-equipped with half a dozen Land Rover Defenders.' He laughed. 'Maybe it's just a story, but I heard a rumor that he wanted those Hum-Vee things but the city council wouldn't spring for the two hundred grand apiece they cost.'

'How do the other cops treat him?'

'He went to school with half of them. The older

ones know better than to get in his way. They've got
pensions to hang on to.' He grinned. 'I guess it
depends on whether you drive one of the new Land
Rovers, or one of the old cruisers.'

'And you?'

'Like I said, I don't have much to do with him.
He's never stepped on my toes and I keep out of his
way.'

'What if he did step on your toes? Interfered with
an investigation?'

'Is this for your article?' Wren was suddenly wary.
He had the same look on his face as Halloran when
he'd handed Rachel the alumni newsletter.

'Just curious,' said Rachel, holding up her hands.
'No need to get all paranoid on me.'

'It's not paranoia,' Wren answered. 'It's how a small
place like this works. Everyone knows everyone else.
You don't badmouth someone like Skelton too loudly
if you know what's good for you.'

The first big drops of rain were smacking down on
the roof of the porch and Rachel could hear growling
thunder. 'Sounds like he's got quite a lock on things.'

'Like I said, it's how a place like Prosper works.
The people here look after their own.'

*And keep each other's dirty little secrets.*

Michael Parker stood in the bathroom doorway,
drying himself with a large, dark blue towel. 'So how
are you going on the golf course deal?'

'Pretty well,' said District Attorney D'Arcy Quinn.
She rolled over on the bed, propping herself up on

her elbow, watching her cousin. Outside it was almost completely dark and the rain had begun falling in serious quantities. She tried to pull her mind away from the Alberoni killing and back to the business at hand. 'We've given you all the easements, all the paperwork is in place.'

Michael swiped at his armpits with the towel, still standing in the doorway. He was posing of course. Ever since she'd known him, Michael had always been vain about his body. She smiled. With good reason; even in his middle forties he looked magnificent – Tarzan going a little gray, tight, firm and muscular, with a full head of salt and pepper hair and enough testosterone in his system to cut the mustard with her a couple of times a week and still keep his wife Gwen happy and oblivious. Not that it took much. According to Michael all it took was five minutes once a month.

He started towelling his groin, drawing her attention between his legs. Her smile broadened. She wouldn't be surprised if he'd spent a few minutes working himself into semi-turgidness before stepping out of the shower, just so he'd have something to display. Which was ridiculous, of course, given the length of time they'd known each other.

Michael padded across the room and sat down on the edge of the bed, ruffling the towel through his hair. D'Arcy reached out with one hand and traced the hills and valleys of the muscles in his shoulder and side. Brown as a nut, thanks to his personal training machine in the workout room of that monster house of his across the river in Federal Heights.

'You're sure we're not going to be disturbed?' D'Arcy asked.

'Gwen and half a dozen of her stupid fucking drama society friends are in New York seeing *Showboat*. Again. The kids are with a sitter. It's almost nine thirty. It's raining cats and dogs,' Michael answered. He nodded toward the rain-streaked window at the far end of the master bedroom. 'Who looks at houses in the middle of the night in the middle of a thunderstorm?'

'I guess you're right.' She pinched a tiny ridge of flesh on his hip. 'I could always cry rape if someone walked in on us.'

'You think anyone would believe you?' Michael grinned. He dropped the towel on to the floor, then laid the flat of his palm across her belly, moving it slowly downward, pressing hard, but not quite hard enough to qualify as pain.

'Statutory rape.' She drew in her breath as he rolled his hand and slid the pad of his thumb between her legs and then inside her. 'How old was I the first time we did this? Twelve, thirteen?'

'Something like that,' said Michael. He began moving the thumb in a slow, circular motion and her thighs drifted open to accommodate him. She wasn't thinking about Alberoni any more. 'And you were the one who tip-toed into my bedroom if I recall. You wanted it as much as I did.' He pushed in deeper, the ball of his thumb pressing hard against her. She

141

brought her hips up into his hand, grinding softly, her movements a mirror to his own.

'Doesn't matter,' said D'Arcy, her breath turning ragged. She moved her hand across his thigh, trying to reach him. He shifted slightly, moving up the bed and she gripped him hard. 'I was too young to make the judgment. No informed consent from a minor child. I could make a case for rape. These days I'd probably get farther on a sexual abuse charge.'

'Christ!' said Michael, 'Don't you ever stop being a lawyer?'

'Only when I think about being Governor,' she said, pulling him forward. As usual he entered her in a rush and began to move. He never lasted very long, but that was okay; about all she had time for these days was a premature ejaculator.

Chief of Police Robin Skelton peered through the rain-smeared windshield of the unmarked police car. A hundred yards away, at the far end of the half-completed, muddy road through the brand new development, he could see the blazing upstairs lights in the display home. Michael Parker was tearing off a piece on company time again. The real estate developers' Mercedes was discreetly hidden away in the attached garage, but D'Arcy's silver-gray Porsche Carrera was clearly visible in the driveway. Skelton shook his head. You think she'd know better by now. He grinned broadly. She'd had hot pants since high school, and if any one thing was going to keep her out of Albany it was going to be that.

He rolled down his window, then picked up the Sharp Hi-8 video camera from the seat beside him and zoomed in on D'Arcy's license plate. It was getting dark now, and the rain made it darker still, but the little palmcorder worked on almost no light at all. He kept the plate in focus, then zoomed out slowly, panning across to the brass numbers on the front door of the house. Finally he zoomed out even farther, pausing to record the large sign on the freshly sodded front lawn: 'Glen Eden Place – The Future is Now with Parker-Welles Developments.'

Satisfied, Skelton rolled up the window, put down the camera and took out the thick spiral notebook he carried with him everywhere. The time and date would appear on the videotape he'd just recorded, but he liked to have a written record as well, especially when it involved the scandalous, adulterous and legally incestuous behavior of the Chancellor of Oneida College and the President of the Farmers' Union Bank, one of Prosper's leading citizens, consorting with his first cousin, Prosper County's District Attorney and potentially a gubernatorial candidate for the State of New York.

His work completed, the police chief swung the car around and drove out of the high-priced housing project nestled in the trees just off Route 25. Reaching the highway he turned toward the town. Nothing like having a little hi-tech insurance policy, just in case, especially now that Alberoni was gone.

Rachel sat at the small writing desk in her room,

going over the alumni newsletter by the light of the desk's old-fashioned gooseneck lamp, checking off names by using the Prosper telephone book as a cross index. There were thirty-eight names mentioned in the newsletter, and of those sixteen still lived in town. One of them was Jerry Weems, the high school photography nut who, not surprisingly, now ran a store called the Lens and Shutter on State Street. Of all the names, his was probably going to be the most useful. She'd gone through the stolen yearbook half a dozen times, but except for Skelton she didn't recognize anyone.

Yawning, Rachel lit a cigarette, got up and went to the window seat. The thunder was fading into the distance and the rain was beating down steadily now, thumping and banging on the roof, rattling on the sheet metal eaves and tapping against the glass of her window. At Brockhurst she'd loved the rain best of all, because somehow all those sounds combined to make her feel safe, binding her up in a soft cocoon, insulating her from all the surrounding terrors.

She dragged on the cigarette and stared blankly out into the rain-filled night, assailed by every lonely thought she'd ever had, willing herself to believe that somehow, what she was doing now would lay all those memories to rest, all the what-ifs and might-have-beens. All the possibilities and potential. The love she'd lost and the hate she'd gained instead, hauling it down through all these years like the chains of ledgers bound to Jacob Marley's ghost in Dickens' *A Christmas Carol*.

Rachel could feel the tears welling up in her eyes and the familiar tightening of her throat. In Brockhurst she'd lived with madness beyond imagining, but after her release she'd discovered that there was something even worse – a feeling of overwhelming sadness and despair that was with her constantly and that sometimes set her weeping at the slightest provocation. At first she'd thought it was sadness for Lauren, dead and gone now for so very long, still so very strong in her heart, but as time went on she realized that who she wept for was not her daughter, but herself, and the lost life she'd never had, and never would.

From the room next door Rachel could hear Wren moving around again and listened to the small metal sound of coat-hangers sliding on a closet bar. The walls between the rooms were that thin. A few seconds later she heard the sagging sounds of bedsprings and then the sharp click of his bedside lamp. She knew it was that lamp because the lamp bedside her own bed made exactly the same noise. Wren was lying in bed, in the dark, listening to the rain.

Rachel stubbed out her cigarette, then gently pressed her index finger against her lips. Still soft, still warm and sitting there she felt the sadness well up again and tried not to think about the fact that no man had kissed her or touched her out of love in more than twenty years.

*How long has it been since you kissed a woman, Detective Wren?*

But she knew that Wren wasn't thinking about that, or anything close to it; Wren was lying in the dark and listening to the rain and thinking about the person who'd used a single knife stroke to snuff out the life of Dr Amos Alberoni, one of the citizens of Prosper who had been instrumental in the theft of half her life more than twenty years ago.

*He's thinking about murder, not about me.*

And she wept, silently.

# CHAPTER TEN

Robin Skelton awoke to the first glimmer of dawn light bleeding weakly between the slats of the Venetian blind on his bedroom window. He briefly considered having intercourse with his wife, Amanda, but rolling over, he saw that the other bed was empty and then he remembered that she was down in Florida with their son, Eric. Two weeks of peace and quiet and he had other ways to get his rocks off than his wife. He grinned. Fuck her, so to speak.

He yawned, swinging his legs off the bed. Being married to a Parker wasn't all it was cracked up to be. Most of the time Amanda was drunk and when she wasn't sloshed and showing her ass cheeks to the tennis pro out at the club she was bitching about having married 'beneath her station'. He picked up his father's old Hamilton *Clark* from the bedside table and strapped it on. The watch was small and rectangular, dating back to the thirties.

His old man had given it to him when he graduated high school. It was the kind of sentimental crap his wife adored and Skelton loathed.

He dressed then went downstairs to the kitchen

and made himself a cup of instant coffee. He stood at the sink, staring out into his back yard, watching the early mist rise and swirl through the line of maples that separated his house from the one behind it.

The house was the one he'd grown up in, a two-story *Leave it to Beaver* house in a *Leave it to Beaver* neighborhood on the eastern edge of the business district called Overbrook, where Carteret Street fanned into a 1950s grid of streets all named after trees with the exception of the ones named after various members of his wife's family: Parker Drive, Hamilton Avenue, Bonnie Lane, Amanda Street. Once upon a time there had actually been a brook and a small bridge over it, but both had vanished when Amanda's father began developing the area.

Amanda had been appalled at the thought of living in Overbrook, but Skelton had insisted that they move into his father's house, vaguely promising that they'd move to her preferred location on the Bridle Path, once the 'dust had settled', whatever that meant. The truth was, he wanted to keep to his own turf; at one time or another during his career as a high-school quarterback he'd screwed half the cheerleading squad at parties on the Bridle Path and the Crescent, but the thought of living there made him uncomfortable. Better to keep his booze-sodden wife down among the real people and out of the way of the Parker-Quinn ménage. It also wouldn't look good if the Chief of Police looked too prosperous.

He took a last sip of coffee, then tipped the dregs

into the sink. Who was he trying to kid? He didn't live on the Bridle Path because he hated the whole pretentious, egotistical lot of them. He'd spent his adolescence screwing their daughters, and in the end he'd even married one, just to even the score a little. He rinsed out his cup, then let himself out of the house, carefully making sure that the screen door didn't slam. It was damp and cool and he hunched his shoulders against the chill.

He climbed into the Land Rover, backed down the driveway and turned out on to Lauren Street. The mist was still rising in ragged strips and the pavement was wet with it, hissing softly under the wheels of Skelton's vehicle. He turned on to Oak, then Pine, then Cherry Blossom Drive, and finally found his way out of the maze, turning west on to Carteret, heading downtown.

Skelton loved this time of day; not for the peace and quiet, but for the sense of ownership it gave him. When they were empty, these were his streets, his houses, his trees and sidewalks. At dawn, with all the drapes drawn and the signs on store windows saying Closed, Please Call Again, this was his playing field. Not Little League or basketball, or football any more though; now it was Monopoly, and the stakes were much higher than a trophy in the display case in front of the Principal's office.

He stopped at the intersection of Carteret and Kennikill, waiting for the light to change, even though there wasn't another car in sight. You never knew who might be watching, even at this hour.

Glancing to his right he saw the big black and white sign in front of the Glades and thought about Alberoni. He frowned. Just like his old man had told him – old wounds bleed the most.

The light changed and he continued on towards Madison Street and Courthouse Square. The mist was almost completely gone and he spotted the Baxter kid with his fat-tired bike, delivering plastic-wrapped copies of *USA Today*. The kid waved and Skelton hit the switch operating the wig-wags hidden in the front grille. Baxter's old man was Chief of the Prosper VFD and the kid wanted to grow up and be a cop on the Prosper force. Skelton smiled again, then laughed out loud. There were worse things to be in a small town. After all, he'd done pretty well for himself, hadn't he?

Instead of parking in his private spot at the rear of the old building on Courthouse Square, he parked in front and went through the main door into the lobby. He nodded to the duty clerk at the information desk, then went up to the second-floor Operations and Communications Center and got a copy of the shift sheet from the Night Commander. A break-in at the Cheesery on Water Street, two domestic violence calls into Mechanicsville, a false-alarm burglar in Federal Heights and a beer bust at a party in his own neighborhood. Just about right for a mid-week night this time of year. At least there were no murders.

He looked up from the shift sheet and glanced around the brightly lit room. The OpCom was his pride and joy, a step beyond state-of-the-art command center complete with a huge, backlit status map of the whole town, a large multi-head log recorder for incoming police emergency, medical and fire calls, a computer providing a direct link to the contract alarms systems, most of them installed in Federal Heights and on the Bridle Path, radio monitors, a panel showing county building fire and entry alarm status and a vehicle monitoring system linking every car in the Prosper Police Department to a satellite global positioning system.

At the time it had been a lot of money, but as far as Skelton was concerned it was money well spent if for no other reason than its value as a benchmark of his tenure as Chief of Police and a signal that he was a very different man than his father had been.

After a look into the empty Detective Room he went to his private offices at the far end of the building. As usual, Freddie Ziner was there before him, sitting behind his desk in the outer office, the living image of Walt Disney's Ichabod Crane in *The Legend of Sleepy Hollow*.

Ichabod Crane in a spit and polish uniform, reed thin, eyes like saucers, ears like Dumbo, nose big enough and hooked enough to open a long-neck beer bottle, feet the size of small boats. Tiny teeth like small, gray pearls. Lips that were always wet and usually flecked with spittle at the corners. Essence of nerd. As far as Skelton knew, Frederick C. Ziner had never been seen in the social company of a man or a woman.

In other words, Freddie was the kind of person no one in their right mind would confide in, yet somehow he seemed to know everything that was going on in town before anyone else did, as though those big ears were tuned in to some frequency beyond the range of normal human hearing, and that giant nose could smell a secret a mile away.

'What's new, Freddie?' It was his standard greeting. Ziner was going through the big ring-clipboard of circulating memos from the Prosper City Council. He looked up at Skelton's question.

'Not much, boss.' His head bobbed and the wet lips curled down into a frown. 'Except God wants you to call.'

'Gadsby?' said Skelton. God was what they'd called him at Woodrow Wilson. He doubted that he'd exchanged more than a dozen words with the man in his entire lifetime. 'The Monsignor?'

'None other,' Freddie nodded, his head bobbing up and down. 'Only one in town.'

'Call him back,' said Skelton. 'Find out what he wants. Make an appointment.'

'You got it,' Freddie nodded again. Skelton headed into his office.

*What the hell does that old penguin want?*

After breakfast and a telephone call, Rachel drove from the Wax rooming house to downtown Prosper. She found an empty parking spot on Snelling Street, in front of the public library, fed the meter, then walked back up to State Street and turned right. As instructed, she headed for the big old-fashioned marquee that marked the Roper Theater a block to the west, enjoying the cool breeze and the shade of the neatly trimmed maples planted every twenty-five feet or so along the sidewalk. The trees were young, no more than ten or twelve years old, a pleasant upscale addition since her days at Morningstar, even if they were just a little contrived, complete with old-fashioned wrought-iron enclosure collars supposedly meant to keep Fido from marking his territory.

The Lens and Shutter photo store was squeezed between McPhee's Drugs and the White Tower restaurant on the corner, opulent with its trademark art deco plasterwork in white and gold. There was a framed family portrait on one display window of Jerry Weems' store and a 'ONE HOUR PHOTO' display in the other. Rachel opened the door that stood between them. A buzzer sounded distantly as she entered the store and closed the door behind her. There was nobody behind the counter. Rachel waited, glancing at the rows of cameras and accessories on the shelves around the store. There was another big 'One Hour' sign by the cash register and from the stacks of 35 mm film that seemed to be everywhere it looked as though Jerry made most of his money from the passing tourist trade.

A moment later a balding man came through a curtained doorway at the rear of the store. Rachel smiled. Jerry Weems was still pudgy and still wearing a cardigan that was a match for the one in his high-school yearbook. He had one of those open, genuine faces that immediately foster trust and friendship.

'You gotta be Miss Kane. I'm Jerry Weems,' he said. He extended a fat little hand across the counter and Rachel shook it.

'How did you know?'

'I know everyone in town, so I knew you were a stranger in Prosper, and you don't look like a tourist.'

'What does a tourist look like?'

'Like me,' Weems grinned. 'Except usually *he*'s carrying an expensive camera around his neck and *she* has a straw hat on and sandals, like this was the Caribbean instead of the Catskills.'

'See a lot of people like that?'

His grin broadened. 'Another few weeks and the place will be drowning in them.' He paused and looked around his store. 'And thank God for each and every one.'

Weems flipped open a pass-through in the counter, stepped across the store and flipped the hanging sign from Open to Closed. He threw the latch on the door and came back to the pass-through. 'You said you wanted to talk about old times at Woodrow Wilson High. I thought we'd be more comfortable upstairs.' He ushered her through the pass-through then led her back through the curtained doorway. Rachel found herself in a narrow hallway piled high with crates and boxes marked Agfa, Kodak and Fuji. At the rear of the storage area there was a stairway.

'What's up here?' Rachel asked.

'My place. I live over the store,' Weems answered.

154

He went ahead and chugged up the steps, puffing a little as he climbed. Rachel followed, noticing that the store owner had a very high-tech looking beeper clipped to his belt as well as a compact cell phone in a little holster.

'Why do you have a pager?' Rachel asked. David had worn a pager for his work at the hospital, years ago, but coming back into the world she'd discovered that the portable phones and the little signaling devices were common as shells on a beach now.

Weems looked back over his shoulder and smiled pleasantly. 'Pager's for the newspaper, phone's for the Volunteer Fire Department and the Police. Gotta keep in touch, stay ahead of the game.'

They reached the top of the stairs and Rachel found herself in a loft that covered the length of the building's upper floor. The walls were white and hung with scores of photographs and the wide-planked soft-wood floors had been lovingly stripped and varnished. In the center of the room there was a couch, a big steel and glass coffee table and a pair of comfortable looking armchairs. It looked as though she was in the middle of an art gallery. Sunlight streamed in through the big windows fronting on to State Street and the mid-section of the loft had been turned into a studio, complete with light tables, projectors and had a dozen large, gray metal sliding filing cabinets. The last third of the floor at the rear had been partitioned off, probably as a kitchen and sleeping area.

'I'm impressed,' said Rachel, which was true enough.

'Me too. Did all of it myself,' said Weems, obviously proud. 'Mr Waterman would be astounded.' He pointed Rachel toward one of the chairs and she sat down.

'Mr Waterman?'

'Shops,' Weems answered. 'He used to bring me up to the front of the class with my projects and show them off to the rest of the kids as an example of everything *not* to do.' He looked around the room. 'Fooled him, didn't I?' He smiled. 'Coffee?'

'Sure.'

Weems disappeared into the rear of the apartment. Rachel got up and checked out some of the photographs on the wall. Most were black and white enlargements but there were a few color ones as well. The most prominently displayed was actually a *Life Magazine* cover blown up three times its normal size: 11 October 1969. Almost twenty people were gathered in a narrow forest glen, a Plains Indian tipi incongruously squatting lopsided in the background. Rachel vaguely remembered seeing the cover a month or so after she and David left the commune, not long after Woodstock.

Two little girls, long-haired and blonde, crouched in the foreground, smiling up into the camera. Beside them another blonde child and two adults also beamed into the lens. The woman had dark hair, wore a plain, homespun dress and had a handful of daisies in her hand; the man was balding but wore a beaded headband anyway. Behind the couple and to the right was Paul Goodman, bearded, wearing his trademark, skin-tight doe-skin pants and high leather boots, long hair streaming down across his broad tanned shoulders, one arm holding a wooden stave, the other wrapped around the waist of a pretty girl of sixteen or seventeen, a single daisy threaded into her long black hair. Behind them, older than the girl but not as old as Goodman was another woman with flame red hair and freckles, her face turned from the camera, but somehow familiar. In the center of the photograph, a young couple, both dressed in long white robes, stood together, their foreheads wreathed in more daisies. The rest of the people were ranged behind Goodman and the girl all the way back to the tipi.

*Morningstar.*

'My one big claim to fame.'

Rachel turned, startled by the sound of Weems' voice. He set a tray loaded down with coffee fixings and smiled broadly.

'You shot this?' asked Rachel.

'Yup.'

'You must have been just a kid!'

'Thirteen,' Weems nodded. 'Summer before I started at Woodrow Wilson. Or Woodwork Wilson, that's what we used to call it.'

'Amazing,' said Rachel. She turned away from the blown-up photograph and came back to her chair.

'Not really.' Weems shrugged. 'Just lucky. Did you see the guy in the tight leather pants?'

*Paul. Play dumb.*

'Yes.'

'Paul Goodman, teaches psychology over at Oneida College. Back then he ran a commune a few miles outside of town called Morningstar.'

'Interesting.'

'I suppose. Not to me. Not then. Anyway, my big brother Andy was sort of baby-sitting me and he had to go up to the commune for some reason. I'm not really sure but I think he was buying dope, or maybe even selling it. Who knows? Well, they were having a wedding – the two people in the middle of the picture wearing white. They were about to go back into the tipi and . . . you know.' Weems actually blushed. He cleared his throat, took a sip of coffee and went on. 'They had a guy taking pictures but his camera screwed up. I had my old Pentax with me, so I wound up taking the wedding pictures for them. I made up some copies of that one and a bunch of others I shot.'

'How did it get to be on the cover of *Life*?' Rachel asked.

'More luck. A friend of my dad's worked for Dick Pollard, the *Life Magazine* Director of Photography back then. He knew that Ralph Graves, the Managing Editor, was doing a hippie commune story and the rest is history.' Weems shook his head and sighed. 'I guess Andy Warhol was right. You get your fifteen minutes and then it's all over. I haven't had anything even close to that kind of success ever since.' He grinned. 'Burnt out at thirteen, good for nothing except the Woodrow Wilson High School yearbook.' Weems put on a solemn expression and let his voice drop a couple of octaves. 'Oh, how are the mighty fallen!'

Rachel smiled back. 'Some people never even get their fifteen minutes,' she said. 'And there are worse things than taking pictures for high-school yearbooks.'

'True enough,' Weems laughed. 'But my early success really ticked off old Shitty O'Shea.'

'The teacher? I saw his picture in the yearbook.' Rachel nodded. 'The one with the lab coat.'

'There was a rumor that he wasn't wearing anything underneath it,' said Weems. 'He never took the damn thing off. Probably wore it to bed. He thought he was Eisenstaedt or something.'

'Most of the credits in the yearbook had your name on them. Didn't anyone else from the photo club take pictures?'

'Yeah, but not as good as mine.' He shrugged. 'My dad was staff photographer at the *Prosper Advance* until he got sick. He started up the shop downstairs back in the forties. I grew up with cameras.' The smile flashed again. 'I took unfair advantage, I guess you could say.' Weems finished up his coffee, then leaned back in his chair. 'You said on the phone you wanted to talk to me about pictures I took back then. You're writing an article you said?'

'That's right.'

'So what pictures are you interested in?'

'It's more than just pictures,' Rachel said slowly. 'I'm trying to put a time-line together.'

'Then and now? That kind of thing.'

Rachel nodded. 'Something like that.'

'Sounds reasonable. Anything in particular?'

'A kid named Robin Skelton,' Rachel answered. 'From the looks of things he was a big wheel back then.'

'Big jerk,' said Weems.

'So I hear,' said Rachel. 'One of his old teachers didn't seem to like him much.'

'Who was that?'

'Mr Halloran.'

'Halitosis Halloran. He hated everyone. I see him wandering around. Reminds me of one of those science projects you used to get – leaf collections waxed down on a sheet of cardboard. A dried leaf covered with wax, that's Halloran.'

'Barney Benechuck wouldn't let him on the football team.'

'He wouldn't let me on either,' said Weems. 'Barney the Bear taught me PE. Never fell for the fake cough I used to try and get out of class.' Weems snorted. 'But now the worm has turned, I wouldn't buy a used car from him if my life depended on it.'

'I did.'

'You're kidding!' Weems laughed. 'Just make sure you check your brakes every time you go down a hill, that's all I can say.'

'Back to Robin Skelton.'

'Really? Why?'

'Because he's beginning to sound like a villain, and villains make the best stories.'

'Villain's too good a word. He's no Joker or Two

Face. Pardon my French but Robby Skelton was, and
is, a world-class asshole.'

'If he's so thoroughly unliked, how come he got to
be top cop?'

'Good question,' said Weems. He leaned back in
his chair, tapping at the thickly padded arms. 'I guess
it's a local hero kind of thing. Went off to the Army,
turned himself into a cop.' The pudgy photographer
gnawed on his lower lip for a moment, brows
furrowing. 'You ever live in a small town?' he said
finally.

'Not really.'

'Well, it's a small-town thing. His father was the
Police Chief and, when he died, it just seemed kind
of natural for his son to take it on after him. Like me
taking over as photographer for the *Advance*. See
what I mean?'

'Traditions passed on.'

'I guess you could say that.'

'But it's not an elected position, is it?'

'No. He was voted in by City Council.'

Rachel smiled. 'Lot of his friends from Woodrow
Wilson on the Council?'

'Not really. Just Donny Hale, City Clerk. Council's
pretty much made up of geezers. The Judge, D'Arcy
Quinn's old man, Junior Parker's dad, over at
Farmers' Union. Rawley Higgins, the City supervisor,
he's in his seventies.' Weems sat forward and nodded
toward the framed *Life Magazine* cover. 'We're still
waiting for the revolution I guess.' Weems dropped
back into the chair again and lifted his shoulders.

'When you get right down to it, I guess you could say he hasn't done a bad job. He got the city to put in parking meters and he came up with the idea of only giving out tickets during June, July and August so the tourists pay the freight for clogging up the town during the summer. He updated Police Headquarters, put in some fancy communications gear that seems to be keeping petty theft down. All small potatoes I guess, but it adds up.'

'Doesn't sound like a world-class asshole to me,' Rachel said.

'I said I thought he hadn't done a bad job as Chief,' Weems answered. 'As a human being he's a son-of-a-bitch and he always has been.'

'Give me an example.'

'You saw the pictures in the Wilsonian. I was the fat kid, he was the jock, hunk, stud, call it what you want. He and his friends used to call me Pork Chop, or Fat Worms.' The photographer shook his head. 'They always had to say something to make you feel like shit.'

*'Maybe the retard will wet her little panties.'*

*'Mommy wouldn't tell on me, would she?'*

Suddenly Rachel's nostrils were filled with the sick sweet smell of spearmint gum and vodka. She swallowed hard and tried to concentrate on what the photographer was saying.

'One day Skelton comes to school with a dozen eggs, you know, in one of those cardboard cartons. He puts three or four into the pockets of his sweater, and then he comes after me.'

'After you?'

'Yeah,' Weems nodded. 'Like some kind of stalker. I come around a hallway and bam! He smashes one down on my head. All of a sudden I've got raw egg dripping down my face.' The man's face was flushing, but with anger now, not embarrassment. 'Said I acted like an egghead, so I should look like one.'

'A prank,' said Rachel.

'Yeah. Fine. One egg is a prank. But he kept on doing it. I cleaned up, went about my business. Next period, there he is again. Bam! Another egg.'

'You didn't tell a teacher?'

'Sure. Three of them. I even wound up telling Katz and the Frog.'

'The Principal and the Vice Principal.'

'Yeah.'

'They didn't do anything?'

'After the third egg they called Skelton down to the office. He denied it.'

'That's all?'

'By the fifth egg they did a locker check.'

'And they didn't find a thing,' Rachel guessed.

Weems bobbed his head. 'You got it.'

'He moved the eggs to a friend's locker?'

'Yup. And walking home from school he drove by in that truck of his and threw the rest of them at me. For no reason.' He shook his head as though he still couldn't figure it out, even after all these years. 'For no reason at all.'

'So why did he do it?'

'Because he knew he could get away with it.

Because he knew I wouldn't fight back. Because he was the king and I was nothing.'

*King Bone.*

'Did you know his girlfriend?'

'In senior year? Sue Marsden?' He nodded. 'Sure.'

Weems got up out of his chair and went back to the studio section of the loft. He puttered around for a moment, opening and closing doors. When he came back to his seat he had a pile of large manila envelopes in his hand. He dropped them on to the coffee table, then pawed through the pile, sorting them. He opened the flap on one of the envelopes and poured out a handful of snapshots. He picked them up and began flipping them across to Rachel's side of the table. She picked them up, one by one.

'Sue at the Senior Prom.' The same dark-haired girl as in the band photo, this time dressed in a long gown with very adult cleavage, Robin Skelton at her side in a pale tux of some kind, complete with a frilly shirt. The picture was posed in front of a gigantic punch bowl.

'Sue as cheerleader.' Sue Marsden in a very short, pleated skirt, standing in a classic cheerleader pose, legs outstretched, arms above her head, the WW on her chest pushed out by the curve of her breasts, her eyes shining, looking straight into the camera.

'Sue at the beach.' A lakeside scene, Sue Marsden and half a dozen others making faces at the camera, standing on a floating dive platform fifteen or twenty feet out.

'Osculating Sue.' Sue Marsden and Robby kissing

deeply, a row of lockers in the background.

'Sue tying up her shoes.' A candid shot, obviously done with a zoom lens, of Sue Marsden kneeling at the running track, doing up a sneaker.

'You had a thing for her,' said Rachel.

He smiled. 'We all did. Every geek and goog and nerd at Woodrow Wilson High. And a bunch of jocks and average Joes as well. She had the greatest *eyes*.' His own eyes seemed to glow behind his glasses. 'She was an inspiration to us all.' He laughed.

'They didn't last after graduation?'

'He went off to join the Green Berets or whatever the hell it was. She went to New York and that was that.'

'He had other girlfriends. Before Sue Marsden?'

'Before, during and after,' Weems snorted. 'If Skelton still screwed around the way he did back then he'd have been dead of some dread disease by now.' He put the pictures of Sue Marsden back in the envelope, none of them familiar. She picked up an eight-by-ten color shot. A beautiful blonde girl in her twenties, seated on a throne in the back of a candy-apple-red pick-up truck.

Robby's truck.

The blonde girl was dressed like a pink, frilly, fairy princess, carried a wand and wore a diamond tiara. The back of the truck was filled with red and white and yellow roses, and there was a sign above the fairy princess's head: HOMECOMING PRINCESS. Through the truck cab window she could make out a young male face. Rachel felt her mouth suddenly go dry.

'Who's the princess?' asked Rachel. She cleared her throat, trying to dredge up enough spit to keep her throat from closing.

'Toby Hale. Donald Hale's big sister.' Weems pointed to the face in the truck cab window. 'That's Donny.'

Donald Hale. Finally. A face and a name. The City Clerk.

*Maybe she wants King Bone. Slip her the snake, Robby, come on!*

The blond one.

*Oh, you son of a bitch, I've got you now.*

Something else.

'When was this taken?' Rachel asked.

Weems took the photograph from her and flipped it over, checking the scrawled notation on the back. 'Uh, Indian Summer Festival, 18 September 1974.'

The day after it happened.

'Do you have a magnifying glass?'

'Sure.' Weems nodded. He bounced up out of his chair, went back to the studio section of the loft and came back with a plastic loupe. He handed it to Rachel. 'See something interesting?'

'Maybe.' She put the loupe down on the photograph and peered through it, squinting at the rear of the truck carrying the Homecoming Princess. The taillight on the left clearly had the word FORD scrolled in white across the red plastic; the one on the right didn't. It was just plain red and Rachel thought she could see a faint grayish line around the edges of the scarlet oval – duct tape. The taillight she'd kicked in, hastily repaired for the festival.

Proof.

Her lawyer's words at the preliminary hearing, coming back to her like aural ghosts, Luteki, the investigating cop, reading from the deposition he'd taken from Robby Skelton.

*'Mrs Lucas said she kicked in the taillight on Skelton's truck when it was parked outside Miggs' store.'*

*'The boy says she didn't, because he wasn't at Miggs' store when she was there. Miggs corroborates his statement.'*

*'Did you check the truck?'*

*'Sure.'*

*'What did you find?'*

*'Nothing.'*

*'You didn't see any damage to the right-side taillight of the truck?'*

*'No.'*

*'When did you check the taillight?'*

*'When I took the deposition from the witness.'*

*'When was that?'*

*'September twenty-third.'*

Almost a week later.

Rachel set her jaws together, trying to keep back the tears she could feel welling up in her eyes, wondering if it was anger or relief that she was feeling. It might not stand up in a court of law, but it was good enough for her.

'Something wrong?' asked Weems, concerned.

'I'm okay,' said Rachel. 'An allergy thing.'

'Oh.' Weems started gathering up the pictures.

Rachel put out her hand, laid it across the one of the Homecoming Princess. 'Could I borrow this?'

'Sure, I guess.' Weems frowned. 'How come you want that one?'

'I'm not sure,' Rachel lied.

*Because after all this time it proves that I'm not insane.*

# CHAPTER ELEVEN

There were six men in the Prosper PD Detective
Division, broken into three two-man teams – more
than enough to handle a town and gown population
of 30,000. During the summer months, with Oneida
College empty, the population fell by at least five
thousand, putting even less pressure on the small
group of detectives; it was usually an easy time and
on the day the Alberoni investigation began, Wren
and Kenny Spearing were the only game in town –
the two other senior detectives were on holiday and
their younger partners were both on courses, one at
the FBI Academy in Quantico, the other doing a
summer session in criminology at Columbia.

Wren sat with his big feet up on his cluttered desk
and sailed a dart-shaped paper airplane through the
air, skimming it over the back to back metal desks
that made an island in the middle of the spacious
office on the fourth floor of the old Municipal Building
in Courthouse Square. The airplane crumpled against
the back of Kenny Spearing's head as he stood at the
coffee machine at the far end of the room.

'It stinks,' said Wren. He lit a cigarette, a long,

looping thread of smoke wafting up to tangle itself in the old-fashioned four-vaned ceiling fans thumping overhead. Spearing brought two mugs of coffee from the machine, set one down in front of Wren, then took his own to the desk butted up against his partner's.

'What stinks?'

'Alberoni.'

'He's dead, of course he stinks.' Spearing grinned. 'Corpses do that after a while.'

'Ha ha,' Wren said dryly. He took a sip of his coffee.

'What's your problem?' Spearing asked.

'I keep on going back to motive,' Wren answered. 'Why shank a small-town doctor?'

'Greed, revenge or crime of passion. Aren't those the classic motives?'

'I think we can rule out crime of passion,' said Wren.

'Because of the way it was done?'

Wren nodded. 'That, and the fact that he was an old man.'

'Pedophile aced by an enraged parent?'

'Doesn't fit. He wasn't a pediatrician and if he was a pedophile there'd be some kind of backtrail.' Wren smiled. 'Or do you have something from your past you'd like to talk about?'

The younger man ignored the dig. 'Okay, so you don't like passion. What about greed?'

'Nobody tossed the house. He's got a life insurance policy, but the beneficiary is his sister down in Florida. She's eighty-one years old.'

'You don't see her hopping a plane to stick a shiv

in her brother to pay off her bingo debts?'

'You're a real comedian today; you stay up late and watch *Letterman* or something?'

'I'm bored,' Spearing confessed. 'It's a nice sunny day out there; I could be fishing Cold Mountain Creek right now.' The younger man sighed. 'You know as well as I do that Sloane is our man for this. We can put him at the scene anyway. Maybe it was a drug thing.'

'I don't think so.'

'You have somebody else in mind?'

'Not yet.' Wren dropped his legs off the desk. He butted his cigarette and took a swallow of coffee. 'I want to take a look at the crime scene again.'

'I guess you want me along, right?' Spearing sounded resigned.

'No,' said Wren. 'You go fishing. I'll check it out by myself and let you know if I come up with something.'

Spearing sighed. 'You must know my mother.'

'Excuse me?'

'Same shit, different pile. My dad calls her Queen of the Guilt Trip.' The younger man raised his voice an octave or two. 'No, no, you just go fishing, dear, I'll clean up the garage, even if it means I'll have to go to the chiropractor – again.' Spearing shook his head. 'The thing is, even though I knew she was doing it to me, it always worked. Just like now.'

'You think I'm trying to guilt-trip you?' Wren asked innocently.

Spearing snorted. 'I know you are.'

'You're right.' Wren grinned. 'So instead of going

fishing, why don't you go down to the *Advance* and feed some dimes into that photocopier of theirs; I'd like as much background on Alberoni as you can get. When you've done that call Prine at the Medical Center and see if the autopsy report is ready.'

'I'm on it,' Spearing nodded.

'Good,' Wren said. 'I'll meet you at the crime scene.'

Leaving Jerry Weems' place, Rachel went back to her car, fed another pair of quarters into the meter, then climbed the flight of stone steps that led to the front door of the Prosper Public Library. There was a group of youngsters on a play-group field trip in the Children's section, but other than that the place was empty. She found the card index for the library clipping file and looked up the name Hale. There were two folders, one for Donald Hale Sr, the other for Donny Jr. Rachel ordered them both from the same lacklustre librarian who'd helped her with the microfilms and a few minutes later she had them on the table in front of her. She started with the file on Donald Hale Jr.

There wasn't a lot in it. Woodrow Wilson High, a B. Comm from the University of Wisconsin at Madison, a wedding announcement, a short feature article on Donny Jr as the new accountant in town, handling small businesses and specializing in medical-dental practices and then, in 1985, a 'pleased to announce' advertisement placed by the Farmers' Union Bank, announcing Donny's appointment as a Vice President.

*The same bank that handles the Chester Miggs trust.*

Curious, but not at all surprising since the Farmers' Union was probably the only bank in town. The last date in the file was a clipping about Donald Hale Jr winning the office of City Clerk in the 1990 municipal elections; not quite a win by acclamation, but there hadn't been any serious contenders for the job, which, according to the article, had been held by Donny's father since the late fifties. Rachel shook her head; first Skelton, now Hale. The whole town was starting to look as though its wheels were greased with nepotism.

More out of curiosity than any real interest, Rachel dumped out the clippings on Donny's father. Donald Sr's file was like an inflated version of his son's and came with a handy, condensed life story in the form of a black-outlined obituary from the *Prosper Advance* dated in 1989. Donald Hale Sr had also taken a B. Comm at the University of Wisconsin, went off to fight WW2 and came back to set himself up as a business consultant and tax advisor. By the late forties his interests turned to local politics and for the next ten years he was, by turns, Executive Director of Prosper County Social Services, Prosper County Purchasing Clerk, Director of Prosper County Supply and Services, County Clerk, and then City Clerk the same year the town of Prosper incorporated as a city. Along the line he'd managed to marry a local beauty queen and produce a son – Donald Jr.

From the looks of it, Donald Sr had been a joiner –

Knights of Columbus, Rotary, Lions, Elks, Chamber of Commerce. He'd also sat on the advisory committee that had established Oneida College and had been on its first Board of Regents. The charities listed at the bottom of the obituary were predominantly Catholic, which was a bit of a surprise, since he'd only had the one child – not the usual Catholic marriage from the fifties.

Rachel went back to Donald Jr's file and sorted through it until she found the wedding announcement. It was dated 1988 which would make Donny thirty or thirty-one if he'd graduated Woodrow Wilson at the same time as Robin Skelton. In the photograph his blond hair was sweeping back into a noticeable widow's peak and even in his tux and frilly front shirt it was fairly clear that he was developing a bit of a spare tire.

She read through the announcement and a few things started to become a little more clear. The plain-faced, heavy-breasted girl he'd married was one Becky Joan Parker, daughter of Hamilton J. Parker, President of the Farmers' Union Bank. It appeared that Donny had lucked out and married into the business. According to the announcement the couple were married by ex-Prosper Mayor, Judge Randall Quinn in an open air ceremony at Stoneacres, the Parker estate on the Crescent, wherever that was. The best man had been Michael Parker, and Becky's maid of honor had been D'Arcy Quinn. From nepotism to near incest.

Rachel stuffed the clippings back into the folders

and took them back to the librarian. She found a pay phone close to the front doors of the library, flipped to the blue section in the front of the phone books listing city and municipal offices and punched the number for the City Clerk's office. She reached Donald Hale's secretary, told her she was from *Life Magazine* and waited on hold for thirty seconds. The secretary came back on the line and offered Rachel half an hour with Mr Hale after lunch. She took it.

It was no secret among cops that homicide was the easiest of all crimes to solve. Walk in on a domestic dispute where a man lies dead in bed with his head bashed in and his wife is sitting in the kitchen with a bloody ball pean hammer from his Christmas tool chest in her hand and you didn't have to look far for your perpetrator. Most murders were like that, a corpse with a clear-cut killer not too far away. There was almost never any mystery about who'd done what to whom, and clues were usually of the more blatant variety, like a blood-stained shirt or a big fat thumbprint on a gun butt. Of the two or three hundred murder cases Wren had been involved with, more than half of them had been solved within the first twelve hours and virtually all the rest within the first twenty-four.

Which was why he found the Alberoni case so irritating. He drove up to the dead doctor's house and sat there for a moment, smoking a cigarette and staring out at the big Victorian mansion. Spearing was right of course – everything pointed, circumstantially anyway, at Allan Sloane, the Vietnam veteran with the chip on his shoulder.

But Spearing was playing it by the book; Wren had half a lifetime of cop intuition setting up an itch he just couldn't seem to scratch into submission.

Fact – Sloane was the last patient to see Alberoni, at least as far as the official record was concerned.

Fact – The murder was a dead bang professional job. Whoever stuck the doctor knew exactly what he was doing.

Supposition – Sloane was a soldier, almost certainly trained to use something like a Sykes-Fairbairn commando knife.

Ergo – Sloane was the killer.

On the other hand –

—There was no apparent motive.

—Would Sloane have left his name on the computer if he was the last patient logged in?

—And if he had killed Alberoni, for whatever obscure reason, wouldn't he have run like hell?

Murderers were predictable. For Wren that was as much a truism as the fact that homicide rarely had any mystery to it. Except for now. The craggy-faced detective blew out a cloud of smoke, opened the car door and flipped out his cigarette butt. He climbed out of the car suddenly realizing what was really bothering him about the killing. *Mystery* was the key word. And that's what Sloane would be if he was the killer – a mystery. People didn't kill other people without a reason, no matter how bizarre, and unless they were complete and utter lunatics, they

176

usually came up with an alibi of some kind. Somehow Wren didn't see Sloane as a psycho and far from having an alibi, he'd stonewalled Wren about why he'd gone to see Alberoni in the first place.

So it had to be someone else, and that someone had to have a reason for sticking a knife in the old man's heart. Which took Wren, frowning and annoyed, right back to where he'd started, which was nowhere. He went up the walk, climbed up on to the porch and used his Swiss Army knife to slice through the paper seal left by the Prosper DA's office. He took out his keys and opened the real-estate lock-box attached to the doorknob, took out Alberoni's housekey, and let himself in.

Nothing had changed since he'd first stepped into the house the day before, except that now he was alone. There was a faintly putrid scent in the air but with the doctor's body long gone it was either his imagination or else someone had left the refrigerator door open and food was spoiling. He went back to the kitchen and found that someone had done exactly that. The refrigerator door was open a crack and the inside light was out. With no sound from the compressor that probably meant a fuse had blown. He pulled open the refrigerator door wide and found the culprit almost instantly – a quart of milk gone sour. He took it to the sink, poured the curdling mass down the drain, then flushed it with a blast of water from the tap.

Wren walked back down the hall and turned into the living room. Yesterday he'd stood here and the first thing that had popped into his mind was the possibility that Alberoni was gay; simple, old-fashioned ingrained prejudice of course, not too surprising for a kid who grew up in the fifties. All interior decorators, hairdressers and ballet dancers were gay, and there wasn't one queer in the NFL. Yeah, right. Live and learn.

He stood in the middle of the living room and did a slow turn again. Still the same as yesterday. Black bookcases full of art books, a litter of architectural models and the collection of old birdcages. He went to the bookcases and flipped through a few of the volumes. Everything from Hockney to Goya; Alberoni had catholic tastes. After five minutes Wren knew the room was going to give him nothing. He left the living room and went up to the second floor.

There were half a dozen bedrooms, most of them small and most of them looking unused. A lot of guest rooms and not a lot of guests. The master bedroom was the one containing the turret, which meant it was directly over the waiting room downstairs. Once again, the decor was a little exotic for a town like Prosper; a four-poster eighteenth-century bed hung with hand-painted tree-of-life fabric in pale green, a close match for wallpaper, Queen Anne bedside tables and a set of botanical prints in expensive looking frames. On a small table by the window there was a single architectural model done in several different woods. It looked like a Shinto shrine, complete with complex, steeply curved pagoda roof with generous eaves and its own tiny set of stairs leading to a dark interior. On the far side of the room there was a plain wooden pedestal desk.

Wren went through the drawers. A lot of personal paperwork, none of it very meaningful; letters from his sister wrapped in a brittle rubber band, half a dozen old-fashioned decal-edge photographs that looked like family pictures from the fifties, bundles of paid bills, old tax forms. The detective went through all of it, but by the time he'd tossed it all back into the drawers, Alberoni was still a cipher. Wren went to the big free-standing mahogany wardrobe on casters that stood in one corner of the room and pulled open the double doors. A dozen expensive looking suits, a stack of white shirts in plastic wrap, fresh from the Gold Coin Chinese Laundry on Carteret Street, four pairs of brogues on the floor of the wardrobe and one pair of Nike Airs that looked as though they'd never been worn. He checked the pockets of the suits. Not so much as an errant speck of lint. He closed the doors of the wardrobe and went to the adjoining bathroom where he checked the medicine cabinet over the sink; Alberoni had hemorrhoids, high blood pressure, an enlarged prostate and corns; not a bad score for a man of his age. He still shaved with a Gillette safety razor and a boar bristle shaving brush and he still used Wildroot Cream Oil. All very fifties. Wren smiled; he remembered watching the old World Series games when they were sponsored by Gillette; Look Sharp, Feel Sharp, Be Sharp with Gillette Blue Blades. The first time he tried them he cut the shit out of his face and went directly to an electric razor and stayed there.

But this wasn't a nostalgia tour. He went back to the bedroom and rummaged through the bedside tables; nail clippers, a litter of pens and pencils and two paperback books – one an old Nero Wolfe, the other an orange covered, well worn P.G. Wodehouse 'Jeeves' book. Nothing tell-tale like K-Y Jelly or a half-empty box of Trojans. On the closest bedside table there was a silver-framed black and white photograph of a pretty looking woman in a thirties dress standing on the deck of the *Queen Mary*, smiling into the camera. You could tell it was the *Queen Mary* because the cloche-hatted girl was standing beside a rope-wound lifesaver with the name written around the edge. Alberoni's sister? An old flame? Either way the picture had no connection to the present day.

On a whim, Wren got down on his hands and knees and checked under the dust ruffle. No hidden sex toys or freak magazines, not even a pair of slippers or a dust bunny. Wren clambered to his feet and plopped himself down on the salmon-colored damask bedspread. Wren pulled his cigarettes out of his pocket and almost lit one before he realized that he hadn't seen an ashtray anywhere in the house. He put the cigarettes back in his jacket pocket, frowning. Amos Alberoni M.D. was pure as the driven snow.

Which was utter bullshit of course. Wren had been a cop long enough to know that everyone had secrets. He heard the screen door slam downstairs and then Spearing's voice.

'Wren? I've got the package on Doc Alberoni!' The younger man called loudly. Wren levered himself up off the bed and headed back downstairs.

The two dozen employees of the City Clerk's Office occupied half a floor of the Stairway to Heaven, but Donald Hale Jr maintained the huge office his father had kept in the old municipal building across the street. That office was an enormous corner suite that came with waist-high burled walnut paneling, three big fans whirring in the ornately plastered ceiling and a view overlooking the main steps leading up to the courthouse. The only bigger office in the building was the Mayor's, directly over his head on the top floor and since Prosper hadn't officially had a mayor since Benny Carlisle blew his brains out and they adopted a committee governing structure, that didn't count. The big, high-ceilinged room still smelled of cigars and the green leather chairs and massive pedestal desk all screamed male chauvinism on a grand scale.

When Rachel Kane stepped into Donny Hale's office, the City Clerk rose grandly from behind the desk and offered the woman his hand. He gave her a quick once over, all you could get away with since sexual harassment had suddenly become a litigator's dream. She looked to be in her mid-forties, with a lean, almost dangerous look about her. When he shook her hand he was surprised at the strength of the grip. She was wearing a dark, musky perfume that it took him a while to identify; he finally figured it out. She was wearing patchouli oil; an old-fashioned hippie who'd kept her body from going to ratshit like most of the other middle-aged broads he'd gone to school with.

'You're from *Life Magazine*?'

'That's right.'

'How come you want to talk to a boring old bureaucrat like me?' He'd practised the 'boring old bureaucrat' phrase half a dozen times before she arrived and he was pleased when he saw her jot it down in her notebook.

'We did a story on small-town America a long time ago; this is a reprise. Small-town America grows up. Prosper was one of the towns we used back then, so we decided to come back.' She could trot out the canned explanation smoothly now, without any hesitation. If anyone asked for her credentials she'd tell them she was working freelance. So far no one had bothered to check.

'I can think of more interesting people to talk to than a City Clerk.' Hale smiled widely; he was playing the self-effacing routine to the hilt. Rachel smiled back at him. He'd put on a few more pounds since the wedding photograph in the library clip file and his hair was even thinner, the pale blond of his youth changed to something closer to the color of nicotine. There were crows' feet around his eyes and she could see a patch on the thick flesh below his chin where his razor had missed.

*Slip her the snake, Robby, come on!*

She wanted to kill him but she smiled instead. 'The

City Clerk is right in the middle of things in a small town.'

'City,' Donny Hale corrected, returning her smile. 'That happened quite a while ago.'

'That was back when your father was Town Clerk, wasn't it?' Rachel asked, knowing the answer.

'You've done your homework.'

'Your dad was Town Clerk, Chief Skelton's dad was Chief as well. Your County Court Judge used to be the Mayor and you married the banker's daughter.'

Hale's smile wavered slightly. 'Are you trying to make a point?'

'Sort of.' Rachel nodded. She turned her own smile up a notch or two, not wanting to spook him. Not yet anyway. 'Some people might call it nepotism, but in a small-town environment like this I'd call it continuity.'

'Is that your personal or your editorial opinion?' Hale asked.

'Both.'

'Good.'

'What exactly does a City Clerk do?' Rachel asked, pen poised over her pad.

*Slip her the snake, Robby.*

'If Prosper was a motion picture, I'd be the Production Manager,' said Hale, smiling. Rachel wondered where he'd come up with the analogy; *Premiere Magazine*? 'The City Clerk's office manages the budget, sees to it that things get done.'

'Garbage pick-up, sewers, that kind of thing?'

'Not directly, that's actually the Public Works

Department, but our office oversees the contracts, makes sure things are done on time, registers changes.'

'Superclerk,' said Rachel, willing herself to smile.

She remembered him, standing with the other two boys at the rear of the car, still wearing blue and green high-school jackets, watching the girl crouch down beside the gas tank, and then the flick of the lighter in her hand and the bright flare of light as the rag hanging from the tank ignited, lighting up their faces for a single hellish instant before they ran.

'I guess that's as good a description as any,' Hale grinned. 'I don't wear a cape though, and I can't jump tall buildings in a single stride.'

She saw the group photograph on his desk and played to it, tearing her mind back from memory with a conscious effort. 'You're married.'

'Yes.' He saw her looking at the picture and turned it slightly toward her side of the desk. A pudgy wife in a dress with a frilly collar and two blonde girls, one six or seven, the other a few years older. Both as plain as the wife. 'My wife Becky and the two girls, Sarah and Colleen.'

'Nice old-fashioned names,' said Rachel.

'Nice old-fashioned family,' he said. He paused, looking at Rachel carefully. 'They're all down at Disney World for the next week or so,' he added. 'They went down with Gran and Gramps.'

Rachel knew that both his own parents were dead, but she asked the question anyway. 'Your parents?'

He shook his head. 'Becky's family.'

'She's a Parker, isn't she?'

'That's right.' He smiled, but the eyes were cold and a little suspicious. 'You really *have* done your homework.'

'They're a prominent family in Prosper; it's hard to avoid them.'

'You're telling me?' said Hale. There was a trace of bitterness in his tone. 'The Parkers and the Quinns are Prosper's version of *Mayflower* mainliners.'

'Are there any conflicts between family and your work as City Clerk?'

'No.' The answer was flat and unequivocal. Dangerous ground again. Rachel backed off.

*Time to bait the hook.*

'Are there any decent restaurants in Prosper?' The question came from out of the blue and startled Hale for a moment. He shrugged, leaning back in his chair.

'A few.' He smiled again. 'More than the first time *Life* came to town, that's for sure!' He paused. 'I thought we were talking about my role as City Clerk.'

*Get him to bite.*

'I'm looking for a nice place to have dinner tonight; I thought you might give me some advice.'

Hale gave her a long, thoughtful look and then his eyes flickered toward the family picture on his desk. He looked back at Rachel. 'Instead of telling you, why don't I show you?' he said slowly. He cleared his throat nervously.

*Reel him in.*

'Sounds great. What time?'

\* \* \*

Kenny Spearing's 'package' on Dr Amos Alberoni was a thick one, made up of newspaper clippings and documentation going back to the old man's birth in 1912, and stretching forward in time to the autopsy report the young detective had picked up half an hour before at the Medical Center morgue.

Wren settled himself into the couch in Alberoni's living room and went through the autopsy report first. The only mildly interesting facts in it were the notation that Alberoni had been circumcised and a mention of what was described as a scar from a 'late-corrected' cleft palate, neither of which seemed to have any bearing on the man's murder. Wren flipped to the opinion Dr Prine had offered at the conclusion of the report.

'It is my opinion that the subject, Dr Amos Quentin Alberoni, an 85-year-old male, died as a result of a stabbing wound to the ventral portion of the abdomen which proceeded up into the thoracic cavity, bisecting the pulmonary artery, piercing the periocardal sac and slashing the myocardial and coronary vessels, causing massive internal hemorrhage. The mechanism of death was loss of blood and shock secondary to traumatic hemorrhage of the heart. The manner of death was homicide.'

It was signed – George Prine, M.D./Chief Pathologist, Prosper County District Medical Center/ Prosper County Coroner/Prosper County Medical Examiner. Stapled on the last page of the report was a standard county Death Certificate, also signed by Prine.

'No help there,' said Wren, dropping the report down on to the coffee table. Spearing nodded silently, sitting across from Wren on one of Alberoni's uncomfortable looking Stickley chairs. Wren picked up the stack of photocopies the young detective had prepared for him and went through them quickly, scanning the text, looking for something he could use in his investigation. Given the doctor's advanced age it wasn't surprising that the *Prosper Advance* kept a boilerplate obituary on Alberoni which gave Wren a reasonable overview of the old man's life.

According to the obituary, Dr Amos Alberoni had been born in New York, 16 August 1912, the only son of Dr and Mrs Nathan Alberoni of Brooklyn New York. Alberoni's father and mother died in the 1917 flu epidemic and Alberoni had been sent to live with his aunt and uncle in California. Graduating precociously from UCLA with a Bachelor of Science Degree at the age of nineteen, Alberoni then returned to the east and received his medical degree from Harvard in 1934, followed by a year at Bellvue Hospital before marrying Miss Jennifer Wax of Prosper in 1937.

Wren looked up from his reading and looked across the coffee table at Kenny Spearing. 'Says here that Alberoni was married to someone named Jennifer Wax. Any relation to Eileen at the rooming house?'

Spearing thought for a moment, then nodded. 'Eileen's sister-in-law I think. Went to school with my Aunt Norma. She died.'

'Jennifer Wax or your Aunt Norma?'

'Jennifer Wax. Suicide, I think. Big scandal anyway.'

He paused. 'Want me to ask my aunt about it?'

'Yeah,' Wren nodded. Spearing got up and left the room. Wren went back to the obituary.

After three years in Prosper, Alberoni seemed to have carved out a healthy piece of territory for himself, establishing a private practise as well as sitting on the Prosper Town Council committee to establish a regional health facility for the town, and the county in general. According to the obituary, it was this committee that had been instrumental in setting up what eventually became the Prosper Medical Center. Alberoni was also a joiner and by 1940 he was a member of the Prosper Chamber of Commerce, the Lions, Rotary and the Knights of Columbus. He was also the doctor of record for the St Anthony's Boys' Camp, the St Anthony Parish Catholic Services Bureau and something called the Maryhill Children's Village. In 1943 Alberoni became Prosper County Medical Examiner, a title which he kept until his retirement in 1989.

In the years between the end of the war and his death, Amos Alberoni had sat on dozens of committees, joined everything including the Prosper Rose Grower's Society, the Prosper Heritage Association and the St Anthony Parish Meals on Wheel organisation. In 1985 they'd named a wing of the Medical Center after him, and in 1989 he'd endowed a special room in the Prosper Library for books relating to Prosper County.

Wren finished the obituary, then went through the other clippings, all of which simply bore out what he'd already read – Amos Alberoni was a medical knight in shining armor, Sir Lancelot with a caduceus instead of a sword.

But in the end, Lancelot had wound up screwing King Arthur's wife, right? Wren dropped the pile of clippings back on to the coffee table. Everyone had a secret sin and Alberoni was no exception, Wren was sure of it. Spearing came back into the room.

'Well?' asked Wren. Except for the mention of his marriage to Jennifer Wax there'd been no other mention of Alberoni's wife in the obituary.

'I remembered right,' said Spearing, sitting down again. 'It *was* suicide. Less than a year after they were married.'

'How?'

'Mixed herself a cocktail of molasses and lye. Apparently it was pretty ugly.'

'A note?'

Spearing shook his head. 'Nope; not that my aunt remembers.'

'Who found her?'

'Alberoni. She got up early one morning and did it to herself. He found her sitting at the kitchen table when he came down for breakfast.' The young man grinned ghoulishly. 'According to Aunt Nora, she made the doctor a pot of coffee, then went and dosed herself.'

'Does your Aunt Nora have any opinion about why she killed herself?'

'Nope.' Spearing's smile broadened. 'Except she said, at the time, just about everybody in town came up with one reason or another. Best bet is she got herself pregnant by someone else when the doc's back was turned, and did herself in out of guilt and remorse. Aunt Nora says she was a Catholic, big time, and so was Alberoni.'

'Catholics don't suicide,' said Wren. 'It's a sin.'

'Right,' nodded Spearing, 'Which means whatever reason she killed herself, it was an even bigger sin.'

Wren smiled; odd logic, but in the end he'd probably turn out to be right. From Wren's experience, people did strange things for even stranger reasons. He took a deep breath and let it out in a series of thoughtful little puffs, glancing around the room. 'Not an ashtray anywhere, no booze in the cupboards, no sign that he was writing himself prescriptions.' Wren tapped the pile of photocopies. 'Nothing here that points to anything scandalous. It all adds up to a good man and a good life.'

'Looks that way,' Spearing agreed.

'Then how come he winds up getting stabbed to death in his own examination room?'

'We're back to Sloane. A whacked-out vet with some kind of monkey on his back.'

'I'm beginning to think you're right,' Wren answered. He looked up suddenly, his eyes tracking around the room. He frowned.

'What?' Spearing asked, frowning back.

'Why only one upstairs?' Wren said quietly.

'One what?' asked Spearing.

His older partner climbed to his feet and walked out of the room. He headed for the stairs and went up, Spearing right behind him. Wren went directly to the master bedroom and stepped into the room. He stared at the large, dark wood architectural model of the Shinto shrine, sitting in lonely grandeur on a small table close to the slightly curved windows of the turret.

'I don't get it,' said Spearing.

Wren crossed the room and squatted down on his haunches in front of the exquisite reproduction. 'It's special,' said Wren, speaking half to himself and half to his partner. 'It had some special meaning to him.' The older man stared at the model for a long moment, then carefully used the nail of his right index finger to ease open the perfectly modeled little doors leading into the shrine's interior. He fished around in the little space behind the doors and pulled out a tiny, yellowing strip of paper three inches long and half an inch high. He pulled his reading glasses out of the pocket of his jacket and used them like a magnifying glass, squinting through one lens to read the inscription on the paper.

'What does it say?' asked Spearing.

'Left 22, Right 90, one full turn, right to 34.'

'A combination.'

'Which means there has to be a safe around here somewhere.' Wren came upright, knees clicking. He winced at the sharp pain that lanced through his thighs and turned to Spearing. 'Who does that kind of work in town?'

'Mark Danby on Roper Street,' Spearing answered promptly.

'He been a locksmith long?'

'Ever since I can remember,' Spearing said. 'And his old man had the store before him.'

'Give him a call. Ask him if he or his old man ever installed a safe for Alberoni and if so, where the hell is it?'

Spearing nodded and went downstairs. He was back up in the bedroom in less than five minutes. 'Dandy checked his records. His old man installed it in the floor in the northeast corner of the master bedroom.'

'Underneath the wardrobe,' said Wren.

Wren and Spearing rolled the heavy piece of mahogany furniture to one side, revealing a flush-plate jewelry safe set into the hardwood floor. Using the ring tab in the door, Wren pulled it open, revealing the combination dial inside. He knelt down, the reading glasses on his face now, and worked the combination. He pulled open the inner door and lifted out the only thing inside the safe – a shoebox, held closed with knotted parcel twine. Wren took the box over to the bed, laid it down and took out his penknife and a small, plastic evidence bag. He sliced through the twine, careful to leave the knot intact, then used the penknife to lift the twine into the evidence bag. He handed the bag to Spearing, then used the knife to pry open the box, revealing its contents.

Photographs. Each one about one inch by two inches, like ones you'd use on a passport, or get from a bus-station photo booth.

'Babies,' said Spearing, staring down into the box.

'Babies,' Wren agreed.

Hundreds of them.

# CHAPTER TWELVE

The middle-aged City Clerk had made a joke about it. 'The best restaurant in Prosper is ten miles out of town.' But Rachel knew the real reason Donny Hale had chosen such an out of the way spot was to ensure that he wasn't seen by anyone he knew. Appollonia's was a small Italian dining room attached to a four-star one-time fishing lodge located on the banks of the Kennikill River. By the time they reached dessert it was almost dark outside and close to ten o'clock.

They'd driven to the restaurant in Donny Hale's Lincoln Town Car, and from the moment she stepped into the vehicle's nauseatingly plush interior she'd pushed herself to make light conversation with the man, trying to keep up the pretense that it really was an interview for *Life Magazine*, but becoming more and more aware of the man's growing physical interest. He was nervous, guilty, horny and, most of all, he was inept. In 1974 he'd been Robby Skelton's yipping little sidekick, obviously in awe of the taller, stronger, better looking boy. Now, hair thinning and waist thickening, he was on his own and not doing very well at all. The worst of it was that he was trying to drown his fears in alcohol; a Harvey Wallbanger before the meal, an entire bottle of Valpolicella during, and a double brandy with his zabaglione. Donny was pissed.

'So, what do you think?' he asked, grinning broadly. He was smoking one of Rachel's cigarettes, tapping his ash into the half-empty dessert dish.

'About what?' asked Rachel, trying to keep the smile steady.

'This place,' said Hale. He waved a hand around the small room, his voice too loud. There was only one other couple in the room, too young and too in love to notice.

'Nice,' said Rachel.

*Let's get on with it. Make your move, asshole.*

He grinned widely. 'Better than a piece of liver with a nice Chianti and a few fava beans.' He made a particularly revolting, slithering sound with his lips and tongue.

'True enough,' said Rachel.

*What is he talking about?*

'A nice Chianti and a few fava beans,' Hale repeated.

'You said that.'

'It's a joke.'

'Oh.' She didn't see the humor.

'You never saw *The Silence of the Lambs*? Anthony Hopkins, Jodie Foster?'

'I guess I missed it.' Rachel shrugged, trying to sound off-hand. She could feel her stomach knot as it always did when she was forcibly reminded of the terrible, nightmare hole in the center of her life. The last television show she could remember watching before she fled with Lauren was an episode of *Marcus Welby MD*. These days the only medical shows she could find were dark and moody with half the doctors being either suicidal or alcoholics.

'How could you miss something like that?' Hale asked, his tone irritated. 'It won Oscars. It was huge!' The blond-haired man spread his arms wide, almost knocking over his wine glass. 'Huge!'

*Let's get this show on the road.*

Rachel leaned back in her chair. 'I'm hot,' she said.

'Oh yeah?'

'When I was doing research for this story I came across an article from the sixties on communes. There was one around here, wasn't there?'

'Sure,' Hale nodded. He brushed crumbs off the front of his shirt. 'Morningstar.' His brows knit together and he looked a little uncomfortable. 'What's that got to do with being hot?'

'Is it around here?'

'Not far.' Hale shrugged. The apprehension was stronger now. She could see his Adam's apple popping up and down his neck as he swallowed. Dry mouth.

*Old memories, Donny? Bad dreams maybe?*

'There was a picture of a pond. A swimming hole.'

'Yeah?'

'I'd love to go for a swim.'

'Too many bugs out there this time of year. You wouldn't like it.' Hale's eyes had gone small and she could see little beads of sweat in the pale pockets of skin below the lower lids. 'Besides, we don't have any suits.'

Rachel smiled, stretching out the moment like a hot wire. 'I haven't gone skinny-dipping in years.'

The Prosper County Health Services Medical Center was located just south of the city limits, just past the Beechwood old folk's home. The sprawling, five-story poured-concrete building was screened by tall stands of cedar and was barely visible from the road. Wren parked his car in the mostly empty lot and headed for the big sliding doors of the emergency entrance. Sitting on benches outside the doors, half a dozen men and women in their night clothes were smoking cigarettes. One of them had an IV unit on a stand with him, and one of the women, dressed in a floral robe, had a wheeled bottle of oxygen with her as she puffed. A nurse in a crisp white uniform and big, boxy white shoes was standing as she smoked.

Wren went through the doors, cut across the small, brightly lit and deserted lobby, then went down a short, yellow-walled hall that led to the blood labs and the x-ray department. He stopped in front of one of the service elevators, stabbed the down button and waited. The Prosper morgue, like every other morgue Wren had ever visited, was in the basement. The elevator came, the doors opened and Wren stepped inside. When he stepped out two levels down, the air was at least ten degrees colder and tinged with a suspiciously overpowering scent of pine needles.

He went down a long, narrow, tile-floored corridor,

ducked his head into Prine's office and saw that the pathologist wasn't there. He went farther down the hall to the autopsy room and pushed through the swinging doors.

The room smelled like a hideous combination of rotting meat and underarm deodorant. Somebody had used a pine-scented spray to cover the ghastly stench of the bloated body on the autopsy table. Prine was standing on a short stepladder beside the table, taking photographs of the just-opened corpse like an artist documenting a work in progress.

Wren was alone in the room with Prine and the putrefied cadaver. The detective stood well back, not wanting to get too close to the body. 'George?'

'With you in a second,' replied the Medical Examiner. He was dressed in a white lab coat over surgical scrubs and a T-shirt. After office hours Prine liked to dress down.

'Who's on the table?' Wren asked. From where he stood the body didn't look like anyone he'd ever known, although given the gaseous bloat and the purpled flesh it was hard to tell.

'I think it's Ed Zuckerman,' said Prine, taking a few more shots, the flash popping brightly. 'No ID on him, but there's monofilament line wrapped all over the body and the clothes fit the description of what he was wearing when he went out fishing.'

'That was more than two weeks ago,' said Wren, recalling the name. 'His wife called him in as missing.'

'Body just turned up in Stoney Creek. Caught under a log in an eddy, that's why he didn't show up sooner. Scared the living shit out of Charlie Boatman's Scout troop. They went up there on an overnight to roast some weenies and marshmallows. One of the kids went looking for kindling and found this.' He took a final shot, then climbed down from the ladder.

'Any sign of foul play?'

'No.' Prine pushed the rewind button on the camera and it began to make a high-pitched whining sound as the film was reeled back into the cassette. He nodded toward a collection of glass fragments on the stainless steel table beside the one that held the putrefying remnants of what had once been the owner of Zuckerman's Five and Dime on State Street. 'You can still read part of the label. Jack Daniel's. Ed's lubricant of choice.'

'You think he was drunk?'

'I bet the tox scan comes up showing him pissed to the eyeballs. He probably got tangled up in his own line, slipped, fell into the water, banged his head on a rock and drowned.'

'One less for me to handle,' said Wren.

Prine nodded. 'You wanted to talk to me about the Alberoni report?'

'Yeah, if you don't mind. I've finished for the day, but this one's going to keep me up all night unless I can get a grip on it.'

'My office or the cafeteria?'

Prine's office was awash in eight-by-ten glossies of dead bodies in varying states of decay. 'The cafeteria,' said Wren. He glanced at the thing on the autopsy table. 'You're just going to leave him there?'

Prine smiled. 'Why? You think he's going to spoil or something?'

The cafeteria was a low-ceilinged, brightly lit rectangle on the main floor with one glass wall facing out into the Medical Center's central courtyard. Wren knew the courtyard was a maze of flowerbeds, hedges and paths, but at this time of night it was dark and the glass was reflecting the empty tables of the cafeteria's interior. The loudest sound in the room was the faint humming of the vending machines beside the main entrance. Prine bought himself a Coke, an egg salad sandwich and a bowl of Jell-O. Wren poured himself a mug of decaffeinated coffee.

'So tell me what bugs you about Alberoni?' Prine asked, seating himself at a table close to the glass wall. Wren sat down across from him and took a sip from his mug of coffee. Wren started his meal with a plastic spoonful of the red gelatine dessert. 'I thought I was pretty clear.'

'You were,' Wren nodded.

'Those baby pictures you told me about when you called?' Prine took another spoonful of Jell-O. 'You said you were going to bring them.'

'I did.' Wren patted his jacket pocket. 'A few of them. But it's not just the pictures.'

'What?'

'You said in your report that he had a cleft palate.'

Prine nodded. 'That's right. You could see the scar on his upper lip. Lots of people have them.' He smiled. 'I can take him out of the cooler and show you the surgical scar inside his mouth if you want.'

'No thanks,' said Wren. 'You said it was "late-corrected". What does that mean?'

'Just what it says.' Prine shrugged. He finished off the Jell-O and began unwrapping his sandwich. 'Late-corrected. From the looks of the inside of his mouth and the breadth of the scar it was probably done when he was thirteen or fourteen. Maybe even later.'

'Why would you wait? Isn't it better to do it early?'

'Sure, but it's expensive. Maybe his family didn't have the money.'

'According to his obituary his father was a doctor in New York.'

'Maybe he was a doctor of philosophy.'

'It was MD.'

'Weird,' said Prine, taking a big bite of his sandwich. He washed down the bite with a slug of Coke.

'What about the circumcision?'

'What about it?' Prine responded.

'You mentioned it specifically.'

'Part of the autopsy protocol. Nothing peculiar. Lots of people are circumcised.' He took another swig of Coke. 'I'm circumcised as a matter of fact.'

'He was eighty-five years old. I didn't think they circumcised people back when he was born.'

'If you were Jewish they did.'

'Sure,' said Wren. 'But Alberoni was a Catholic.'

'Who says?' Prine asked. He finished off the first half of the sandwich and began the second.

'He was doctor of record for St Anthony's Parish among other things.'

'So what?' Prine answered, shrugging again and speaking around a lump of white bread and egg salad. 'Jews can't work for Catholics?'

'He was a member of the Knights of Columbus,' said Wren. 'Not a lot of Jewish KCs, I think you'll agree.'

'True enough.'

'His father's name was Nathan. Maybe he *was* Jewish.'

'Look him up, find out,' said Prine.

'How?' Wren asked.

'I'll do it for you,' said Prine. 'The AMA will have a listing for Alberoni and his father. Give me a day or two.'

'Appreciate it,' said Wren.

'The pictures,' Prine reminded him.

Wren dug into his pocket and brought out a handful of pictures he'd taken from the box in Alberoni's bedroom. The rest of them were locked securely away in the property room back at the station. Wren pushed the photographs across the table. Prine picked one up, examining it as he finished his sandwich.

'What do you think?' asked Wren.

Prine picked up a second photo, then a third. 'All newborns, none of them more than a day or two old.'

'How can you tell?'

'Shape of the head. Gets squished coming down the birth canal; one of nature's miracles, you know? Takes about a week for the head to get all round and cute – unless you're like this one.' He handed one of the pictures back to Wren. The child in it had a perfectly shaped head.

'Caesarean?' Wren suggested.

'Smart boy,' Prine nodded.

'There's writing on the back of each photograph,' said Wren. 'They all have the initials CSB or MCV. The numbers are dates.'

Prine picked up a photograph and flipped it over. He peered at the writing. 'MCV 6.24.39.' He chewed his lip thoughtfully. 'We can presume the date refers to the date of birth. What about the initials?'

'I think they stand for Maryhill Children's Village. CSB probably stands for Catholic Services Bureau. The dates go from the mid-thirties up to the late sixties. The ones after 1959 don't have any initials.'

'What's your problem with all of this?' Prine asked. 'Alberoni was a doctor in Prosper for more than fifty years. He delivered a lot of babies. So what?'

'Why would he keep pictures, and why so meticulously dated, and why keep them hidden in a safe?'

'What's this Maryhill Children's Village?' Prine asked. 'I've never heard of it.'

'I think it was some kind of maternity home. I'm not sure.'

'Unwed mothers?'

'Something like that.' Wren looked down at the pictures on the table and thought for a moment. He picked up a photograph of the Caesarean newborn and turned it over: CSB 9.9.44. He looked at Prine. 'If you gave birth by Caesarean section back in 1944, where would the surgery have been done?'

Prine frowned, thinking about it. He shrugged. 'If there was time you probably would have sent the patient to the hospital in Newburgh.'

'What about an emergency, or if you wanted to keep it private?'

'Alberoni's office I guess. I think I read something once about him having some kind of clinic and surgery back then.'

'Where would the records be?'

'Not here,' said Prine. 'Long gone presumably.'

'But the birth would have been registered.'

'Sure. With the Town Clerk's Office. Back then you had to register the child within seven days of the birth.' Prine swallowed the last of his Coke and put the empty can down on the table. 'Where are you going with this? Alberoni had a speech impediment when he was a kid, a clipped dong and he liked to keep pictures of the babies he delivered. I wouldn't like to see you take that to D'Arcy Quinn as a motive for murder.' The pathologist belched primly and stood up. 'I have to get back to work on Ed,' he said. 'Anything else before I go?'

'No, thanks,' said Wren absently, looking down at the pictures on the table. 'Appreciate your help.'

'No problem,' said Prine. He stood with his hands gripping the back of the chair, looking down at Wren. 'Word of advice,' he said after a moment.

'Sure,' said Wren.

'Don't look for a needle that never got dropped in the haystack in the first place.'

'What's that supposed to mean?'

'You've got a suspect – this Sloane character; so go and arrest him before he bugs out and disappears into the woods.' He gestured at the pictures on the table. 'The motive for Alberoni's murder is in the present, not the past.'

Donny Hale piloted the Lincoln down the humped track that led to the old Morningstar commune site. He winced every time the oil pan smacked into a hidden rock and kept his eyes glued to the twin cones of light boring through the narrow darkness ahead. He had the air conditioning in the big pimp car cranked up enough to give Rachel goosebumps on the exposed skin of her legs and arms but Donny was sweating. It occurred to Rachel that he probably hadn't been here since the night Lauren died. He was returning to the scene of the crime and it was getting to him.

*Me too.*

'Me too what?' asked the blond-haired man.

*Christ! I said it out loud!*

'I didn't say anything,' she bluffed.

*Too far, too much, I'm losing it. We should go back.*

'How much further?'

'Not much.'

She knew exactly how far it was. Another hundred feet and they'd be out of the deep brush and into the clearing. She could see the car, parked at an angle to the right, almost seeing Lauren, sleeping in the comfortable back seat, cozy under her blanket.

*Blinkie. She called her blanket Blinkie.*

Rachel bit back the tears, forcing herself to stay calm, focusing her eyes on the built-in, back-lit compass set just above the rear-view mirror. It read north and barely wavered.

They reached the clearing, the headlights swooping in a wide arc across the site. 'Here we are,' said Hale. There was a frog in his throat. He cleared it, turned to Rachel and smiled at her. She could smell the wine on his breath.

Vodka and chewing gum, that's what Robby Skelton's breath smelled of – vodka and chewing gum.

*Mint.*

She wanted to vomit.

'Well?' said Donny Hale.

Rachel opened her mouth to scream, to yell, to spit in his face. She lifted her hand to claw his face and stopped and said nothing, and smiled. She turned away, popped the door and stepped out into the warm night, out of the too-cool automobile. The smell of sun-hot straw filled her nostrils from the tall, untended grass that had grown up everywhere like sheaves of wheat and barley. She stared into the night, looking across the gently sloping pasture that led up to the bracken and the line of trees that marked the edge of Paul Goodman's Wildwood. It was dark enough to take the color out of the night, but still light enough to see. Lauren had died less than fifty feet away from where she stood, on the right, between the parked Lincoln and the unnatural rectangle of darkness that marked the old Chicken Coop, where the bachelor quarters had been.

Two sets of memories tried to prevail. The smoky insides of her first visit to the Coop and the sight of half a dozen naked men with drooping scrotums and swinging dicks, all clustered around an old napthalene cooking stove, arguing about how it was supposed to work . . .

And.

The light and heat and blast from the rising ball of flame that had consumed the car, turning every detail of their faces into stark, etched shadows. Her scream. 'Penny for them,' said Donny Hale. He was standing in front of the headlights which, like some kind of huge night light, he'd left blazing.

*He's frightened. He thinks he's going to see a ghost.*

'You're going to run down your battery,' said Rachel.

'It's brand-new,' said Hale.

'Which way?'

'I'm not sure.'

Rachel knew, but she wasn't going to let him know that, not yet. 'I can hear running water,' she lied.

She headed off across the old cow pasture, veering slightly to the right just beyond the Coop and the big flat oval of hard-packed earth where nothing grew even after all this time, marking the spot where they'd parked the old school bus, its leaky oil pan scouring a no-grow zone for twenty feet in all directions. The old wood-working shop was nothing more than a hump in the ground, but Rachel knew it was there.

Skirting it, she headed into the trees, walking the narrow ridge edged with whispering birch trees that ran alongside the little stream a dozen feet below. Passing the slight falling away of the land on her left she kept her eyes turned the other way, trying hard not to think and failing, feeling the old, old pain, and a soft choking in her throat.

*That's where we buried Matthew.*

She could hear Donny Hale flailing around in her wake, his breath coming hard as he tried to keep up. She heard him trip and fall and snarl out an expletive and she smiled, enjoying even that small pain.

*It's going to get worse any minute now, Donny Boy.*

She smelled the pond before she saw it. Cold and fresh with that deeper, darker tang of old, rotting earth, like soil from an old battlefield, rich with blood and mealy bone.

*Stop it.*

That kind of thing had been Paul Goodman's stock-in-trade, stories to make their own mythology he'd called his tales of how the ancients had lived and walked here a hundred thousand years before. Smells and tastes and love and lives taken an eon in the past, but still echoing in their collective unconscious.

Anthropological gobbledegook to spook the girls and boys. She had a brief flashing memory of Beth, the big-eyed blonde she'd seen with Paul a few days before. Was he using the same ghost stories on her to get between her shaking, eager little thighs? Did he have a cute *Lord of the Rings* name for her as well?

She stopped at the top of the ridge and looked

downward. The oval pool was like a black hole in the earth, swallowing light, reflecting nothing. She heard Donny Hale panting just behind her and she stepped down between the trees to the bank of the pond, and walked quickly halfway around it, putting the pond between her and the approaching man. She saw his shadowy figure reach the top of the ridge, outlined against the purple light of the sky. He stopped.

'Where are you?' he called. There was a worried catch in his voice, almost as though he knew that there was something wrong. And he was right.

'Down here.'

His shadow disappeared from the top of the ridge and she heard him sliding down toward the pool. 'I can't see you.'

'You will,' she said. 'Just watch.' She put down her heavy shoulder bag and quickly kicked off her shoes, peeled off her jacket, dark T-shirt and her jeans. Finally she stepped out of her panties, knowing that her nude body would pick up all that was left of the light and make her a beacon.

Thirty feet away, across the pond, she heard Donny's indrawn breath and then the sound of him stripping off his own clothes. The more clothes he removed, the more visible he became until she could make him out quite clearly. A long way from where he'd been – Robby Skelton's pretty-boy sidekick. From where she stood she could see the droop of his middle-aged gut over the stubby jut of his penis, rooted like a tiny bird's egg in a nest of pale pubic hair. His legs were skinny and china white, his shoulders dropped and his chest was sagging.

Rachel tensed the muscles in her back and buttocks, feeling the hard loops and skeins of tendon and muscle. The best therapy she'd been able to find over all those years at Brockhurst and the other hells was constant, obsessive exercise, working out using the most basic equipment from climbing endless stairs, to leg lifts with the steel bars of her bedframe for a partner. They had a word for it now. Hardbody, and that's exactly what she was. She'd never been very tall or muscular, but now, at least, mind and body, she was hard.

As stone.

Rachel dived into the pond, cutting down into the water like a knife. It was black and freezing, like diving into the past. Consumed by the headache then, she'd watched the bubbles rise and felt her hair against her back like seaweed, but now her hair was chopped short and what she felt was the cold tightening of her skin, her nipples hardening, her vulva swelling, sealing and protecting her. She came up in almost the exact center of the pool and shook the water out of her eyes and hair, making long ripples with outstretched arms like the wings of some black angel as she moved to keep herself afloat. 'Come on in, Donny,' she called out quietly. 'The water's just right.'

She watched him step slowly into the pool, up to his knees, skinny arms wrapped tightly around his chest. 'Jesus! It's freezing!'

'Good for the soul,' she said. 'Come on.'

He stepped forward, wincing as his feet touched the algae-covered rocks that ran around the edge. 'Gross,' he muttered.

'All the way, Donny. Swim to me.'

He shivered, his whole body caught up in it, his head turtling down into his shoulders. He took a deep breath, puffing out his cheeks, then flopped forward into a shallow dive, the pale moons of his buttocks offered briefly to the air. He came up a few seconds later, no more than a few feet from her. She could see his legs churning under the water and his arms frogging back and forth in perfect summer-camp swimming-lesson form.

'Been a while,' he puffed.

'You're doing fine,' said Rachel. She waved her arms just below the surface of the water, knowing that he could see her breasts and hips and thighs. 'Why don't you come closer?'

'Gimme a second.' He was still puffing. His slightly goggling thyroid eyes were wide and round and his thinning hair was slicked back against his skull, revealing what would be a monk's tonsure within a few years. Donny was going downhill fast. Rachel inhaled, the sour smell of the man's breath mixing with the quick clean scent of the forest and the darker, richer tang of the black water they were floating in.

'Come on, Donny,' she repeated. 'I'm waiting.'

He struggled forward a few feet, half his mind concentrating on keeping afloat, his other senses tracking Rachel's ghostly figure only a foot or so away. He reached out and let the fingers of one hand touch her belly, then moved the hand up to her small, hard breast. She didn't mind, or care. She'd endured much worse from patients and staff alike at Brockhurst and her body had long ago given up any thought of pleasure at another's touch.

'Nice,' he muttered. Rachel reached down and found his cold-shrivelled organ, shrunken to a short, fat sausage in the nest of the man's pubic hair. There was barely enough to grasp. 'Too cold in here,' he shivered, trying to explain the diminution. She reached down a little further and found the small, thick-skinned sack of his scrotum. She gripped it lightly and felt the first tapping of his growing penis on the back of her wrist. 'Sweet,' said Hale. She watched as his head tilted back and his eyes closed. She kept her fingers lightly moving and heard him sigh.

Rachel spoke softly, almost a croon. 'We used to come here to make love on the banks of the Rivendell. Sometimes just like now, in the water.'

'Huh?' Hale's head came up out of the pool and he looked confused. 'What are you talking about?'

'This was everybody's favorite spot.'

'You said you saw this place in an old *Life Magazine*.'

'I lied.'

Hale tried to back away from Rachel, but she kept her grip on his testicles, squeezing just a little harder. 'What the fuck is going on?'

'We were the Children of the Flowers,' said Rachel. 'That's what Paul called us.'

'Who the fuck is Paul?'

Even now she could remember the lines he'd spoken. Beautiful, perfect lines. 'The tide is sweeping inland, the ancient sea walls crumble before the cleansing sea. We are the Children of the Flowers, and the Children of the Flowers are . . . now.'

'This is nuts,' said Hale. He pushed hard with his feet, bicycling them under the water. Rachel twisted her hand slightly and he yelped. 'Hey!'

'Who was the girl?' Rachel asked. 'The one with the Zippo lighter.' She knew it was a Zippo because she'd seen the plain steel glint and heard the familiar 'click' as the girl in the high-school jacket flicked it open.

'What?'

'She was with you and Robby and your other friend at Miggs' store that evening, remember?'

'What the fuck are you talking about?'

She squeezed harder and Hale screamed, his face jerking down under the water. She kept her grip hard on him, keeping her wrist slightly twisted, and waited for him to surface. 'There were four of you.'

'Let go of me!'

'Four of you in the store.'

'Let go!'

'But she had the lighter. She was the one who torched the car.'

'Whaa?' The pain was cutting through the alcohol fog and he was beginning to get it now.

'What was her name, Donny?'

'I don't know what you're talking about, you

fucking bitch!' He tried to get away again and this time Rachel squeezed her hand as tightly as she could, feeling the hard boiled pigeon eggs of his testicles almost bursting between the scissor grip of her thumb and fingers. This time the sound of his scream was so loud it sailed up past the surrounding, smothering wall of trees and echoed dimly in the distance.

The scream ended as he forgot where he was and his face slipped under the water again as he doubled over. Rachel let go with her hand and with a quick, strong stroke, pushed herself back to the far bank. She climbed out of the water, feeling the warm air all around her, and bent to open her shoulder bag that lay beside her clothes. She turned back to the pond just in time to see Donny Hale surface again, retching and gagging, his head spinning around, searching for his tormentor.

He coughed, spitting water. 'I'll fucking kill you!' He flailed at the water, swimming toward her.

'No you won't.' She fired the big handgun she'd pulled out of the her purse, feeling it buck hard into her palm, the soft-nosed bullet *thripping* sharply into the water even before the cracking thunderclap of the shot went yodelling off into the night. Donny Hale stopped moving except for the tiniest fluttering of his hands beneath the water.

'Oh God.' It was barely a whisper.

Keeping the gun trained on him, Rachel reached down into the bag and picked up the expensive cassette recorder she'd bought in town that afternoon.

She clicked it on. 'It was going to be a red truck fuck wasn't it, Donny?'

'Oh shit.'

'You were going to slip me the snake, big time, right?'

'Please. I don't . . .'

'You were going to make me scream for the cream, weren't you?'

She fired again, taking aim and making sure that it went well wide, knowing that even through the water the bullets could still do terrible damage if they struck flesh and bone and soft organ.

'Dear Jesus God!' She watched his face screw up and the tears flow and his hands spasmed towards his groin to cover his shame as he lost control of his bladder and passed water into the pond. 'You're fucking crazy!' he whispered, horrified by the raw, obvious truth of his statement. But he still didn't really know.

'Come on, Donny, think!' She fired a third time and he made a horrible little mewing sound like a kitten being drowned in a bag. 'Red truck fuck, scream for the cream, moan for the bone. You were the asshole who tried to rhyme "weep" with "meat", remember?'

'Who the fuck are you!' he screamed, his voice cracking. 'Why are you doing this to me!'

'I've got a real thing for Clint Eastwood movies, did you know that? Nice simple morality plays; nothing too complex. You remember one called *High Plains Drifter*?'

'No, please, I . . .'

'A guy gets whipped to death and then comes back to haunt the townspeople that did it to him. He makes them paint the whole town red.' She paused, lifted the gun again and aimed it at the pale blob in the water that was Donny Hale's head. 'That's me,' she whispered. 'Or maybe I'm the Count of Monte Cristo. I didn't go to the Chateau D'If and I didn't escape by winding myself into an old man's shroud, but it was pretty close, Donny. I spent twenty years in a bunch of mental institutions where the male nurses idea of having fun was putting a female inmate in restraints in some back room then fucking her up the ass until she bled, or taking out an old lady's dentures so she wouldn't bite down when they forced her to give them oral sex.' Rachel took a long shuddering breath. 'Nightmares, Donny. Endless nightmares. Locked, stinking rooms. The smell of piss and shit and puke and drugs so often and so much you didn't know if any of it was real, you only knew that it was hurting.'

'Oh, please . . .' It was a whimper now. She cocked the gun and Donny Hale began to sob and weep.

'You and Robin Skelton and two other people harassed my daughter Lauren and I in Miggs' store back in 1974, can you remember back that far, Donny? Ford was pardoning Nixon that day, but I haven't forgiven you for what you did.'

'No,' said the frightened blond man in the pool.

*Now you remember.*

'That's right, Donny. There were four of you, all

wearing Woodrow Wilson High School jackets. I kicked in the taillight of Robby's truck and you followed me when I went up here. You put a rag into my gas tank and the girl used a Zippo lighter to set fire to the car and the only benefit of the doubt I'm willing to give you is to think that none of you knew my daughter was in the back seat sleeping, and that you didn't know you were murdering an innocent child.'

'We didn't know.' The tears were streaming down his cheeks. 'Oh Jesus, we didn't know!' The cold water was taking its toll as well. He was weakening. 'Can I get out now?'

'I want the names of the other two. The girl and the other guy.'

'What are you going to do?'

Rachel shifted her aim a foot to the right and squeezed the trigger. Hale yelled out loud and flailed off to one side, trying to escape the shot that had already passed him by. 'It's none of your business what I'm going to do to them. All you have to worry about is what I'm going to do to *you* unless you tell me their names.' She cocked the gun again, the bright, stainless steel cylinder clicking around another notch. 'Ask me what I'm going to do to you if you don't tell me, Donny.'

'What?' He choked. 'What are you going to do?'

Rachel smiled. 'I'm going to blow your fucking cock off, Donny. I'm going to punch you an up-front asshole and watch you bleed to death through it, right here and now. So tell.'

'I can't. We didn't mean . . . Oh shit, I *can't* tell you.' Hysteria was setting in.

'Sure you can. Two names.'

'You're going to kill me, aren't you?' he moaned.

'Risk you have to take. I'm going to give you to the count of one to tell me the names, Donny. No more screwing around, okay.' She paused. 'One.'

He barely hesitated. 'The guy was Mike Parker.'

'His father owned the bank?'

*Set up a trust to pay off Miggs. Making sense now. Father covering for son.*

'That's right. He owns it now. A bunch of real estate too, and he's also the Chancellor of Oneida College. Real big wheel.' Hale was shivering constantly now, his teeth clicking together. 'I'm freezing. Please. I just want to get out of here.' He shook his head, sobbing. 'I'm sorry, okay. I'm really fucking sorry! We didn't mean it!'

*I was chust following orders! Not good enough, Donny.*

'The girl?' She'd always been fascinated by that; the vision of the girl, in the light of the first small flame, looking up at her boyfriend for approval. It always seemed so strange to her that the person who actually started the fire had been a girl. Strangely, sadly now, it really didn't seem to matter any more. 'Who was she?' Her voice was flat, energy draining from her like blood from a mortal wound.

*I really don't want to know.*

*I'm so terribly tired of it all.*

*They murdered my daughter.*

217

*They have to pay.*

Hale's voice was a chattering whisper. 'Quinn. It was that little bitch D'Arcy Quinn.'

Wren lay on top of the sheets, stripped to his Jockeys in the dark, his window open, the fan clicking as it reached the end of its swing, then started back again, stirring the hot air and giving him one cooling second out of five. Maybe Prine and Kenny Spearing were right, maybe he should stop looking for mystery where there was none. Allan Sloane had been the last person to see Alberoni alive and Wren knew the man had lied to him at least once. Sloane had said he was forty-one years old; if that was true he'd turned eighteen some time in 1974, long after there were any outer perimeter firebases like the ones in the photographs on his wall. In fact, if he was telling the truth about his age it was unlikely that he'd shipped out to Vietnam at all – the last troops were already on their way home by then and everything was almost over except those last, horrible days as Saigon was overrun.

He rolled over on his side, staring across the room. Tomorrow he'd start some real checking on his so-called Vietnam veteran. He heard the door open and shut in the room beside his and then the soft sound of creaking floorboards. The wall between his room and the dark-haired lady journalist was like cardboard. He glanced at the glowing dial of his watch. One in the morning. What had kept her out so late. Oddly, he felt a twinge of jealousy and wondered where *that* had come from? He heard the ticking sound of coat hangers tapping together in her closet and for a few seconds he had an image of the woman's body as she stripped down for bed. The crows' feet around her eyes said she was in her forties, but in jeans and a T-shirt she looked like a small, well built woman ten or fifteen years younger. In the old days the short, shaggy hair and the boyish body would have had her described as 'gamine'. A female Peter Pan.

A sense of humor too, and old enough to know exactly what she was doing in bed.

'Enough,' he muttered softly to himself. He padded his head against the pillow with his hands and closed his eyes, concentrating on the soft humming of the fan.

# CHAPTER THIRTEEN

Police Chief Robin Skelton stared down at the body on the rubber sheet. 'This is bullshit, Wren.' He was dressed in a perfectly tailored uniform, his cap perched just so, tilted slightly to the right. Wren had set up a crime scene perimeter with yellow tape, roping off an area around the body. There were four vehicles parked beyond the tape, just off the road: George Prine's dark green Miata, the Glades dark-windowed Chevy wagon, Wren's unmarked Caprice and the Chief's exotic, cherry-bar-topped Land Rover. Twenty feet to the right, down a steep bank, the bright water of Stoney Creek babbled happily downhill in the early afternoon sunlight. The sky was flat blue and cloudless, but there was a faint whiff of ozone in the air, as though there was a storm closing in. Wren could hear Kenny Spearing slogging around in rubber boots at the foot of the bank, going over the spot where the body was found. Prine was silently giving the body an on-site once over before it was loaded into the stationwagon by the waiting Boris and Igor.

'Total bullshit,' Skelton repeated angrily.

'Why's that?' asked Wren, coming up out of his crouch, not wanting to talk to Skelton while looking up at him; he preferred it the other way around.

'Two murders in less than a week,' Skelton snapped. 'Not on my patch, Wren, no God damn way that's going down. I want some answers, and fast.'

Nice, clipped, ROTC tones but not a lot of force behind the words. Bluff and bluster, thought Wren. It was a good thing he'd been an MP and not in combat; that kind of bad ass act would have had him fragged within days.

'I can give you one answer,' George Prine said, standing up and wiping his hands on his L.L. Bean fly-fisherman's vest.

'What's that?'

'He was stabbed to death, exactly the same way as Alberoni.'

'Shit,' said Skelton. He looked down at the body. There was a neat, vertical slit about three quarters of an inch long just under the base of the ribcage.

'Same knife?' asked Wren.

Prine lifted his shoulders. 'Hard to tell. Knives don't have grooves like bullets, but there are a few indicators.'

Skelton's jaw hardened. 'I don't want indicators for Christ's sake! I want somebody under arrest.'

Prine looked Skelton in the eye. Wren thought it was an odd confrontation: the dapper Chief with movie-star good looks and the frowzy, curly-haired pathologist in a rumpled seersucker suit with sweat marks under the arms. 'I don't work for you, Chief,' said Prine, his voice cool and even. 'I work for the County, so back off.'

The good looking Police Chief glared at the pathologist. 'Sorry.' He didn't sound sorry at all. 'This thing has me rocked.'

'Then why don't you let Detective Wren and I get on with our jobs,' said Prine. Skelton scowled, then silently turned on his heel and went back to the Land Rover. He backed and filled with a lot of tire spinning, then headed down the logging road towards the main highway.

'Thanks,' said Wren. 'I needed a little breathing room there.'

'He's an arrogant little prick,' said Prine. 'You have to put up with his crap, but I don't.'

'I'm still not sure what he was doing here.'

Kenny Spearing came slogging up the riverbank, clumps of mud all over his boots. 'Told me he heard it go out on the scanner. Came to see for himself.' The younger detective scraped the mud off of one boot with the toe of the other.

'Anything down there?' Wren asked.

'Nothing,' Spearing answered, shaking his head. 'Just the skid mark in the mud where he slid down the bank.'

Wren rocked back on his heels and looked down at the pale, naked body of Donald Hale. 'Riddle time,' said the detective sourly. 'What ties together an old man doctor and a naked City Clerk?'

'All you've got so far is cause of death, and that's only probable,' Prine cautioned.

'You take Country 18 half a mile farther, then turn left on the old Mountain Road and wind up in Allen Sloane's back yard,' said Kenny Spearing. He had his boots pried off and he was wringing out his socks, seated on the grass a yard away from the body.

It was too easy. 'You think Sloane did Hale?'

'He's the obvious suspect for Alberoni and, like Doc Prine says, they're tied together by cause of death.' He grinned at the pathologist. 'Sorry. Probable cause of death.'

Wren frowned. 'So out of nowhere this weirded-out guy who lives in the woods turns into some kind of serial killer?'

'Why not?' countered the younger man. 'To his neighbors the Unabomber was just a weirded-out guy living in a shack until the Fibbies got their break.' He grimaced at his feet. 'Damn boots leak.'

'Kenny's right,' said Prine. 'Nobody knows you're a serial killer until you get caught and show up on CNN. Jeffrey Dahmer was just a bad tenant with a smelly apartment until they nabbed him.'

'I hate to quote our recently departed Chief of Police, but as far as this case is concerned, that's just pure, unadulterated bullshit.' Wren paused, looking out over the babbling water to the wall of trees on the far side. The opposite bank of Stoney Creek was part of the Stoney Mountain Forest Preserve. If the City Clerk's body had been dumped on the other side of the narrow river the whole thing would be the State Police's problem.

'Why bullshit?' asked Spearing, wiggling the mud out from between his toes.

'In the first place, Alberoni's case has no clear motive, and neither does Mr Hale's death, at least not yet.'

'So what?' said Spearing. 'Since when does a psycho need a motive?' He shrugged. 'Leave *that* kind of bullshit to the shrinks.'

'Even psychos have motives,' Wren answered. 'They also have patterns. Dahmer ate his victims, for instance. Jack the Ripper disemboweled prostitutes. Except for the wounds there's no pattern here. Alberoni's found in his house, Hale is found dumped by a river. Alberoni is fully clothed, Hale is buck naked.'

'That is strange,' Prine agreed. He got down on his hands and knees and peered at the slit-shaped wound. 'I can't really tell just by looking, but it's a good bet he was naked when he was killed. There were visible traces of fiber in Alberoni's wound – from the shirt; there's nothing here.'

'But he wasn't killed here.'

'No. Definitely not,' said Prine, getting to his feet again. Kenny Spearing got up and padded back across the grass to the Caprice, boots and wet socks in hand. 'There's no blood traces anywhere, but there were a few small shards of plastic. Looks like green garbage bag material. I found it under his toenails.'

'No sign of the bag?'

'No.'

'So somebody killed him, bagged him and brought

him here to dump.' Wren shook his head. 'I still don't buy Sloane though.'

'Why not? Kenny says he doesn't live too far from here.'

'That's the point,' said Wren. 'Somebody goes to the trouble of shifting a body from where he does the deed, you think he'd shift it a little farther away from home.'

'If he's crazy, maybe he doesn't care,' suggested Prine.

'Sloane's not crazy, that much I'm sure of.' He paused. 'What are these "indicators" you were talking about?'

'The knife?' said Prine. 'I'm pretty sure it was a Buck knife from the shape of the bruise the tang left when it was rammed into the bodies.'

'There's got to be a million Buck knives out there.'

'Not with a little V-shaped notch in the tang,' said Prine. He drew it in the muddy soil. 'Like a deep scratch.' He stood up. 'Find me a Buck knife with that scratch and I'll give you a definite match to both Alberoni and Hale.'

Kenny Spearing came back from the Caprice, his bare feet pushed into his street shoes. 'Just came over the radio,' he said. 'A uniform just found Hale's car.'

'Where?'

'Parked in front of Blackie Lewis' Smoke Shop on Madison,' said Spearing. 'Half a block from Courthouse Square.'

\* \* \*

226

Rachel sat in the window seat of her room, cigarette in hand and a cooling cup of coffee on the window ledge. She had the Woodrow Wilson yearbook in her lap and, going through it, she'd realized why she hadn't spotted Parker, Hale or D'Arcy Quinn. Both the young boys in the graduating class had been absent when the photographs were taken, with nothing but the standard silhouette with mortarboard blank beside their name. It had taken her longer to find D'Arcy Quinn in the yearbook because she hadn't been in the graduating class at all and, in fact, had been a junior. Knowing the names now, Rachel had eventually picked them off from their pictures in the school annual; Hale had been a member of the Math Club and D'Arcy Quinn had been on the Junior Debating Team and the Junior Ski Team as well. That evening in Miggs' store the girl had obviously been wearing someone else's jacket.

*Sue Marsden.*

Skelton's girlfriend. The name popped into Rachel's head and she frowned, dragging on her cigarette. It was a possibility of course; Robby Skelton could have given his girlfriend a letter jacket as some kind of going steady pledge of his affections then taken it back when they broke up, ready to pass it on to someone else; he was just the type. She stubbed out her cigarette, crossed the room to her desk and flipped open her spiral-bound notebook and checked the name of the Marsden girl's sister. Rachel went back to her perch on the window seat and flipped through the pages of the yearbook. Presumably Anne

McConnel had been Anne Marsden back then. As it turned out she was also listed in the graduating class, right above her sister, except in this case there was a picture. Not as pretty as Susan, but sweet-faced and smiling.

Anne Marsden
'Che Sera, Sera'
Our own Little Orphan Annie has three main ambitions: get out of Woodrow Wilson High, picket the White House and become the first woman President of the United States.

Rachel slapped the yearbook shut and lit another cigarette. She looked out the window, across the street to the overgrown land that ran along the old railroad right of way. From where she sat she could see across to the old feed mill buildings and the big brick structures marking the long abandoned dairy and cheese factory. Everything was shimmering in the heat and there was no breeze to stir the air. It was mid-afternoon and dark clouds were beginning to gather on the northern horizon. A storm coming down from Lake Ontario. It would rain by evening, one of those classic Catskill thunder and lightning storms they used to say meant that the giants were playing skittles in the hidden valleys and hollows. Rip Van Winkle Time. *The Legend of Sleepy Hollow* and Ichabod Crane. Robby Skelton as Beau Brummel.
*What does that make me?*
*The Headless Horseman, of course.*

228

Rachel gathered up her things and left the room, pausing only long enough to look up Anne Marsden McConnel's address in the Prosper telephone directory. Rachel went out to her car, popped the glove compartment open and pulled out the street map that had been part of Barney Benechuck's 'Welcome to Prosper' package. According to the directory, Woodrow Wilson's Little Orphan Annie lived on Brock Street, not too far from downtown.

The Brock Street house turned out to be a pleasant looking two-story brick colonial squeezed on to a narrow lot between its neighbors, screened on both sides by trees and landscaped with a lot of low-maintenance shrubbery. She knocked, made her introductions and explanations to the pretty, dark-haired woman who answered the door, and was led into a living room of grays and beige and white on white, set off here and there by bursts of color. All of it was right off the pages of *Martha Stewart Living*, and so was Anne McConnel. It was the middle of the afternoon and the forty-something woman was a Liz Claiborne version of perfect unobtrusiveness. Who wore that much careful makeup just to run a vacuum cleaner around the house? Rachel felt slightly awkward in her jeans and T-shirt and out of style leather jacket.

'*Life Magazine*?' the woman asked, sitting down on a couch striped in alternating bands of gray and deeper gray.

'That's right.' Rachel nodded, dropping down into the big wicker chair across from her, a gray granite

229

coffee table between them. The only thing on the table was a bowl of carved wooden fruit. 'Mr Halloran at the high school suggested you might be an interesting person to talk to.'

'He never thought I was interesting in his music class.' Anne McConnel smiled. 'I couldn't even play the triangle.' The smile went a little chilly. 'Not like Sue. She could play anything.'

'Your sister?'

'That's right.'

'Older or younger?'

'Older.'

'I saw both of you in the yearbook; you were both in the same graduating class.'

Anne frowned. 'Susie was kept back a year.' The smile broke through again, a little more brittle now. 'She was pretty and popular. I was just smart.' She cupped her knees, then pulled nervously at the hem of her skirt. 'Can I get you anything. Coffee, tea?' She paused. 'Something cold?' Rachel saw the pink tip of the woman's tongue dart across her carefully colored lips.

'Whatever you're having,' said Rachel.

Anne flashed her smile, and slipped gracefully out of the room. A few seconds later Rachel heard the sound of ice cubes crackling into glasses. She looked around the room, trying to get some feeling for the people who lived here. It didn't amount to much; pale, expensively framed prints on the walls, flowers in terracotta planters and a gleaming, jet black Steinway baby grand in the far corner without any music on the stand or any other sign that it was ever used.

Anne came back with a tray set out with two glasses of iced tea and a cold-sweat glass jug three quarters filled. She put the tray down on the granite coffee table and handed Rachel a glass. Rachel saw that her glass had a sprig of mint tucked down between the ice cubes while Anne's glass went without. The woman lifted her glass and took a long swallow and Rachel saw an oily swirl as the vodka in Anne's glass went gliding around the ice cubes. Afternoon boozer; it didn't look as though Little Orphan Annie was a happy camper.

Rachel quickly went through her standard explanation and description of the article she was writing, letting the vodka in the woman's drink soothe whatever anxieties she might have about talking to a total stranger about her past. She started slowly, moving through the basics of what it had been like growing up in Prosper, then moving on to the more dangerous ground of high school, her sister, and Robin Skelton.

'I understand he's the Police Chief now.'

'That's right,' said Anne. 'Just like his dad.'

'According to Mr Halloran at the school, he and your sister were quite an item.'

'For a long time,' she nodded.

'When I went to high school there were all sorts of groups that kids hung around in. Cliques. Was it the same for you and your sister?'

'For her.' Anne took another long swallow of her

drink, then put the glass carefully down on the coffee table. She settled herself on the couch, tucking one knee up under herself, adjusting her skirt, then holding on to her ankle. She looked like someone modelling in a Sears catalog or a chatelaine in a *Good Housekeeping* article. 'Like I said before, Susie was one of the popular ones. She ran with people like Robby and Mike Parker and all the rest of them.'

'Donny Hale?'

She nodded. 'Sure. He was one of that bunch.'

'D'Arcy Quinn?'

'No,' she said, shaking her head. 'She was too young. I think she was a junior when we all graduated.'

'Didn't she go with Robin Skelton after he broke up with your sister?'

'No.' Anne reached out and picked up her glass, cupping the bottom so she didn't drip condensation on the couch fabric. She took a delicate sip and looked into her glass as though she expected to find something more down there among the ice cubes. 'Like I said, she was too young for that crowd.'

'You weren't part of it either?'

'Robby and his friends valued cup size, not IQ.'

Rachel laughed. 'I guess most boys are like that when they're teenagers.'

'I suppose.' Anne took another look into her glass, then downed the remainder of her drink. 'Everything comes around though.'

'What do you mean?'

'Things have a way of working out,' the woman

said, smiling a small, secret smile. 'Back in high school Susie and Robby were the magic couple; Susie was going to be a movie star in Hollywood and Robby was going to be a war hero.' She made a little snorting sound. 'At best I was going to wind up being Annie Activist, political as hell but unlucky in love.' She looked around the room and shook her head. 'It never occurred to anyone that I'd be the one to wind up marrying the rich doctor and having two perfect children.'

'Your husband's a doctor?'

'Superdoc,' she said, without any humor. 'But he doesn't save people's lives, he shaves budgets. He's the chief administrator of the Prosper Medical Center.'

'You must be very proud.'

'More like alone most of the time,' she answered. She straightened herself on the couch and grabbed her ankle a little more tightly. 'But I don't suppose any of this is going to be of any interest to you.'

'You'd be surprised.'

'I assumed this was going to be one of those breezy, nostalgia, Norman Rockwell kinds of things.' She smiled. '*Life Magazine* isn't known for its depth of coverage.'

'It's not I.F. Stone if that's what you mean,' said Rachel. The hip, left-wing newsletter had been just about the only periodical that came into Morningstar.

'Now those were the days,' said Anne McConnel. She stood up, half-filled her glass with iced tea from the jug, then disappeared into the kitchen. She came back with the glass full to the brim and arranged herself on the couch again. 'God! I wish I had a cigarette!'

'I've got some.' Rachel opened her bag and took out her Tareytons.

Anne waved them away. 'No. I quit years ago. Phillip won't allow it. I've had too many lectures on second-hand smoke to endure another.'

'There's always air freshener,' said Rachel, smiling. Anne smiled back. There was a long silence and then Anne climbed to her feet a little unsteadily, disappeared again, returning with a chipped saucer and a spray can of pot-pourri-scented Glade.

'Light me up,' said Anne, eyes shining. Rachel lit a cigarette, then slid the package and her lighter across the table. Anne lit up herself, drawing the smoke deeply into her lungs, eyes closed, without the slightest sign of a cough. She let the smoke out in two long streams from her nostrils and a third, uptilted from her pout-lipped mouth. 'Fantastic!' she said. She switched the cigarette to her other hand and took a sip of her refreshed iced tea. 'So tell me,' she said, smiling, smoking and drinking, 'what's the article really about?'

'I told you. It's a retread of an old thing we did on small-town America a long time ago.'

'I don't believe you.'

'Why not?'

'What I said. *Life* is Norman Rockwell. You look more like *The Village Voice*, or maybe *Rolling Stone*.' She shook her head and drew on her cigarette. 'You're doing something else, I can tell.'

Rachel took a deep breath; she'd known that something like this was bound to happen and now here it was. She let the breath out slowly. 'In the late summer of 1974 a woman supposedly set fire to her car at the old Morningstar commune site. Her five-and-a-half-year-old child was inside the car. The child burned to death and the woman was committed to an indefinite term in a New York mental institution. She was drugged by the police doctor throughout her interrogation and her preliminary hearing. Her name was Renee Lucas.'

Anne frowned and took another long drag on her cigarette. 'What month?'

'September.'

*No more. She'll blab it all over town.*

Anne nodded. 'Susie and I were in Europe. Dad's graduation present.' She shook her head. 'We weren't here when it happened but I remember people talking about it.' Her frown deepened. 'I still don't get it.'

'The woman didn't kill her child. She didn't set fire to the car.'

'I still don't see the point. It was all a very long time ago.'

'That *is* the point,' said Rachel. 'The woman spent more than twenty years in high security institutions for the criminally insane, and she was innocent.'

'You have proof?'

'Yes.'

'And that's what the story is about?'

'Yes.'

'If the woman didn't set fire to her car, who did?'

'I'm not sure,' Rachel lied. 'I'm still investigating.'

'All these questions about Robby Skelton and my sister.' Anne stubbed her cigarette out in the makeshift ashtray. 'You don't think she was involved do you? My God!'

'No. Not your sister,' said Rachel.

'Robby?' she whispered. Her eyes widened. 'Robby was involved?'

'It's beginning to look that way.'

'That's crazy! Robby wouldn't do a thing like that!'

'Really?'

'He was pretty mean when he was younger, but that doesn't make him a killer.'

'That's not what the woman says.'

'You've talked to her?'

*Frequently.*

'Yes, I've talked to her.'

'She said Robby set fire to her car?'

'He was involved.'

'But she must have had a trial. Didn't any of this come out?'

'Robby was never called as a witness. He just had a signed affidavit offered into evidence. There was no trial, just a preliminary hearing. The woman was bound over for an indefinite period.'

'Did Robby have an alibi?'

Rachel nodded. 'He said he was visiting a friend of his.'

'Who?'

'His name was Allan Sloane.'

The proper looking woman on the couch opposite let out a barking laugh. She reached out to the coffee table, tapped another Tareyton out of the pack and lit up again. She blew a cloud of smoke at the ceiling, then looked at Rachel, shaking her head.

'Not a chance?'

'Why not?'

'Robby hated Allan Sloane. Allan Sloane read books, for Christ's sake! When he went on trips with his old man the dentist he visited museums!'

The reading of Robin Skelton's affidavit into evidence was one of the few clear memories Rachel had of the hearing; there was no doubt in her mind – Allan Sloane had sworn that Robin Skelton had been with him all evening. That affidavit and Miggs' testimony that Rachel had come into his store alone had put the last nails in her coffin. The irony of it was that if she'd simply pleaded guilty to the murder of her child she would have been given a life sentence that would have seen her released from an ordinary prison after only eight, or perhaps ten, years instead of the two decades she'd spent in Brockhurst and those other hellholes.

'So who's lying?' Rachel asked finally. 'The records show that Allan Sloane said Robin Skelton was visiting him that night; if Skelton hated Sloane, what was he doing there in the first place?'

'Why don't you ask him?' said Anne bluntly.

There was a sudden commotion from the rear of the house; screen doors smacking, cupboards banging and children's laughter. Anne quickly stubbed out her second cigarette and picked up the can of Glade air freshener. She spritzed half a dozen times around herself and managed to get the can under the couch and the ashtray slid over to Rachel's side of the coffee table before a twelve-year-old boy with dirty blond hair bounced into the room, his baseball bat turned backwards on his head, a can of Pepsi in his hand. He gave Rachel a quick once over, and then his eyes went to the drink on the table in front of his mother and then to the jug. The boy didn't look convinced.

'Tom, this is Miss Kane. She's here from *Life Magazine*.'

'Cool,' said Tom, even though Rachel could see that he didn't think it was cool at all. His eyes brightened as he turned his attention back to his mother. 'I was talking to Petey Cairns, his old man is a cop you know?'

'Don't say "you know",' Anne corrected, smiling. 'And yes, I know. Go on.'

'Yeah, whatever. Anyway, Petey's old man said they found a body out by Stoney Creek.'

'I know, dear. Mr Zuckerman. He drowned. It was on the early news this morning.'

'Not *him*,' said Tom McConnel, shaking his head emphatically. 'This was whatshisname, you know, the guy who always comes here for those hospital cocktail parties. Dad calls him the consummate bureaucratic ass . . .' The boy flushed brightly. 'You know who I mean.'

'Donald Hale?' said Anne McConnel.

'Yeah! That's him!' said the boy. He took a slug of his Pepsi. 'They just found his car down by the courthouse and there's cops all over the place!' He grinned. 'It's way cool!'

This time he meant it.

# CHAPTER FOURTEEN

There were no criminalists on the staff of the Prosper Police Department so Wren and Kenny Spearing had gone over Donald Hale's Lincoln Town Car by themselves. It was either that or bring the State Police in and then wait for days while whatever evidence they found was sent to the Forensics Lab in Albany. When they were finished with the car Wren went directly to the eighth floor of the County Administration Building. It was well past six by the time he got there, but the District Attorney was still hard at work.

'I thought I could talk to one of your assistants,' said Wren, settling uneasily into one of the chairs across from the big partner's desk in front of the window.

'You don't want to deal with me directly?' smiled D'Arcy Quinn, leaning back in her chair. 'I'm hurt, Detective.'

'I don't want to waste your time.'

'You said you wanted an arrest warrant for this man Sloane.'

'That's right.'

'For the Hale murder?'

'For Hale and Alberoni.'

'You think he killed them both?'

'The evidence is pretty clear. George Prine is pretty sure they were killed by the same knife. It's the same MO anyway.'

'Pretty clear and pretty sure isn't going to make it with the Grand Jury,' said Quinn. She leaned forward in her chair and lit a cigarette. 'Or a Judge for that matter.' She shook her head and snapped her lighter closed. The lighter was a Zippo with the Harvard 'VE- RI- TAS' crest, a gift from her father for getting through the grueling horror of 'One-L' – first year at Harvard Law School. 'What else have you got?'

'The car is pretty much of a . . .' Wren stopped himself. 'The car is a washout. Hale was a blond and we found some dark hair on both headrests, but Hale's wife has dark hair and she used the car from time to time, and no one believes DNA evidence after the O.J. thing, so comparing hair is out too.'

'Fingerprints?'

'All sorts of them, but it's going to take some time to screen out people who have a good reason to have left them there.'

'Just about everyone in town,' said the District Attorney.

'Exactly.' Wren sighed. 'One of whom is probably the killer.'

'So run Sloane's prints,' D'Arcy shrugged.

'I thought that might be prejudicial,' Wren answered. If it looked as though they were zeroing in on Sloane without cause a good lawyer could have any evidence that came as a result of the fingerprinting suppressed.'

'It won't be prejudicial if you run all the other prints you find as well. Go for it.'

Wren nodded. He looked beyond Quinn at the fading light outside, unsure of how to proceed.

D'Arcy smiled. 'You look as though you've got a bone caught in your throat, Detective. What's the problem?'

'I mentioned getting a warrant to Chief Skelton.' He shifted uncomfortably in his chair.

'And?'

'He didn't seem too happy about it.'

'Understandable. They were in school together. I think Robby knew him in the Army as well.'

Wren nodded. 'I thought it might be something like that.' He paused. 'They were friends?'

'I don't think friends is the word, but they knew each other.' D'Arcy tapped her cigarette into the cut-glass ashtray on her desk. 'This kind of thing happens in small towns like Prosper, Detective Wren. Most of the violent crime that happens in a place like this is between people you know, sometimes close friends. Sometimes it's hard to deal with.'

'The Chief isn't someone I'd ever thought of as being bothered by that kind of thing.'

'Don't underestimate Robby,' the District Attorney said slowly. There was an edge to her voice, as though she was passing along some hidden message, or talking to herself. Wren shifted in his chair again.

'He wants an arrest,' said Wren, pursuing the point. 'It just feels as though he doesn't want *this* arrest.'

'Drop it,' said Quinn, her tone a little chilly. 'If you can pile up some more evidence that points to Sloane, bring it to me and we can swear out a warrant.' She sighed and squashed her cigarette into the ashtray. 'What I really want is a smoking gun, Detective Wren, or, in this case, a bleeding knife. Without that, or a fingerprint or two, I don't think you have a case. Not one that I'm willing to proceed with anyway.' She gazed across the desk at Wren; the smile was still on her face, but it looked to him as though it had been welded on. 'Anything else?'

Wren stared back at her. Then he shook his head. 'I guess not.'

D'Arcy Quinn nodded, then picked up her pen and pulled a file folder down from the stack beside her on the desk and opened it. Wren had been dismissed. He stood up and left the office. As soon as he was gone, the District Attorney put aside the file folder she'd used to send Wren out the door and lit another cigarette. Alberoni, Hale, and now things were pointing toward Allan Sloane. She didn't like the way things were shaping up. After two puffs she jammed out her cigarette and called Robin Skelton's office. Robby's assistant, Fred Ziner, informed her politely that Chief Skelton was visiting with Monsignor Gadsby at the Catholic Services Bureau and wasn't expected to return to his office that day. D'Arcy hung up the telephone, scowling. What the hell was Robby doing, going off to visit God?

Appropriately enough, the Church of the Holy Cross was located on Church Street, kitty corner to the Holiday Inn and directly across from the County Services building. Only a block away from the State Street business district, Church Street was narrow and tree-lined, most of its large Victorian houses broken up into apartments to accommodate students at Oneida College.

Several of the large houses on Church Street had also been converted into homes for the elderly as well as professional offices for a number of dentists, lawyers and accountants. Since Holy Cross was the only church on the street, most visitors assumed that the street had been named for it, but in fact it referred to Benjamin Church, a wealthy businessman who lived in Prosper at the turn of the century. Ironically, Benjamin Church had been a Jew.

The original church, a small brick and stone building, had been put up in 1903, but as the years went by and the ivy spread across the chapel walls, the simple place of worship expanded to include an attached rectory and parish house, a gymnasium-style recreation hall and an annex for the Catholic Charities and Social Services office. By the mid-fifties Holy Cross occupied most of the land between Snelling Street and Roper and had right of first refusal on the rest. Of the three Catholic parishes in Prosper County, Holy Cross was the most senior and by far the largest. The parish had been governed by

Monsignor Vincent Andrew Gadsby for slightly more than half a century and there was nothing done in Catholic Prosper that didn't bear his stamp of approval.

Gadsby maintained a small, austere office in the church annex, but the true heart of Holy Cross was his inner sanctum in the rectory. The room was large, the ceiling high and box-vaulted in wine-dark oak. The walls in the north end of the room were given over to rows of towering, custom-fitted bookcases in the same dark wood as the ceiling, the upper shelves reached by wheeled ladders that ran along narrow hidden rails.

Here too was Monsignor Gadsby's massive desk, a huge carved thing of ebony-colored wood, inherited from some long dissolved mission to darkest Africa. The top of the desk was covered in a thick, single sheet of shining glass, the glass in turn covered by Gadsby's leather-edged blotter, an immense Tiffany lamp and a 1940s marble Waterman desk set.

There were always several chairs set around the desk, but most of those invited into Gadsby's sanctuary were ushered to the other half of the 'study'. Here the walls were done in deep blue watered silk, the pegged cherry floor spread with large, richly colored Persian carpets, seating provided by two large Victorian couches and three deep green upholstered chairs set in front of the gigantic polished granite fireplace that took up the entire south wall of the room.

With the exception of one of John Martin's large,

brooding, nineteenth-century mezzotint engravings of the Apocalypse which took up all the room above the mantelpiece, the pictures on the walls were photographs of Monsignor Gadsby at various stages in his life and career, generally showing him shaking hands with a range of celebrities from Jerry Lewis to Gerry Garcia, not to mention Harry Truman, J. Edgar Hoover, Tom Dewey, Jack Kennedy, Fulton J. Sheen and Billy Graham.

His personal favorite was a pair of photographs matted in a single frame, one showing him shaking hands with two Princes of Wales – one, taken in 1950 was Edward, Duke of Windsor, who'd given up the throne of England to marry Wallis Simpson, the other, taken in 1994, showed Gadsby shaking hands with Prince Charles, who'd separated from Princess Di.

Virtually the only photograph of Gadsby in which he wasn't shaking hands showed him being blessed by the Pope on his visit in the fall of 1995. At seventy-nine years of age, it sometimes seemed to Gadsby that he'd shaken hands with almost everyone on the planet.

The priest was seated behind his desk. He still wore the long black robes of his order, his thin, old man's neck cinched in a high canonical collar, the collar itself circumscribed by the heavy chain of the large silver and black crucifix resting on this chest. Just below Christ's feet the long gnarled fingers of Gadsby's hands were loosely entwined, the fingers moving up to form a praying tent, then falling back in slow motion, intertwining again, always in motion like withered, restless snakes.

Robin Skelton sat in one of the leather-covered armchairs in front of Gadsby's desk. A crystal shot glass of neat Laphroaig single malt whisky stood on the desktop in front of him, filled by Gadsby from the decanter which stood on a silver tray by his right hand. The old priest had filled the glass so full that Skelton knew it would be impossible to lift it without spilling some. His father had warned him about the wizened old priest years before: '*Stay out of the black-cassocked son-of-a-bitch's way. He's had his fingers in more pies for more years than almost anyone else in this town and you don't have to be a fucking sheeny to feel his wrath.*'

Skelton looked across the desk. He could believe it; the priest's eyes were like chips of pale blue glass set into deep sockets in the speckled skull of an Egyptian mummy. He looked as though he could stare right into your secret heart and count your old sins like marked cards in a poker game.

'We've never really talked, you and I,' said Gadsby. There was the faint echo of an Irish accent in his voice.

'No,' said Skelton. He stared at the shot glass on the desk in front of him. It looked like a huge amber jewel, just waiting for him to pick up and savor. He glanced up as Gadsby unfurled his hands and picked up his own glass, sipping the honey-colored liquid. He put the glass down on the table and gestured to Skelton.

'Drink up, lad. There's no law that says an off-duty priest and an off-duty Chief of Police can't have a dram together.'

Skelton was double-damned. If he picked it up, the Scotch would almost certainly spill and if he didn't pick it up he'd look like an ingrate. He took a deep breath, let it out and swept up the small glass, almost throwing the whisky into his mouth in a single swallow. He didn't spill a drop. He set the shot glass on to the desk again. The alcohol slid down his throat like molten glass and into the pit of his stomach, burning his insides like cold fire, reminding him that he hadn't eaten since morning. Not surprising after seeing Donny's flaccid little corpse on the river bank.

'That's not how you drink Laphroaig,' chided Gadsby. 'You're supposed to sip it, son.' He picked up the decanter and Skelton quickly covered the mouth of his glass.

'I'm fine,' he said. He sat back in the chair and waited for the old man to speak his mind. Gadsby toyed with the pen set, then touched a large and very ornate glass paperweight beside it. Finally the priest sat forward, tenting his hands again, this time beneath his chin.

'I'm concerned about Dr Alberoni.'

'Donny Hale wasn't a Catholic I guess.'

'I heard about Mr Hale's demise. Tragic. But at the moment I am concerned about Dr Alberoni.'

'He's dead,' Skelton answered. 'Not much either one of us can do for him now, Father.'

'Quite so.' Gadsby nodded. 'Quite so.' He paused. 'How much do you know about him?'

'He was the County Medical Examiner when my father was Chief of Police.' Skelton smiled pleasantly, exercising a little of his own power. 'You might say I inherited him.'

'Did you know him personally?'

'No. He wasn't my family doctor or anything.'

There was a long silence. Skelton could hear the muffled sound of a vacuum cleaner from somewhere outside the study.

'Is there some problem I can help you with?' said Skelton at last. He nodded at his empty glass. 'You didn't really invite me over here for a drink, Father.'

'No,' said Gadsby. 'I suppose not.'

'Is it something about Dr Alberoni?'

'I find myself in a somewhat delicate position here,' said Gadsby. The priest sighed. 'The doctor was a Catholic, did you know that?'

'I assumed it,' said Skelton. 'If I remember correctly he was Medical Director for the nursing homes you operate.'

Gadsby smiled and shook his head. 'I don't operate them, Chief Skelton, the Church does.'

'Whatever.' They both knew who the Church was in Prosper.

'My problem isn't with the nursing homes. My problem is Dr Alberoni.'

'What about him?' Skelton shrugged. 'If it's about releasing his body for burial there's nothing I can do until Dr Prine has finished with him.'

'It's not that, I'm afraid, Robin,' said the priest. Skelton frowned. The use of his first name was like biting into a candy bar with a bad tooth. 'I understand there were some . . . photographs,' Gadsby continued.

Skelton tried to keep his face blank, but he was impressed. The old bastard clearly had some very good sources of information; Bob Wren's preliminary report on his search of Alberoni's premises had only just reached his desk and he'd barely had a chance to read it himself. It occurred to him that it might be worth his while to go through the PD's computerized personnel files to pinpoint Catholic members of the force.

'Yes,' Skelton nodded.

'The pictures exist?'

'Yes.'

'Is there any evidence of any . . . indiscretions related to the photographs?'

'Not that I know of.'

'Are the photographs evidence?'

'At the moment.'

'And the disposition of those photographs when your investigation has been completed?'

'I'm not sure,' said Skelton. The old son of a bitch wanted the pictures, but why?

Gadsby leaned back in his chair. His right hand gripped the crucifix that lay over his heart, thumb rubbing across Christ's chest and tortured, miniature face. 'As I am sure you're aware, the Church is going through troubled times these days; my parishioners have enough to contend with.'

Skelton could almost see the capital letters when Gadsby referred to 'the Church'. 'I told you, Father, we don't have anything concrete.' Somehow the baby pictures had stirred something up.

Monsignor Gadsby nodded. He glanced at the thin gold watch on his wrist, then pushed back his chair and stood. 'Almost time for evening mass,' he said. 'You'll let me know how the investigation is proceeding?'

'Of course,' Skelton nodded. The meeting had obviously come to an end. He pushed back his chair and stood up as well. 'You can count on it.'

Monsignor Vincent Gadsby saw Skelton to the door, then returned to his desk. Frowning, he sat down, then poured himself another tot of Laphroaig from the decanter. He sipped it thoughtfully. Young Skelton was no fool and potentially he was even more dangerous than his father had been, although not quite so accomplished a liar. His father had been a stone wall; the son was transparent as glass.

The old priest sighed and put down his glass. He'd been around for far too long and was the keeper of far too many secrets, not the least of which were his own. Alberoni's secrets, however, were much more likely to be revealed in the near future. It was an impossible situation and one which couldn't simply be forgotten about or covered up. He shook his head and quietly cursed Alberoni's memory.

'Damn him,' said the old priest. 'Damn him to hell.'

'You young people don't know when you're well off,' said Eileen Wax. She was seated at the head of the dining table in her 'fancy room' beside the kitchen.

Most of the dinnertime conversation had revolved around the murder of Donald Hale, and Eileen hadn't managed to corner very much of the conversation. With dessert and coffee long over with, there were only two people still at the table – Bill Wren, and the new boarder, Rachel Kane. The detective smiled. He was getting closer to sixty every day and Rachel looked to be at least thirty-five or so, but to Eileen, anyone who hadn't gone through the Depression and 'Double-You, Double-You Two' was a youngster. He'd heard every one of the old woman's stories a hundred times in the four years he'd been living at the House of Wax, but he'd stuck it out longer than usual tonight, intrigued by the Kane woman.

And it wasn't simply a question of the woman's dark good looks. There was a hardness to the woman, and something in her eyes that seemed to be setting his cop-antenna twitching.

He pressed one of Eileen Wax's favorite buttons, wondering how Rachel would react to the inevitable response. 'It's a different world than the one you grew up in.' He'd heard her reminisce a hundred times about the days when 'men wore hats and women were called ladies'.

'How in hell would you know that?' snorted the old woman. She lit another cigarette with one of the kitchen matches she kept in a little container beside her place at the head of the table. She put out the match by poking it head first into the remains of the grape Jell-O in front of her. There were four other charred matches already in the dish and four soggy

253

butts to match in the saucer of her coffee cup. Smoke lay like a fog a foot or so off the surface of the table.

The detective smiled. 'Everyone's got a tale to tell,' he said. He lit a cigarette of his own and glanced in Rachel Kane's direction, but the woman's attention was on Eileen.

'Sometimes I think the war was the best thing that ever happened to this town,' she began. 'Before Pearl Harbor everything was slow and sleepy. You worked at Dexter's Diary, or you drove a truck for Triple D. You bought a house from Quinn and you borrowed money to do it from Amos Parker. You wanted anything better than that, you packed your bags and left town. We all knew that.'

'Did you stay, or did you pack your bags?' asked Rachel.

'Both.' The old woman smiled. She coughed, butted her cigarette and lit another. 'In 1941 I was nineteen years old, out of school and working at the bottling plant across the way there in Mechanicsville.' She nodded her head in the direction of the railway tracks to the south. 'I was already going out with my Frank by then. Steady.' She winked in Wren's direction. 'He figured there was a war coming so he enlisted instead of being drafted and got into the Marines. We got married in October and he shipped out to the Recruit Depot in San Diego two weeks later.'

'You went with him?' Rachel asked.

The old woman nodded. 'You bet. I got a little place in Cabrillo Heights and played house for a couple of months.' She shook her head. 'I spent a total of nine days with him; three weekend passes and a three-day pass just before he left for K-Bay.'

'K-Bay?'

'Kaneohe Bay Air Station,' said Wax. 'Hawaii.' She sighed. 'Arrived at Pearl Harbor on a Saturday, died on a Sunday.'

'December seventh,' put in Bob Wren. He'd heard the line a hundred times and knew the appropriate response.

'That's right,' said Eileen Wax. She drew deeply on the cigarette. 'And that was the end of my marriage to Francis Archibald Wax.'

'You came back to Prosper?'

She nodded and lit up yet another cigarette. 'Pretty much had to. The widow's allowance the Corps gave me wasn't enough to live on. Not to mention the fact that I barely knew a soul out there. A year later and things were booming here anyway. I got a job at Silks right away.'

'Silks?'

'That's what we called it. The real name used to be Ogerman's Silks and Linens. It went bankrupt during the Depression and the bank picked it up for a song. Parker and Quinn went off to Washington and came back with a whole bunch of Defense contracts. Started off making parachutes and then we branched out into all kinds of other stuff.'

The old woman made a little snorting sound. 'I made life-preservers from '42 to '45. Old George Parker used to walk up and down the assembly line, pinching his favorite girls and making stupid jokes;

"Well, this is one way to keep the town afloat". That was his idea of a laugh.' She frowned. 'Nothing funny about that job,' she muttered. 'Nothing funny about that old son of a bitch either, or his cheapskate pals.' Eileen shrugged again, then brightened. 'At least I managed to save my money. Enough to put a down-payment on this place anyway.'

'The virtue of hard work,' said Bob Wren, smiling. Relieved, the detective sat back in his chair; he knew when one of Eileen's stories had come to an end.

'More like the virtue of keeping your mouth shut,' said Eileen, stabbing her cigarette into the remains of the Jell-O. She made a low, grumbling noise somewhere in the back of her throat. 'Why don't you two get out of here and let me clean all this mess up.' She lit another cigarette, planted it squarely in the center of her mouth and stood up, rattling dishes and cups together as she gathered them on to a huge plastic tray she kept on the sideboard behind her.

Wren stood up, gave Rachel a broad, conspiratorial wink and tilted his head towards the front porch. They went outside and sat down on the padded wicker chairs Eileen kept for her guests. Storm clouds had been building steadily all day and there was the smell of electricity in the air. Rachel lit a cigarette of her own and leaned back against the flower-print cushions. 'Can you tell me what that story had to do with the murder case you were talking about?'

'Eileen's way of putting her two cents in I think,' Wren answered. He was sitting less than a foot away from his next-room neighbor and he could feel the tension coming off her in waves. He couldn't help wonder what was causing it.

'What do you mean?'

Wren smiled. 'Eileen's a gossip among other things, and a bit of a crime groupie. She would have been hell on wheels on the O.J. Simpson jury.' He paused, his smile widening. 'She'd love to know something about the Hale murder, or Alberoni, but she doesn't, so she tells a story instead.'

'But what's the point of the story?' Rachel asked.

'It's the old Beatles song – everyone's got something to hide . . .'

'Except me and my monkey,' Rachel said, completing the line.

'Secrets; that's what she's talking about; the fact that a town like Prosper is built on them, one on top of the other.' He laughed out loud. 'I've heard that story about ten times since I moved in here. I've also heard rumors about it from a few other places too. I think it has something to do with the Silks company using defective, or second-grade material in their life-jackets.'

'So?'

'You haven't heard the rest of the story.'

'There's more?'

Wren nodded, laughing lightly. 'It's like something out of a cheesy operetta. A government inspector comes to town and is about to blow the whistle on them, but the head of security for the company kills the inspector and hides the body. The inspector is never seen again and, in gratitude, or maybe because he's blackmailing them, the people who own the company get the security man elected Chief of Police for the town.'

'You're kidding me,' said Rachel.

Wren shook his head, then held up his hand in a three fingered-salute. 'Nope. It's true, Scout's honor,' he said. 'At least the bare bones of it. I checked the records. An inspector *did* disappear back in April of 1945, and in June of 1946 George Skelton *was* appointed Police Chief of the town of Prosper.'

'And the owners of the company?'

'Parker went back to being a banker and a businessman. Quinn became the mayor of the town and eventually a judge. His daughter's District Attorney for Prosper County.'

'Very neat and tidy,' said Rachel.

Wren shrugged. 'It's just a story,' he said, leaning back against the couch, tasting the electric air and smelling the faint, herb-sweet scent of his companion's shampoo. 'One of Eileen's tall tales.'

They sat together silently in the growing darkness, both of them waiting for something neither one of them was sure would happen. Eventually the first lashes of lightning began to snap and crash around the hills surrounding the town. Rain began tapping at the roof of the porch and darkening the concrete walkway leading up to the front steps.

Wren sighed, then yawned. He stood up, knees popping, and said goodnight to Rachel. 'Got to get some sleep,' he said, yawning again. 'I've got a murderer to catch in the morning.'

'Your Vietnam veteran?'

'He's all I've got.'

'Good luck.'

'Thanks. Goodnight, Rachel.'

''Night, Bob.'

He stood, looking down at Rachel for a long moment. She waited, wondering what he was going to say, but in the end he said nothing. He smiled, then turned away and went back into the house. Rachel stayed on the couch. She lit another cigarette and stared out at the hardening rain and the lowering night sky.

It was all starting to unravel. Hearing about Donny Hale's murder from young Tom McConnel had almost made her faint. Leaving the woman's house she'd spent a long twenty minutes sitting in the car, convincing herself that she wasn't going crazy all over again, telling herself that someone else had murdered Donny Hale, not her, blowing his brains out in some dissociative trance, and not quite believing it until this evening when she heard from Bob Wren himself that Hale had been killed by a knife and not a gun. A knife, just like Alberoni. It had taken every ounce of strength she had not to scream out her own complicity to the detective while they sat around the dinner table.

The rain was coming down in great solid sheets now, a gray wall, obscuring everything. Rachel smoked and let the list form in her head, mentally drawing a line through the names of the murdered men.

Robby Skelton
~~Donny Hale~~
Michael Parker
D'Arcy Quinn
Allan Sloane
~~Dr Alberoni~~

Donny Hale had been one of the four who set fire
to her car and murdered Lauren. Alberoni was the
pet doctor Robby Skelton's father had used to both
keep her in a drugged haze throughout the trial and
to provide the necessary authority to have her sent
to Brockhurst. Allan Sloane was the young man who'd
given Robby Skelton his alibi for that night, even
though, according to Anne McConnel, Sloane and
Skelton hadn't been friends. Now Sloane was Bob
Wren's chief suspect for the two murders.

Thunder crashed behind the pouring curtain of
the rain. Rachel flicked her cigarette butt out into
the downpour. None of it made any kind of real sense;
both Alberoni and Hale were linked directly to her,
but they were obviously linked to someone and
something else as well. What did make terrible sense
was the fact that she'd left her fingerprints all over
Donny Hale's Lincoln, both when she'd been a
passenger and also when she'd taken the big boat of
a car back to town the night before. She wasn't sure
how fingerprints were retrieved these days, or how
quickly criminal files could be accessed, but she knew
that it wouldn't be long before Bob Wren matched
the fresh prints on the murdered City Clerk's steering

wheel to the prints of Renee Lucas from two decades before. All of a sudden she was going to take the place of Allan Sloane as the detective's prime suspect, and all she had to back up her story was an audio tape punctuated with gunfire and a confession from Hale obtained under seriously compromising duress.

Rachel stopped herself from lighting another cigarette and stood up. She'd give herself another twenty-four hours to find out what she needed to know about that last, black night before the end of her life and then she'd leave Prosper once and for all.

The rain had turned the roof over her head into a tin drum and after half an hour the windows were fogged up completely. She moaned on the seat beside him, feeling the two rigid fingers of his right hand digging up under her panties and deeply inside her, his thumb spreading the lips of her vulva and pushing painfully against her. Her pelvis lifted up off the fabric of the seat and she used her free hand to pull up the fabric of her skirt.

'Let's get into the back. I don't have much time,' she panted into his ear. His thumb pushed harder and she gasped. He was still angry from his audience with Gadsby.

'There's always time.'

'I have to be home when he gets there; you know what he's like.'

'I know what he's like. He's like an asshole.'

'Now. Please,' she whispered. She put her hand

on to his leg and felt the long thick bulk of him under the fabric of the uniform. 'I want you.'

'Sure you do, Annie.'

She pulled away from him, feeling his finger slide wetly out of her. The skirt was a wraparound and it only took a few seconds to get it off. Lifting her legs she stripped off the panties, then crawled back into the back of the vehicle. The two jump seats on either side were pushed back and there was just enough room for her to stretch out on the floor. She heard him stripping off his clothes in the front seat and then he was in the back with her, looming over her. She reached forward and gripped the club-like length of his organ, feeling its stony hardness and its heat.

'Do you want me to . . .' she whispered.

'No.' He settled down between her legs and pushed himself into her in a single stroke. 'You said it yourself, there isn't much time.'

She rose up against him hard, taking his entire length inside her, marveling, not for the first time, how men could be so different; sex with her husband was a well planned act, as structured and predictable as one of his annual reports about his stupid hospital; this on the other hand, was sex as raw power. He began to move, pumping in and out steadily, pushing hard against her pubic bone on each downstroke, one hand grabbing her hair, the other under the small of her back, levering her lower body up into him.

'I met someone today. A reporter . . .' she began, her breath coming in ragged little puffs. 'She was asking about you.'

'Shut up,' he answered, pulling her hair even harder. Threads of pain arced down through her scalp and neck. 'You talk too fucking much, just like your sister.'

'But I'm better than Sue was in the back seat of a car, right?' teased Anne McConnel, feeling him swell even larger inside her. He moved his hand from her back to her breast, the fingers squeezing hard.

'I haven't decided yet.'

'Bastard,' she groaned. He twisted her nipple between his thumb and forefinger and she squealed. 'That hurts!'

Outside the rain was smashing down even harder now, which suited his mood perfectly. 'It's meant to,' said Robin Skelton. He pulled himself halfway out of her and stopped, the break in rhythm making her draw in a shivering breath. He didn't move a muscle. 'So tell me about this reporter,' he said softly.

# CHAPTER FIFTEEN

'This is starting to piss me off,' said Wren, seating himself behind his desk and uncapping a tall cup of coffee from the Beanery, the trendy coffee shop around the corner from the police station. He handed the other cup across his desk to Kenny Spearing. 'I've got a suspect my chief doesn't want me to arrest, a dozen sets of fingerprints from a murdered man's car, none of which I can get a computer hit from, and two bodies in the morgue with toe-tags but no motives to attach.'

'Not to mention no murder weapon,' grinned Spearing. 'And all the baby pictures.' He sipped his coffee and winced as the hot black fluid burned his mouth.

'Serves you right for drinking your coffee black,' said Wren, adding two creamers and two sugar packets to his own brew.

The younger man made a small snorting sound. 'Well at least I'm not going to get clogged arteries and adult-onset diabetes.'

Wren ignored the remark and stirred the coffee with a pencil from his desk. 'I still don't buy Sloane for Alberoni, let alone Hale.' He sipped his coffee, then added another packet of sugar from the little hoard he kept in his desk drawer. Kenny Spearing shook his head and raised his eyebrows simultaneously. Wren stirred his cup again, then took a long, satisfying swallow. He leaned back in his chair. 'When you dug into the old records this morning did you find anything at all to connect Hale to Alberoni?'

'Nada,' said Spearing. 'Alberoni had no record at all. Hale has never had anything worse than a parking ticket.'

'Domestic?'

'It doesn't look like it. Nothing obvious, anyway.'

'The suicide. Jennifer Wax.'

'Yeah,' said the younger man.

'She must have been young.' He remembered the photograph of the young woman on the *Queen Mary*.

'She was,' Spearing nodded, flipping through the pages of his small black notebook. 'She was twenty-one.'

'I forgot to ask Eileen about it last night,' said Wren. 'I should get on to that.'

'Why? That was what? Sixty years ago.'

Wren shrugged. 'Sometimes the past can sit up in its grave and bite you on the ass.'

'Sounds pretty far-fetched.'

A primly uniformed constable clerk peeked into the Detective Room and knocked on the doorframe. She had a long fax trailing from her other hand. 'Detective Wren?'

'That's me,' said Wren, rocking forward in the

chair. The constable came across the room and handed him the scrolling roll of paper. 'This just came to you from Communications.'

Squinting, Wren managed to read the nametag on her blue-shirted chest. 'Thanks, Maggie.' The woman gave him a little half-smile and trotted out of the room. Wren took his reading glasses out of his breast pocket and slipped them on. He read for a few moments, nodding to himself every few seconds, but saying nothing.

'What?' Spearing asked finally.

Wren looked at him over his glasses, smiling. 'It's just what I thought. Our friend Sloane is a bullshitter.'

'What kind of bullshitter?' asked Spearing.

'The kind who lies about his military record.'

'Really?'

Wren rattled the long strip of paper in his hands. 'According to this our boy got bounced out of Parris, six, six and a kick. Big Chicken Dinner.'

'Big Chicken Dinner? Why don't you translate that?' asked Spearing.

'Six months in the brig, six months without pay and then you get thrown out with a Bad Conduct Discharge. Parris Island, South Carolina is the Marine Corps boot camp.' Wren dropped the fax roll on to his desk. 'Allan Sloane never even made it through basic training.'

'So maybe he joined the army or something.' Spearing shrugged.

'Nope,' Wren answered, shaking his head.

'According to this there's no record of Allan Sloane
ever having been a member of the United States
armed forces anywhere or any time. Our Vietnam
veteran never went to Vietnam at all. He's a phoney.'

That morning, Rachel spent an hour in the Prosper
Public Library filling in the blanks between 1974 and
the present in the life of Michael Thomas Parker.
Outside, the drizzling rain slowed, then stopped
altogether, the overcast breaking up to let the sun
shine again. It was going to be a nice day after all.

Rachel worked her way through the clippings on
Michael Parker, stitching the events of his life
together. After graduating from Woodrow Wilson
High School he'd spent one year in an exclusive prep
school in Cambridge, Massachusetts, then went on
to get a Harvard MBA before returning to Prosper
where he took over the reins of the Farmers' Union
Bank after his father retired.

In 1983 he married Gwen Kennedy, an imported
Boston blueblood he'd met in Cambridge, who began
breeding infant Parkers, stopping with the fourth
child, a male heir to the Parker fortunes. From the
clippings it appeared that Michael Parker had taken
the not inconsiderable fortune he'd inherited from
his father, invested it in various kinds of real estate
and now had the bulk of his resources tied up in a
sprawling new recreational development that was
supposed to turn Prosper into a latterday version of
Vail or Aspen. Three years previously, Parker had
added another feather to his cap, taking over as

Chancellor of Oneida College, taking his place on the Board of Regents with people like D'Arcy Quinn's mother, the judge's wife. There wasn't a single breath of scandal in the entire clipping file under Parker's name.

*Maybe we can change that.*

She stuffed the clippings back into their envelope, gave the file back to the librarian, then went to the pay phone and made several calls, eventually tracking Parker's location down to his Oneida College office. On the way out of the library she ran into Bob Wren and, for a single, heart-stopping instant, she thought he was there to arrest her. Instead he just smiled.

'You look a little frazzled,' he said, pausing at the top of the concrete steps leading into the building. He gestured toward the doors. 'Doing some research?'

'Background for an interview,' she said.

*Not really a lie.*

'I've got some work to do in there myself.' He seemed to hesitate and then he spoke again. 'Look, I've been thinking . . .' He let it dangle.

*He's going to ask me for a date.*

'Umm?'

*What kind of stupid response is that? Help him out.*

'Unless you've fallen in love with Eileen's cooking I thought we could go out to dinner, maybe take in a movie.'

'That sounds nice,' Rachel answered quickly, and it did.

'Great!' Wren beamed, looking proud of himself. 'Uh, I guess I'll talk to you this evening.' He paused again. 'Six?'

'Fine.'

'Terrific!' He beamed at her again. 'See you then.' He gave her a little wave then went through the doors and into the library.

Weak-kneed with relief Rachel went down the steps to her car. Climbing behind the wheel she lit a cigarette. 'A date with a cop! Jesus! I must be out of my mind!' she muttered, and then she laughed.

*Been there, done that.*

She turned the key in the ignition and headed out of town, the clouds above her continuing to shred like tissue, releasing sunshine and blue skies. Ten minutes later she drove through the ornamental gates that marked the beginning of the Oneida College campus and stopped at the information kiosk to consult the big plastic-covered map again. This time she headed east on College Way until she found the College Administration Building, a low-slung glass and red brick example of nineties architectural restraint with long concrete planters cascading winding cataracts of ivy over everything.

She spotted a parking spot on the opposite side of the road, almost exactly across from the main entrance and did a quick U-turn. She slipped into the space, lit another cigarette and sat there for a moment, staring out her side window at the building across the way. Before learning about Hale's murder she'd planned to confront both Parker and Quinn with the City Clerk's taped confession, but now she wasn't so sure. There had been two murders in Prosper since her return and both of them could be laid at her front door. Skelton, Quinn and Parker, power, politics and money; all three had a great deal to lose and it had occurred to her that any one of them was entirely capable of setting her up for the murders in an effort to keep the lid on the secret that had bound them together.

She had her fingers on the ignition key when she saw movement out of the corner of her eye. Two people, a man and a woman, were coming through the swinging glass doors of the Administration Building. The man was dressed in a perfectly cut chalkstripe three-piece suit and had thick, salt and pepper hair and a deep even tan; a craggy somewhat better looking George Hamilton.

*Parker, you son-of-a-bitch.*

*'Slip her the snake, Robby, come on!'*

*'Yeah. Let's take her and the retard for a ride.'*

Rachel took her hand off the ignition key. The woman with Parker was in her late forties or early fifties, her gray hair done in a long, thick pigtail. She was wearing faded jeans, sandals, a man's shirt and a dark blue hippie vest done up with fancy beadwork and little chips of mirror that sparkled in the sunlight. Once upon a time the woman would have been called beautiful and she still looked handsome, lithe and fit.

*I know her.*

Parker and the woman seemed to be arguing, or

at least to be in heated conversation although Rachel was too far away to make out anything they were saying. Even from a distance though, her profile was tantalizingly familiar. Then she lifted one hand and tugged at the root of her pigtail in a quick nervous motion that Rachel was sure she'd seen somewhere before.

*Who is she?*

Suddenly the conversation ended as a dark green Volvo stationwagon pulled up and double-parked in front of the main entrance. The familiar woman looked back over her shoulder at the Volvo, then stalked away. The driver of the car was an attractive blonde and the back of the car was alive with children ranging in age from thirteen or so to a caterwauling four-year-old strapped into a complicated looking car seat.

*His kids.*

The hippy woman with the gray hair walked angrily down the sidewalk, then climbed into the ancient looking VW bus. The sign on the side of the van said: 'THE HERB & SPICE CAFE, Naturally Good.' The woman behind the wheel backed the old van out, then thumped and banged back down the road, rattling past the Volvo in a cloud of smoke and giving Rachel a close-up view of her face. It was the VW that did it. She *did* know the woman; in fact she'd had her memory jogged by the framed *Life* cover she'd seen in Jerry Weem's studio. Gray hair now, red hair then.

*Rainbow.*

Michael climbed into the Volvo beside his wife and they drove off. Rachel watched them go and then, on impulse, she wheeled the Golf around and followed the old Volkswagen bus back into Prosper.

Oddly, it had been the report on Sloane that had prompted Wren to dig more comprehensively into Dr Amos Alberoni's past; that and his own suspicions about Eileen Wax's little allegorical story of the night before. Whatever the case, logic said that, contrary to what the pathologist George Prine believed, if the motive for Alberoni's murder didn't lie in the present, it had to lie in the past, and the most obvious fact from the doctor's history was the suicide of his wife.

As Wren had seen from the material Kenny Spearing had gathered for him, there was quite a bit of information about the marriage, but very little about the suicide. The only real mention of it was a brief story about the tragic death of the young Mrs Alberoni.

Wren went back and cross-checked the old obituaries and discovered that while Jennifer Wax Alberoni had been married by Father Vincent Gadsby of the Prosper Catholic Church, she had been buried in the non-denominational Beechwood Cemetery rather than Notre Dame Cemetery on the other side of town; proof enough to Wren that she probably had committed suicide.

Until he had a chance to talk to Eileen Wax back at the rooming house, Wren knew it was unlikely that he was going to find anything more about

Jennifer Wax in clippings from the *Prosper Advance* so he turned his attention back to Alberoni. Wren consulted his notebook. According to the material Kenny Spearing had given to him the doctor had been a member of several service clubs in town, St Anthony's Boys' Camp, the Catholic Services Bureau and the Maryhill Children's Village.

Ignoring the service club connections and the boys' club, Wren went to the librarian and retrieved the clipping files on the Catholic Services Bureau and the Maryhill Children's Village, since they were the two organizations linked to the doctor's collection of photographs. Neither file had much in it. The Catholic Services Bureau was just that – an organization dedicated to providing service to Catholic parishioners in the County, including medical help for the needy, clothing and fuel for the poor and legal advice.

Maryhill Children's Village was a non-denominational orphanage occupying what had once been the Beechwood Tuberculosis Sanitarium and which was now the Beechwood old folk's home. The first clipping in the file dated back to 1934 and the founding of the orphanage; the last clipping in the Children's Village file was the notification of its closing and sale in the late 1960s. The editorial stance of that article was that the orphanage had closed due to the advent of the Pill with a capital P, a mixed blessing since while preventing unwanted pregnancies, it was also promoted promiscuity. The only one of the news stories that mentioned Alberoni was one of the very early ones, which also mentioned his connection to something called the Model Maternity Home and Settlement House. Returning to the librarian, Wren retrieved the envelope of Model Maternity Home clippings and tipped it out on to the wooden table in front of him. Most of the clippings were advertisments and there was even a brochure. Wren chose an ad at random, dated 1933.

MODEL MATERNITY HOME AND
SETTLEMENT HOUSE
'Mother's Refuge'
Also Department for Girls.
No Publicity Infants Home in connection.
Write for literature box 20, this newspaper.

'I'll be damned,' Wren whispered out loud. Alberoni had been the doctor for a home for unwed mothers. He picked up the brochure. It was in black and white, dated 1937. The cover of the trifold sheet of heavy paper showed several pleasant-faced women in nurses' uniforms and caps seated on the lawn of a large, Victorian-style house. In front of the nurses, arranged on several large quilts was an assembly of at least a dozen babies, some of them squinting in the sunlight, others smiling, still more crawling hither and yon across the quilts, barefoot and diapers dragging. Cute as little buttons, each and every one. Wren opened the brochure and read a paragraph at random.

Much of the future happiness of mother and baby is due to the care she receives; therefore, ever since the founding of the MODEL MATERNITY HOME AND SETTLEMENT HOUSE in 1928, its management has put forth great effort to meet every need for the comfort and protection of its patrons to make it truly 'MODEL'.

Wren put down the euphemistically worded brochure. This, at least, explained the baby pictures. Alberoni worked for the Model Maternity Home delivering babies. Some, the ones born of Catholic mothers, had been adopted out through the Catholic Services Bureau while the rest had gone over to Maryhill Children's Village. The detective sighed wearily; the Model Maternity Home and Settlement House explained the baby pictures but it wasn't getting him any closer to a motive for the doctor's murder or a connection between the doctor's death and the murder of Donald Hale.

On the other hand he had the report on Allan Sloane. Wren sighed again and began putting the clippings back into their folder. To get six, six and a kick before he even passed out of basic training meant that Sloane had committed a serious offense of some kind, perhaps even a violent one. Maybe Prine had been right after all; the motive for Alberoni's murder might have come from the present after all.

The detective felt the vibrating hum of his pager and slipped it off his belt. Prine was calling him from his office at the Medical Center. Wren went to the pay phones by the main doors into the library and called. Prine answered on the second ring.

'I checked up on that Caesarean baby picture, the one from 1944,' said the pathologist.

'Checked up?'

'I called the City Clerk's office, that's where all that stuff is filed, births, deaths, all that.'

'And?' Wren asked.

'Zip. Zero. Nada.'

'What do you mean?'

'The birth wasn't registered.'

'How can you be sure?' said Wren. 'I mean there must have been other births during that time period. What did you tell me? Seven days after the birth?'

'There were eleven as a matter of fact,' Prine answered. 'But any child born premature or by a Caesarean section had to be identified as such on the registration back then. You even had to register stillborn children or children who died within forty-eight hours of birth. Maybe it had something to do with the old silver nitrate applications.'

'Silver nitrate?'

'Sure,' said Prine. 'Up until just a few years ago every single vaginally-born child in the country had to have silver nitrate eyedrops administered at birth to prevent syphilitic blindness in case your mother had a dose when you were born. Crude, but effective.'

'So the Caesarean kid would have shown up on the registration?'

'Yup. No sign of him, or her.'

'Maybe they moved right after the child was born.'

'If the birth took place in Prosper County it should have been registered here.'

'Odd,' said Wren, trying to make some sense of it.

'Uh-uh,' said Prine. 'Not just odd. Illegal.'

# CHAPTER SIXTEEN

The Herb and Spice Cafe was located on the ground floor of a warehouse on the corner of State and Water Street; a dozen round tables with checked cloth covering them, mismatched chairs and a chalkboard menu that offered hamburgers and tofu side by side. Behind the ancient cash register up front, there was a bulletin board covered with three-deep postcards from old friends and well-wishers. From the table by the window, where Rachel was sitting, you even got a view of the river. According to the owner, the Herb and Spice had been there long before that end of State Street and the area around Courthouse Square turned trendy in the late eighties. According to the business license on the wall by the door, the woman Rachel had known only as Rainbow was actually someone named Laura Talbot. Both had changed beyond any thought of recognition.

'You really doing a story on Morningstar?' the woman asked.

Rachel nodded. 'A reprise of the one we did back in '68. Sort of a "where are they now" story.' Rachel had used this variation on her *Life Magazine* article theme, assuming that she'd have to work her way around slowly to Michael Parker and Rainbow's argument with him earlier that morning.

'It was all so long ago,' said Laura Talbot. Rachel took out her cigarettes but Laura pointed to the 'No Smoking' sign on the wall. 'Sorry,' said Talbot.

'No problem,' Rachel answered, smiling.

'Where were you back then?' asked Talbot. 'You look old enough to have been one of the tribe.'

'Here and there,' said Rachel. 'I moved around.'

'I came to Prosper in '67, couple of years before Woodstock. Started up here in '71.' Laura Talbot shook her head. 'Hard to believe it was that long ago.' She smiled. 'Be our thirtieth anniversary before you know it; us and the new millennium!'

'I wouldn't think you'd be welcome in a town like this, not back then.'

Talbot laughed. 'I wasn't.' She shook her head again. 'Me and the town went through this kind of "Alice's Restaurant" thing for a while. Public Health people tried to shut me down, Fire Department, Police. I just fed them all slabs of my pumpkin pie and coffee and waited them out.'

'How long did it take?' Rachel asked.

Laura Talbot sat back and pointed down State Street toward the center of town. She shrugged. 'I don't remember exactly, except that it was freezing and there was about ten feet of snow on the ground. Three, maybe four months after I opened. There was a fire at the bakery up there beside Roper's Theater. Real stubborn fire, and there was a ruptured water main to boot. Ice all over the place and power out for most of downtown.' She jerked her thumb toward the ceiling. 'I was living in a kind of loft space upstairs back then, and I saw the whole thing happening, so I came down here and started making coffee and soup and sandwiches and shit. Brought it all down to the firemen.'

'Nice of you,' Rachel commented.

'I guess they thought so too,' Talbot answered. 'Things changed after that. No one really gave me a hard time and some of the straights from the courthouse started coming in.' She laughed. 'I actually dated one or two of them. Even a cop.'

'I asked around and people said you knew more about Morningstar than anyone else in town.'

'Yeah. I was there almost from the start. What was I then? Seventeen, eighteen?'

'I guess you knew a lot of people from the commune.'

Laura smiled, almost wistfully. 'Most of them at one time or another. The serious ones anyway.'

'Serious?'

'The ones who were in it for the long haul, not the drifters. Lots of kids came to Morningstar, stuck around a few days, then moved on.' She lifted her shoulders. 'Word gets around. Morningstar was a groove. Good place for getting laid, having babies, cooling off from the Draft and getting your shit together to head up to Canada. Laid back, no pressure.' She blew air out through her pursed lips, then glanced briefly out through the window.

'Keep in touch with any of your old commune friends?'

'Some.' She nodded at the bulletin board loaded down with postcards by the cash. 'They were good people, a lot of them.'

'All gone their separate ways.'

*Some gone to hell and back.*

Laura Talbot laughed. 'You can say that again. One guy who did nothing but read the Bible and wander around in a loincloth is a big time televangelist now. Pete Arnold's a computer millionaire at Microsoft, Sheila Wells went to Kathmandu and became a Catholic nun, then un-nunned herself a few years ago. Bruce Chester's a professor up in Canada.' She smiled fondly. 'Everything from housewives and school teachers to a plastic surgeon and a gestalt dentist.'

'Were there kids?' asked Rachel, knowing the answer, feeling the knot tighten in her throat.

*Everywhere.*

'Everywhere,' answered Laura Talbot. 'Morningstar specialized in kids. Someone was always pulling up in a banged-up old car, eight months gone.'

Rachel nodded; even now she could hear the children laughing, see them running down the steep hill, arms outstretched, playing 'Airplane'. She could feel the sun on her taut, bulging womb, Matthew turning toward the heat, basking in it.

*Matthew.*

Rachel swallowed hard, then cleared her throat. 'You came here in '67; when did the commune start?'

'I'm not sure exactly. It was already there when I came into town. A version of it anyway.'

'I went up there. Doesn't seem to be much of it left. From what I could see there were four or five main buildings, is that right?'

Talbot nodded. 'Yeah. Hilltop up on the ridge, Mike Taylor's Dome on the far side of the clearing.' She paused, thinking, then nodded again. 'The little place down by the path was called Erewhon after the book by Samuel Butler. That's where Dean and Jill lived. He wanted to be a carpenter. Last I heard he was doing helicopter weather in San Diego.' She paused. 'And then there was the single guys' place out by the road.' She closed her eyes briefly, then opened them. 'The Chicken Coop, that's what they called it.'

'The building in the center of the clearing was the largest.'

'Yeah. The king's castle. Goodman called it the Alamo.'

'Goodman?'

'The guy who started the commune in the first place, Paul Goodman. He was a sociology professor at some university in the Midwest. Very weird. Fell in with Kesey and Leary and that whole trip. One of the original touchie-feelies.'

'Touchie-feelie?' Talbot was slipping back into the argot of the times as her memories took shape. Rachel sat forward in her chair; until now she hadn't known very much about Paul's background.

'A group-groper,' Talbot continued. She squinched her eyes closed and made pawing gestures with her small, delicate hands. She opened her eyes and looked at Rachel. 'It was like a game of "trust me" we used to play when we were kids, except there were no boundaries. If you objected to him grabbing your tit or taking a swipe at your snatch he'd tell you that you were repressed. If you didn't screw him, you were a frigid bitch who hated your mother and wanted to fuck your father.' She let out a short, barking laugh with a lot of history in it. 'He'd put on Jim Morrison and take off his clothes, waving his hard-on at you like it was some kind of magic wand.' Laura Talbot sighed. 'Christ, I can't believe anyone fell for that shit!'

*Neither can I.*

'Did you?' asked Rachel.

Talbot grinned. 'Of course,' she laughed. She paused for a moment, remembering; Rachel couldn't tell if the memories were fond ones or otherwise. Finally the woman looked across the table at her. 'He was from Prosper, you know.'

'Goodman?'

'Yeah. His father was a doctor I think. There was some kind of scandal and Goodman's father blew his brains out. That was in the fifties. Apparently his old man had some idea of using the Stoney Creek land as a summer camp for the kids but he never got around to doing it. Goodman came back from the coast and used it to set up Morningstar.' Talbot let out a long, sighing breath and sat back in her chair. 'All so long ago,' she said softly, still looking out the window. 'Hard to believe.'

'You sound like you miss it,' Rachel said.

'Not really,' said Laura, turning to face Rachel again. She shook her head slowly. 'Sometimes I miss the fun of it all, the uncomplicated sex, the drugs, the music. In the end it got a little boring though, like you were watching someone else's movie. That's why I stuck to the café.'

She looked around the big, airy room, half-filled with customers even after the lunch hour. She was obviously proud of what she'd accomplished. Her expression darkened. 'I could have gone wandering off to Kathmandu like Sheila, or turned into some yuppie driving a fucking Volvo loaded down with kids, but in the end I decided to be true to myself. It's pretty simple. I like cooking, I like people.' She spread her arms wide, grinning broadly. 'It ain't much, but it's mine.'

The reference to the Volvo was clear enough but Rachel still wasn't sure of how to bring up Parker's name. In the end she decided to simply broach the subject bluntly. 'I've been doing quite a few interviews for this article. Even townies who used to go up there, just for kicks.'

Laura Talbot smiled broadly. 'There were enough of those. All the kids from the high school thought Morningstar meant free dope and free sex.'

'Was Mike Parker one of them?'

'Excuse me?' Rachel watched as the blood seemed to drain from the face of the woman seated across from her.

'I was out at Oneida College a little while ago. I

saw you talking to him.' Rachel paused. 'Was he one of the townies who came up to the commune to visit?'

'Not that I can recall,' said Laura Talbot. Her voice had gone brittle and cold, but there was something else there as well. Anxiety? Fear?

'Then how come you were having a fight with him?' Rachel asked flatly.

*Lovers' quarrel maybe?*

'I don't see how that's any of your business.'

*I struck some kind of nerve.*

'Just wondering,' said Rachel. 'Like I said, it's a "what ever happened to" article.'

'Well screw your fucking article,' said Talbot, standing up. 'I don't need this shit.'

*Major nerve.*

Rachel pushed away from the table and stood up herself. 'Sorry if I said something to bother you.' There was more than anger in the other woman's voice; the fear Rachel had recognized before had been transformed into something close to panic.

'I don't like my privacy being invaded, okay?' said Laura Talbot. 'I don't like being spied on.' Customers at nearby tables were beginning to stare. 'And just to satisfy your fucking curiosity, honey, the son-of-a-bitch happens to be my fucking landlord, and he happens to be raising my fucking rent, okay?'

Allan Sloane stood by the fireplace in his A-frame studio by the creek and stared at Detective Bob Wren, seated in the wooden armchair a few feet away. 'You don't act as though you're here to arrest me,' said Sloane. 'So why are you here at all?'

'Because I'm confused,' said Wren, honestly enough. 'You're the best suspect I have for the Alberoni killing, which also makes you a prime suspect for the death of Donald Hale.'

'Donny Hale was a jerk-off,' said Sloane.

Wren smiled. 'You really know how to make friends, don't you?'

The man with the strawberry-blond ponytail heaved a small, exasperated sigh. 'Donny was the kind of guy who held your hand too long when you shook it,' said Sloane. 'Just a little on the slimy side for my taste.'

'But you knew him.'

'It's a small town, Detective. Of course I knew him. We went to the same high school.' He shook his head. 'We *all* went to the same high school.' Sloane dropped down into the chair on the far side of the fireplace from Wren. 'Why don't you get to the point, Detective? I've got work to do.'

Wren turned it around abruptly. 'You said you were in South-East Asia. Cambodia and Laos, I think.'

'What about it?'

'You lied.'

'Really?'

'Really,' Wren nodded. He reached into his pocket and took out his notebook, flipping through the pages until he found what he wanted. 'You signed up for the United States Marine Corps in the late spring of 1974 when a couple of Corps recruiters came to the high school. About half a dozen of you signed up the following week.'

'So what?'

'You shipped out to Parris Island, South Carolina on October seventh, 1974 and entered basic training three days later. On November twelveth of that year they threw you in the brig on a six-month ticket. When you got out they bounced you out of the Corps entirely on a Bad Conduct Discharge. They threw you out in May of 1975 and five months later you came back to Prosper in full USMC uniform with three or four medals swinging from your chest, including a pair of Purple Hearts.' Wren shook his head. 'You did your homework, didn't you, Allan? You knew that in the Marines it takes two Purple Hearts not just one to get rotated home.'

Sloane continued to stare at Wren from across the fireplace hearth. After a long moment he spoke. 'My father had been a Marine. Me getting a Bad Conduct Discharge would have killed him.'

'So you lied for the sake of your father, is that it?'

'My old man was on his second coronary when I signed up. He said me joining the Corps was the proudest moment of his life. I came back just in time to spend a week or two with him before he died. My mother went a year after that. Cancer. Nobody got hurt.'

'Who knew? Alberoni?' asked Wren. 'Is that why you killed him?'

'No.' Sloane shook his head. 'Nobody knew.' He

shook his head again. 'I didn't kill Dr Alberoni, Detective. I had no reason to.'

'You own a Buck knife?' asked Wren.

'No.'

'Mind if I look around?' asked Wren.

Sloane shrugged. 'Be my guest, Detective. You won't find anything.'

'You're sure of that?'

'Yes. You won't find anything because I haven't done anything.'

'Except lied about your military record.'

'Like I said, who got hurt?'

'You wore the uniform falsely, and the medals.'

Sloane shook his head and held out his wrists, pushing them together. 'So arrest me,' he said.

'Maybe later,' said Wren. 'First I want to find out why the Corps bounced you.'

'That's really no business of yours, Detective.'

'Sure it is,' Wren answered easily. 'You're a prime suspect in an ongoing murder investigation. A double homicide in a State that just brought back the death penalty. How do you feel about making the lights go dim in Ossining, Mr Sloane?'

'Save it for Academy Awards night.'

'My boss wants an arrest,' said Wren. 'You're the best I've got.'

'Then arrest me,' answered Sloane, shrugging his shoulders. 'I didn't kill Alberoni and I certainly didn't kill Donny Hale.' The ponytailed man let out a hollow, derisive laugh. 'You've got some freak running around town sticking knives into people and you're wasting time on me?' He shook his head. 'Forget it, Wren, I'm not your man.'

The detective looked around the room and suddenly remembered the pile of courier slips he'd seen spiked on Alberoni's desk and the one in the waste basket; all the slips had been made out for trips to the lab at the Prosper Medical Center. It came together in Wren's mind like a slamming door.

'They threw you out of the Corps because you were gay. The receipt from the courier in Alberoni's office was for your blood test results, wasn't it? You went to him for an HIV test.'

'My private life is none of your affair. And medical records are private.'

'Yes it is, and no they aren't, not when the doctor who made the records is the victim of a murder. Doctor-patient privilege goes out the window, I'm afraid.'

'Why are you doing this to me?' said Sloane.

'Answer the fucking question,' snapped Wren. There was a long silence. Sloane stood up and went back to his position beside the fireplace. He looked around the room, then back at Wren.

'Do you know what the "Moment of Truth" is in Marine Corps jargon, Detective?'

'I was in air force.'

'You arrive at Parris Island in the middle of the night and then you spend the next four or five hours at the Receiving Barracks with a bunch of hard-nosed grunts who run you through the numbers, including telling you which parts of your body you wash first in the shower. The whole process ends up just before dawn at another place called the Recruit Administration Center and the Moment of Truth. It's your last chance to take back anything you've written down on all the forms they've had you filling out. The last chance you have of admitting to any of the things the Corps abhor – conviction on felony charges, drugs and homosexuality. You fill out that last form and swear to it and they find out you were lying, that's it – they give you the kick.'

'You told them you weren't gay.'

'I told them nothing. I just didn't think that Parris Island was the place for me to out myself.'

'Why six in the brig?'

Sloane let out a long breath. 'That's what they call the "Twelfth General Order,"' Sloane explained. 'Don't get caught.'

'Someone caught you . . .'

'That's right.' Sloane smiled. 'Doing it is one thing, getting caught doing it in the head by your Drill Instructor gets you six months in the brig at Camp LeJeune, just down the road.'

'And Alberoni?'

'I went to him twice a year for an HIV test, just in case.'

'Just in case?'

'I haven't been sexually active in a long time, Detective, but AIDS can take years to show up.'

'That's it?'

'That's it.' Sloane shrugged again. 'I was always his last patient of the day. No big secret; but in this

291

town it classifies as top-level gossip stuff.'

'No one's going to hear any of this from me,' said Wren.

'I thought I was a suspect?'

'Some people think so,' Wren answered. 'I was never one of them.'

'All of this was just a roust?'

'I wanted to see if something would shake loose. Something for me to get a handle on.'

Sloane smiled weakly. 'If I didn't kill Alberoni or Donny Hale, then who did?'

'Frankly, Mr Sloane, I don't have the faintest God damn idea.'

Wren's beeper buzzed. He unclipped it from his belt and squinted at the little readout window. The page was coming from Kenny Spearing and it was coded 'urgent'.

Wren stood in the bedroom of Laura Talbot's small apartment above the Herb and Spice Café. Brick and board bookcases in the small living room that overlooked the street, a small neat kitchen, a bathroom with an old-fashioned claw-foot tub, the feet painted blue, and a bright, sunny bedroom looking down to a pocket handkerchief garden in the rear, reached by climbing down an old wrought-iron fire escape. The window leading to the fire escape was open, the white, embroidered curtains flipping and swinging in the light breeze.

The bedroom was a shrine to the past: on the wall at the end of the bed was a floor-to-ceiling photo blowup of a cathedral-like forest. On another wall there was a woven godseye and a framed poster for the rock musical *Hair*. On the wall behind the head of the futon bed was a huge Jimi Hendrix print. The bed itself was unmade and Laura Talbot's nude body was spread across the pale green bottom sheet, barely any blood at all leaking from the single wound just beneath her breasts.

According to Kenny Spearing, Jerry Weems had come and gone with instructions to process the crime scene photographs as quickly as he could. George Prine was seated on the bed, using a narrow pair of surgical tongs fitted with a cotton ball to swab out the dead woman's vagina. Finishing, he dropped the swab into a small, ziplock plastic bag.

'Anything?' asked Wren.

Prine shook his head. 'I don't think so.'

'How long ago?'

'Two, maybe three hours. Could be less, a little more.' He shrugged.

'A delivery guy was bringing her a package,' said Kenny Spearing, checking his notebook. 'Bobby Markstein; works for UPS. He saw the door open. He called but no one answered so he came in and took a look. Found her. Called us.' Spearing flipped the book closed.

'Same knife?' asked Wren, staring down at the body.

'I'd say so,' Prine nodded. He used a surgical-gloved finger to point out a small bruise at the edge of the wound. 'I'll have to do a photographic comparison, but the discoloration here is identical to Alberoni and Hale – find the knife and it'll have a little chip on the outside edge of the tang.'

'I'd need a suspect to find the knife,' said Wren.

'We've got one,' said Spearing. 'Two witnesses down in the cafe said they saw the victim having a serious argument at a table by the window about an hour before Bobby Markstein called it in.'

'Who was she having the argument with?' Wren asked.

'Your roommate at the House of Wax. The lady from *Life Magazine*. Rachel Kane.' He paused. 'Except that's not really her name.'

'What do you mean?'

'While you were off talking to Sloane we got an answer off the AFIS computer. A match on the prints we took from Hale's car. Her real name is Renee Lucas. Back in 1974 she was arrested here for murdering her own child. Torched her car with the kid in it up at the old Morningstar commune.'

'Jesus,' Wren whispered, staring down at the murdered woman.

'Yeah,' Spearing nodded. 'According to the records she just got let out of the loony bin upstate at Brockhurst.'

Rachel sat in the window seat of her room in the House of Wax and smoked a last cigarette. Her suitcases were packed and waiting by the door; the only thing left for her to do was to finish the note to Bob Wren that lay on her desk and slip it under his door along with the tape she'd made of Donny Hale's confession. She dragged hard on the cigarette and stared blankly out the window.

Except for the tape the whole thing had been a bust and she was no closer to justice than she'd been when she returned to Prosper. If she was reading the whole thing correctly, Robin Skelton had somehow discovered that she was back in town and had decided to clean up a few loose ends; perhaps if she simply disappeared again, fading back into the mists, no one else would get hurt. One way or the other, with her fingerprints all over Donny Hale's car, she was bound to take the fall.

Rachel stubbed out her cigarette and went back to the desk. How did you explain what had happened in a few simple words? How did you explain the desperate pain of losing your child and then spending the balance of your life in a living hell?

*How do I convince him I'm not insane?*

'Renee Lucas?'

She looked up from her note. Wren was standing in the doorway. He had a pair of handcuffs in his hand and his face was the color of ashes. 'Renee Lucas, you are under arrest for the murders of Laura Talbot, Dr Amos Alberoni and Donald Hale. You have the right to remain silent . . .'

*Laura? Rainbow?*

*Nightmare.*

*Again.*

# PART THREE

*Then Again*

# CHAPTER SEVENTEEN

Winston Tucker entered the tiny interrogation room and sat down across from Rachel, putting his pigskin briefcase down on the table between them. He snapped the briefcase open and took out a folder, then closed the briefcase and put it on the floor beside the table. The walls were dead, white and bare. There was no other furniture except the table and two chairs.

'I'm Winston Tucker.' He looked at her curiously and offered a small smile.

'I remember,' said Rachel, staring at him. No lumberjack shirt and corduroy jacket now. Tucker looked as prosperous as a banker and as sleek as a seal. 'You've changed.'

'So have you.'

'Why are you here?' Rachel asked.

'I'm your lawyer.'

'I didn't ask for a lawyer and I certainly didn't ask for you.'

'You didn't have to,' Tucker said. His mouth was a prim little line. For the first time Rachel noticed his teeth: small, like perfect little seed pearls. 'It's just one of those things.'

'I don't understand.'

'I was your lawyer back in 1974, *pro bono* or not; I was court appointed, that's a matter of public record.'

'So?'

'So, according to New York State law, since I was your last legal counsel of record, I continue to be your legal counsel until you tell me otherwise.' He paused, smiling. 'Are you telling me otherwise?'

'Do you want me to?'

'It's up to you.' He glanced down at the folder in front of him. 'But believe me, you do need a lawyer.'

'I didn't kill anyone.'

'That's not what the evidence shows.'

'What evidence?'

Tucker took in a long breath and let it out in theatrical little puffs as he scanned the file in front of him. 'They found your fingerprints all over Donald Hale's car. They found a Buck knife in the spare wheel of your Volkswagen that matches the wounds in all three bodies. There were half a dozen witnesses to the fact that you and Laura Talbot had a violent argument in the Herb and Spice Café. An hour later UPS tries to deliver a parcel to Ms Talbot in her upstairs apartment and the delivery guy finds her dead on her living-room floor. When Detective Wren arrested you, your bags were packed and ready by the door – you were leaving. Adds up to a lot of bad news, I'm afraid.'

'It's all bullshit.'

'It's enough to get an indictment from a Grand

Jury.' He paused. 'Mind you, there isn't one sitting for the next two months.'

'Can I get out on bail?' Rachel asked.

'On a triple homicide? Don't make me laugh.'

'So I'm back in the shit, is that what you're telling me?'

'That's exactly what I'm telling you.' He shrugged. 'The District Attorney has it all, Ms Kane, including a terrific motive – revenge.'

'D'Arcy Quinn is the person responsible for the death of my daughter; didn't anyone listen to the tape I made? Hale's confession?'

'It will be ruled as inadmissible since, from the sound of things, you were firing a large-calibre weapon in his direction at the time.' The lawyer pursed his lips again. 'Not to mention the fact that the confession is addressing a previous crime and has no direct bearing on the homicide in question.' He glanced down at the file. 'According to a witness you said that Dr Alberoni had, and I quote, "drugged you throughout your interrogation and your preliminary hearing". Did you say that?'

*The McConnel woman.*

'Yes.'

'Strong motive there, don't you think?'

'And my motive for murdering Laura Talbot?'

'You had a fight with her.'

'It wasn't a fight. It was a disagreement. I saw her having a real fight with Michael Parker earlier, at Oneida College. I wanted to know why. I had no reason to kill the woman.'

'You were following her?'

'I went out there to speak to Parker. She happened to be there.'

'The District Attorney will make it sound as though you were stalking one or the other of them.'

'The DA is a murderer, Mr Tucker.'

The balding, overweight lawyer flipped the folder shut. 'Look Ms Kane, or Ms Lucas, or whatever your name is, all of this is beside the point. You spent twenty-odd years in several institutions for the criminally insane. You were convicted of locking your mentally retarded daughter into the automobile you stole from your husband, then setting fire to that automobile by igniting the gas tank. No jury is going to believe a word that comes out of your mouth.'

'Have you listened to the tape I made?'

'Yes.'

'Do you believe it?'

'I don't have to believe or disbelieve it.'

'But do you?'

'I haven't made up my mind,' the lawyer answered.

'If the tape is inadmissible, then so is my motive,' said Rachel. 'This Quinn woman can't have it both ways. Without the tape there is no motive.'

'Smart,' said Tucker. 'But irrelevant. They've got their eyewitness to your statements about what happened here back in 1974.'

'Cut to the chase, Mr Tucker,' Rachel said quietly. 'Just what is it you're trying to tell me?'

'I'd start thinking about a plea-bargain if I was you, Ms Kane.'

'I haven't done anything.'

'That's irrelevant too, I'm afraid.' He shrugged again. 'The knife ties you to all three murders and you have clear motives for two out of the three homicides.'

'What kind of plea?'

He smiled weakly. 'Not guilty by reason of insanity.'

*It's happening all over again.*

'I'd go back to Brockhurst, wouldn't I?'

'Probably.'

'An indefinite term. Like before.'

'Yes.'

'I won't do that.'

*The rest of my life.*

'The electric chair is hardly a reasonable alternative.'

'That's for me to decide,' said Rachel.

Tucker cocked an eyebrow. 'I'm afraid that's not true,' he said. 'Your previous record shows mental defect. A psychiatric evaluation is mandatory. If the report comes back negative the State takes over and decides your plea for you.'

Rachel stared at him. 'That's insane,' she whispered.

'You said it, not me,' he answered. He brought the briefcase back up on to the table and snapped it open. He looked at her across the open lid. 'You shouldn't have come back here, Ms Kane. You should have left well enough alone. You should have tried to put all this behind you and got on with your life.'

'My life was stolen from me, Mr Tucker. In 1974,

four kids murdered my daughter and got away with it. I just came back to find out why, not to hurt people. And you know it.' She stared at him without blinking. He turned his eyes away.

*He does know it. He believes me.*

*So what?*

The lawyer slid the folder back into the briefcase and closed it softly. 'I'm afraid there's not much that I can do,' he said. He swallowed, his Adam's apple bobbing up and down.

*He's afraid.*

'Who frightens you the most?' asked Rachel. 'Is it Skelton or is it Quinn?'

Winston Tucker cleared his throat. 'I have responsibilities,' he muttered.

'They paid you off,' she whispered, suddenly seeing it very clearly. 'Way back then. You *knew* Alberoni was keeping me stoned. You knew there was a coverup. You were part of it, right from the start.'

'Arraignment is in an hour or so,' said Tucker, standing up. 'If you want to dispense with my services you can do it then and the judge will appoint another counsel for you.' Keeping his eyes averted, he turned away and left the small, featureless room.

Bob Wren sat in the Detectives Room, the battered office Sony cassette recorder on the desk in front of him. It was empty; the tape Rachel Kane had given him had been duly signed for and taken away by Ted Harmon, the DA's arrogant, carrot-topped assistant.

Kenny Spearing sat at the desk opposite, dutifully pecking out a report on the arrest made by his partner.

'What did you think of the tape?' Wren asked, still staring down at the empty recorder.

The pecking stopped as Kenny Spearing looked up thoughtfully. 'I don't think it's worth much,' he said after a moment. 'She was doing most of the talking.' He paused. 'When she wasn't blasting away at the poor bastard.'

'It's not what's on the tape,' said Wren. 'It's where she recorded it.'

'I don't get you.'

'She said she got him to go skinny-dipping in some pond, right?'

Spearing nodded. 'The swimming hole up at the old commune. You can hear him splashing around in the water.' He shrugged. 'I still don't get it.'

'He was found out at Stoney Creek. Naked. What did she do, stab him in one place, then drag him off to Stoney Creek by magic?'

'She's pretty strong.'

'She's half the size of Donny Hale.' Wren shook his head. 'Not to mention the fact that his car was absolutely clean. If she dumped him into the trunk she'd have left some trace, even if she had stuffed him into a plastic garbage bag.'

'You're saying she didn't do it, or Alberoni, or Laura Talbot?'

'I'm not saying that, I'm just saying it doesn't fit.'

Spearing looked at his older partner. 'When we

got the match on her prints from the AFIS people in Albany we got her old file up from the basement, remember?'

'Yes.'

'She incinerated her own kid for Christ's sake! She spent twenty years in a loony bin!'

'She says she didn't do it.'

'Right,' Spearing snorted. 'I was there for the interrogation, remember? She says the people who really burned up her kid just happen to be the Chief of Police, the District Attorney, the City Clerk and the Chancellor of the local college.' Spearing laughed and poked his hand in between the buttons of his shirt. 'Just call me Napoleon.'

'It stinks,' said Wren.

His partner grinned. 'I think you've just got the hots for her, some kind of mid-life crisis thing.'

Wren balled up a piece of memo paper and flipped it across the desk, striking Spearing in the chest. 'Screw you,' he said, but he wondered if the young man didn't have a point. He took his notebook out of his pocket and flipped it open. There, circled on the page was the name Jennifer Wax.

'I'll be back in a while,' he said, and left the room.

Chief of Police Robin Skelton sat in the black leather chair across from D'Arcy Quinn, uniformed legs crossed, smoking a cigarette. Behind her desk he could see the sky darkening as another rain storm blew down from the north. Skelton had arrived in her office cold, with no appointment. Ushering him into the room she'd told Ted Harmon that they didn't want to be disturbed. So far Skelton hadn't said anything beyond asking D'Arcy about her recent vacation trip to Ireland.

'Why don't you get to the point, Robby?' she said finally. 'You're not really interested in whether I kissed the Blarney stone or not.'

'I want to know which way you're going to go on this Rachel Kane thing.'

'There is enough evidence to have her arrested for all three murders. I'm going to bring it to trial.'

'You can't do that.'

'Can't?' She stiffened. 'You're the Chief of Police, Robby, not my boss.'

He uncrossed his legs, leaned forward in his chair and smiled at her. 'Don't try any of that high-class holier-than-thou snob shit on me, D'Arce. Remember who you're talking to here.' He let the smile widen. 'I used to fuck you in the back of my truck in Beechwood Cemetery, remember? We did things together your asshole cousin never even imagined doing. Still can't imagine I bet. Or can he?' Across from him the blood had drained from the District Attorney's face. Skelton sat back in his chair. 'We did some bad shit together, D'Arcy, and you did some on your own, like torching that lady's car and turning her kid into a cinder. Remember that?'

'You were as much a part of that as I was,' said Quinn. Her voice was thick with anger and humiliation. 'I was just a kid. You had me so stoned I didn't know what I was doing.'

'Cheap excuse.' He made a snorting sound. 'Tell it to Alan Dershowitz.'

'You're a bastard, Robby.'

'That's never been in dispute.' He smiled, leaned forward and tapped his cigarette on to the edge of the ashtray on her desk. 'But, like I said, we can't let the woman come to trial. She'll dig up all that other shit.'

'That's more than twenty years in the past,' said the District Attorney.

Skelton shook his head. 'No it isn't, D'Arce. It's right here and it's right now.'

'What's that supposed to mean?'

'In 1974 my old man called in a lot of favors to get us off the hook and send this Renee Lucas woman up the river. He had a whole story tacked down nice and tight within twenty-four hours. Alberoni, Hale's old man, your father and Parker's father were all involved as well. My old man even gave me poor old Allan Sloane on a fucking platter. Between them they pulled every string you could think of, and the four of us walked away from it all, clean as a whistle.' He paused. 'You ever wonder why they went to all that trouble, D'Arcy?'

'To protect their kids,' said Quinn. 'To keep us from having our lives ruined for one stupid mistake.' It was the party line, the accepted truth, the rationale she'd used as a mantra for more than twenty years, a way to cast off the nightmares that had haunted her since the night it happened.

'Stupid mistake?' Skelton laughed dryly. 'You call

incinerating a retarded kid by blowing up someone's car a "stupid mistake"?' He shook his head. 'It wasn't a mistake, D'Arcy, it was murder, pure and simple. And we got away with it.'

'What are you saying?'

'My old man never did anything for me,' said Skelton. He held up his wrist and showed her the old Hamilton watch he wore. 'See this? My old man gave me this, but it wasn't even his to give. He got it from a government inspector who was going to blow the whistle on your grandfather and a bunch of other high mucky-mucks in town. My old man was their straw boss. By the last year of the war they were buying up used navy surplus World War I life-jackets and stripping the kapok out of them for new jackets they were making out at their plant. The war materials inspector tumbled to it.'

'What does that have to do with the watch, or with any of what we've been talking about?' asked D'Arcy Quinn.

Skelton smiled. 'My old man stripped it off the guy after he beat his brains in and buried him out by the tracks leading to the Old Dairy. That was the start of it.'

'The start of what?' asked Quinn.

'My old man's pact with the devil,' said Skelton.

'I still don't understand.'

Skelton sighed. 'For someone who's seriously contemplating running for Governor you can be pretty lamebrained, D'Arce.' He shifted in his chair and took a last drag on his cigarette before screwing it down into the glass ashtray on the District Attorney's desk. 'Our parents didn't come up with that elaborate coverup to protect their children, they did it to protect themselves.'

'From what?' D'Arcy asked. Her voice had thinned and dried, and a vein was beating angrily in her throat.

'There are some things gubernatorial candidates shouldn't know,' said Skelton. 'I think Richard Nixon called it "plausible denial."' He shook his head. 'For the time being me knowing all the secrets is enough.'

*That's twice he's mentioned me running for Governor.*

*Oh shit, he's blackmailing me.*

'You're crazy,' whispered D'Arcy Quinn.

Skelton smiled again. 'No, I'm not, D'Arcy. Renee Lucas, also known as Rachel Kane, is the crazy one, which is why you're going to cut me a court waiver so we can transport her directly to the high security lockdown at Brockhurst right after the arraignment. No one's going to dispute a psych evaluation on this one.' Outside, muffled by the thick plate glass of the window at the District Attorney's back, came the rough, cloth-tearing sound of approaching thunder.

'Tucker won't allow it.'

'Winny boy will do as he's fucking told,' said Skelton. 'I'll take care of it.'

'But why so . . .'

The Police Chief shook his head and put a finger to his lips. 'No more questions, D'Arcy, just give me the waiver and leave it all to me.'

* * *

Outside, the rain had begun to come down hard, splashing darkly against the sidewalks and the road, streaking against the windows. Seated across from Wren in the darkened dining room, Eileen Wax puffed on her cigarette, her breath coming in carefully controlled wheezes from deep in her old, scarred lungs. There was a package of cigarettes, an ashtray and a cut crystal sherry glass in front of her. She'd filled the glass from the decanter of smoky liquid that sat on the Victorian buffet behind her.

'This is official business,' the detective said quietly. 'I'm not looking for gossip, Eileen; I *have* to know this.'

'I don't understand all this interest,' said the old woman. 'It was so long ago. Before the war, before anything.' She glared at Wren accusingly and poked the glowing tip of her cigarette in his direction. 'That creature was in this house all along and you didn't do anything about it!'

*Deflecting. Changing the focus. Bring her back.*

'That's why I'm asking you about Jennifer Wax. I don't think Rachel Kane murdered Dr Alberoni and I do think your sister-in-law's suicide had something to do with his death.'

'That was more than fifty years ago,' the old woman whispered. 'You have no idea.'

*When men wore hats and women were called ladies.*

'Your sister-in-law was a Catholic.' Start with sin.

'Yes.' Eileen nodded, a trace of a smile crossing

her face. Outside, the thunder boomed and a slashing flare of lightning lit the room for a split second. In the brilliant, intense spark Wren could see the curve of bone and gristle underneath the old woman's skin, could see how she'd be in death. He brushed the thought away.

'Was she devout?' asked Wren.

'No more than anyone else.' Eileen shrugged. 'Mass every Sunday, confession every other week.' She shrugged again. 'Gadsby'd had her in the choir and Frank had been an altar boy.' She curled her lip. 'The old pervert.'

'What about Dr Alberoni?'

'What about him?' Eileen said. 'He was from New York. An outsider.'

'How did he meet Jennifer?'

'She was a nurse. At Bellevue. He was a doctor.'

'They settled here?'

'That's right.'

'Why?' asked Wren.

'Because they were married.'

'He was working at Bellevue, living in New York. Why move to a small town like Prosper?'

'They asked him to come,' said Eileen. She butted her cigarette and lit another. It was only late afternoon but the storm had made it dark as dusk outside. In the dining room everything had been robbed of shape and color and Wren could only see Eileen as a dark shape at the end of the table until she dragged on her cigarette, or a stroke of lightning scratched through the sky.

'Who asked?' said Wren.

'The town. Quinn, he was the mayor back then. Parker, Dexter from the dairy. We needed a doctor. Percy Rodman was the doctor before that, but he went senile; wasn't any use to anyone.'

'So they convinced Alberoni to come to town?'

'Yes.'

'He married Jennifer in 1937.'

'Something like that.'

'I saw a photograph of her. On a ship. The *Queen Mary*.'

'They went to England for their honeymoon.'

'Expensive,' Wren commented.

'Part of the deal I think,' said Eileen Wax. 'They paid for the trip.'

'Quinn and Parker and the others?'

'That's right.'

'A year later she committed suicide. She swallowed molasses and lye. A hard way to go.' He paused. 'Especially since it's a cardinal sin.'

'Yes.'

'Why?'

'You don't want to go and raise up dead things,' said Eileen, her smoke-rough voice coming at him out of the shadows. It was almost a plea. 'It's just going to cause more pain.'

'Sometimes bringing it out into the open can stop the pain.'

Eileen let out a phlegmy laugh that was half a cough. 'You've been watching too much talk TV,' she said. 'That Sally woman and her friends.'

'I think your sister-in-law's suicide ties in with Dr Alberoni's murder.'

'So you really don't think our star border did it?'

'No.'

There was a long silence as Eileen pulled on her cigarette in the gloom. The storm was much closer now, gathered all around them, filling the sky with light and rain and crashing noise.

'It was the baby,' she said at last, speaking so softly that Wren barely heard her. She put out her cigarette and slid another one out of the package on the table in front of her.

'She was pregnant?'

'No.' The word came out flatly.

'I don't understand,' said Wren.

'There was another woman . . .' Eileen's voice trailed away, swallowed by the sound of the storm.

'Who?'

'Does it matter?'

'What do you mean by "another woman"?'

'Are you foolish? Just what I said. Another woman.'

'Dr Alberoni had another woman?'

'Yes.'

'A mistress?'

'You couldn't call her that.' Eileen paused. 'It wasn't like that. It was just . . .' Again her voice faded.

'The other woman was pregnant?'

'Yes.'

'Your sister-in-law found out?'

'No.'

He sighed, exasperated. 'Why don't you just tell me what happened?'

'One of the things the doctor did was take care of the girls at the Model Home. Back then it was up on Snelling Street, in the building the Heritage Society's in now.' Eileen laughed dryly, coughed and lifted the sherry glass. She took a short swallow, then put the glass carefully back on the table.

'The maternity home?'

'Yes.' She took another sip from the glass and lit another cigarette. 'There was a nurse there . . .'

'Alberoni got her pregnant?'

'That's what she said. The doctor denied it.' Eileen took a long drag on her cigarette, almost as though she was trying to draw strength from it. 'She said if he didn't do something she was going to go to the newspaper.' Eileen scowled. 'She would've too, the little bitch.' Eileen shook her head. 'Now wouldn't *that* have been something!'

'What do you mean, "do something"?' asked Wren.

'Help her lose it.'

'An abortion?'

'Yes.'

'Did he do it?'

'Yes.' Eileen sighed. 'Three days later she died of septic peritonitis.'

'Your sister-in-law found out about it then?'

'She didn't find out about it; he *told* her. Confessed.' Eileen shook her head. 'She came to me in tears and told me the whole story. She didn't know what to do. She said there was no one she could turn to, she said that everyone else was pretending that it had never happened. To her that was the biggest sin, bigger than adultery, bigger than the abortion – the fact that it was all being swept under the table.'

'Why didn't she go to the priest?'

'Gadsby?' She made the name sound like a foul smell. 'He was just as much a part of it as all the rest of them.'

'I don't get it.'

Eileen sneered. 'The girl? The nurse who died after the abortion? She was Father Gadsby's niece.'

In the District Attorney's office, at four thirty that afternoon, with the rain slashing down outside, Winston Tucker countersigned the court waiver D'Arcy Quinn had prepared, allowing Rachel Kane to be removed from custody and transported to the Forensic Psychiatry Unit at the Brockhurst Institution for the Criminally Insane just outside of Oriskany, New York, a few miles west of the city of Utica.

Shortly after five o'clock, Rachel Kane was duly deprocessed from the holding cells in the sub-basement of Courthouse Square, still wearing a fluorescent orange one-piece Prosper Jail jumpsuit and thin plastic jail slippers. Since the holding cells were usually occupied by drunks and juveniles, there were few facilities for transporting dangerous criminals and Rachel was led out of the lockup handcuffed, but without leg chains.

She was taken across the building's interior

courtyard and placed in the left rear jumpseat of a dark green Prosper Police Department Land Rover Defender. One of her cuffs was removed, then re-attached to the steel D-bolt welded to the side wall of the police vehicle. She was separated from the driver's compartment of the vehicle by a steel mesh screen.

For the next five minutes she sat alone in the vehicle, listening to the rain pound down on the roof like hammers on steel drums, watching as it streamed down the windows all around her. Finally, shortly before six o'clock, a single, uniformed figure wearing a yellow Prosper PD rain slicker got in behind the wheel and started the engine. A few moments later they pulled out of the courtyard, turned left on to Madison Street, then right on to Carteret Street, heading north, out of Prosper.

'I don't suppose you have a cigarette up there by any chance,' said Rachel, speaking to the back of the driver's head.

'Sorry. This is a non-smoking vehicle.' The man behind the wheel turned and glanced back at her through the mesh, smiling. It was Robin Skelton.

# CHAPTER EIGHTEEN

Windshield wipers thumping, Robin Skelton piloted the four-wheel-drive police vehicle out of town, taking the old Jaketown Road west, then turning due north on County 52, heading into the mountains. Rigid on the jump seat Rachel kept her eyes squeezed shut, feeling the terror-driven pulse beating in her throat and in the cuffed wrist binding her to the D-bolt set between her legs. She winced at each lurch and bump, terrified that anything might set off the madman seated behind the wheel. The universe was tied up in a fragile instant and the hot eyes she'd seen searching for hers in the rear-view mirror.

*Don't talk. Don't say anything.*

'Just like old times.'

*Nothing. Not a word.*

'Cat got your tongue?'

*I'm going to scream.*

*No you're not.*

'Funny how things work out, isn't it?' He paused. Rachel opened her eyes and met his again in the mirror. The narrow road was empty ahead, trees like a wet green wall on either side of the rushing vehicle.

319

The smell of gasoline and hot oil was rank in her nostrils. The claustrophobic little compartment squeezed in behind the mesh screen was barren; two jump seats across from her, the rear door, the glass wire-netted and screened on the outside, the floor and ceiling bare metal. 'Forget it, sweetheart.' Skelton smiled. 'You're not going anywhere I don't want you to go.'

'What do you mean?'

*Oh shit, you opened your mouth!*

'You shouldn't have come back,' said Skelton. His eyes raked hers in the mirror again as he looked away from the road. Rain smashed on the roof like bony knuckles knocking on a metal door. 'If you hadn't come back I don't think any of this would have happened.'

*Don't argue with him, that's what he wants.*

'I haven't done anything.'

*Shut up, you idiot!*

'That's what you said the last time.'

*He's dangerous. So far he's killed three people.*

*This time.*

'You murdered my daughter, you bastard.'

*Oh, no.*

*Kick his taillight in.*

'You committed murder because of a broken taillight on your stupid fucking truck.' She paused. 'Asshole.'

His eyes flared in the mirror, but then he smiled again.

'Pick up a few balls in the loony bin?'

'You're a slimy piece of shit, did you know that?'

*Might as well go out with a bang, Renee. He's going to kill you anyway.*

'I don't deny it, sweetheart.' He laughed. 'You know, this is the first time we've really talked.'

*Insane.*

'We're not going to Brockhurst, are we?'

Skelton slowed going into the turn around Black Lake Pond, a long narrow strip of swamp that curved around the foot of Stoney Mountain. At the next crossroads he turned on to Stoney Creek Road and headed deeper into the gloomy hills. Thunder rolled and boomed around them and lightning flashed through the windshield every few seconds but Rachel was barely aware of either sound or fury.

'We're not going to Brockhurst, are we, Robby?' she said again.

'Don't call me that.'

'Why not?'

'It's a kid's name. I didn't like it then, I don't like it now.' He paused, looked at her again in the mirror, his eyes flat and cold and without feeling. 'It's what my father called me.'

'We're not going to Brockhurst, are we?'

'You keep on asking that.'

'And you don't answer.'

'I haven't decided yet.'

'You won't get away with it.'

*Who are you trying to kid?*

'Why not?' Again the eyes glanced back at her through the metal screen. 'What's going to stop me?'

321

'It all comes around, Robby, believe me.'

'Spare me the hippie bullshit, sweetheart.' He laughed dryly. 'It was shit then, it's shit now.' He shook his head. 'I can get away with anything I want,' he said quietly. 'No one at Brockhurst is expecting you, no one back in Prosper cares. You'll just disappear. Vanish from the bureaucracy.'

'Someone will wonder.'

'No they won't. I read through your jacket. Your parents are dead. You legally changed your name. No one's waiting and no one cares.'

*He's right. I thought I wanted it that way. No ties, no obligations.*

*Just me.*

'What about Winston Tucker?'

He laughed. 'Winnie is my tame fat boy. I won't tell and he won't ask.' This time he actually turned and stared at her through the mesh for a split second. 'That's how the town works, sweetheart. That's how it always worked.'

Rachel squeezed her eyes shut again, trying to contain the rising tide of hate that was threatening to consume her and carry her away into its black, silky depths; give in to it now and she would be lost; she didn't have the luxury of madness here. She had to keep it together.

*Keep him talking.*

*Why?*

*Because I can't think of anything else at the moment.*

'Why?'

'What?' Eyes in the mirror again, his face like a mask.

'Why did your father protect you that night? You and the other three?'

'I've already had this conversation once today.' He grinned at her. 'This isn't some B movie where the bad guy tells you everything just before the big rescue.' The smile on his face broadened. 'Face it, sweetheart, you're never going to know.'

He was still looking at her in the mirror when the deer stepped out into the road, jack-lit by the array of fog lamps set into the Land Rover's grille, terrified. Rachel saw it before he did, a split-second glimpse between sweeps of the wiper blades and then it was too late. The vehicle hit the deer across the haunches, spinning the wheel out of Skelton's hands and taking them towards the deep, flooding ditch that ran between the road and the dripping cliff of trees.

The Police Chief managed to get control for a final, single instant and then the outer front wheel tripped into the ditch, pulling the wheel out of his hands again. The Land Rover spun out of control, the rear section lifting back up on to the road, smashing Rachel off her seat and down on to the floor. Turned at right angles to the road, the front wheel still trapped in the ditch, the vehicle tumbled and began to roll, the side window smashing into a thousand little hexagons of safety glass, the transmission howling madly as the engine continued to race, tires spinning wildly, searching for traction where there was none to be had.

Rachel was torn across the rear section of the vehicle, smashing her shoulder into the jump seat opposite her own and then the Land Rover careened entirely into the ditch, flipping again, Robin Skelton's head smashing into the side window of his door, knocking him unconscious. Rachel blacked out for a moment and when she came to she was vaguely aware that the D-bolt holding her to the chassis of the Land Rover had been stripped away by the impact of a huge boulder that was now poking through the side of the truck.

She also realized that she was soaking wet; the rain continued to hammer on the roof and thick, muddy currents of water were now flowing into the Land Rover through the smashed windows and the sprung, driver's side door. Rachel let herself slide forward and down until she was resting against the mesh screen separating the front and rear compartments. Skelton had slumped over on to the passenger side. Blood was swirling out of a wound that had cut deeply into the flesh above his right eye and more ropes of blood tracked down through the hair at the back of his head. Water swirled and gurgled all around him. He didn't look as though he was breathing but it didn't really matter because if the water from the ditch kept pouring in he'd almost certainly drown.

*I want to watch. I want to see the bastard die.*

*Don't be a fool! Move!*

Using the back of the jump seat for leverage, Rachel pulled herself back toward the uptilted rear of the Land Rover. She smashed away what was left of the side window with her elbow, then boosted herself up and out of the vehicle, flipping herself over the side and down into the ooze pushed up from the ditch when the Land Rover dropped down off the road. She was soaked instantly, the thin fabric of the jail jumpsuit virtually no protection at all from the cold, sleeting rain. She wiped water out of her eyes, put up a shading hand and looked down the narrow road. Empty except for the carcass of the deer, broken and steaming in the opposite ditch fifty yards back. There was no sign of the sun; in this weather it was perfectly possible that no other car would come down this old road until well after sunset, or perhaps not at all.

Feeling the weight of the cuff and the chain and the dangling D-bolt, Rachel lifted her arm and stared. If she did manage to get away she'd have to get rid of the jumpsuit and the shackles. Grimacing she stepped back toward the Land Rover, boosted herself up, and pulled open the sprung, damaged remains of the driver's side door. Half of Skelton's face was under water now; another minute or two and it would reach his mouth and nostrils.

*In a car. Fitting.*

*Fire and water.*

*Let him drown.*

She wiped water out of her eyes a second time and stared down at the slumped figure, the yellow rain slicker swirling around him like the wings of some enormous broken butterfly. Even after all this time he was still handsome, the jaw firm, the bones and muscles of his face still strong, his skin uncorrupted by the passage of time.

*Lauren would be a full grown woman now, and beautiful.*

*Matthew would be . . .*

'Bastard,' she whispered, and then she reached down with both hands, grabbed bunches of the slicker at his collar, and pulled him up and out of the water, dragging him out through the half-open door until he was lying across the crumpled side of the Land Rover, raindrops smacking down on to the slicker and his face, bouncing off his closed eyelids, watering down the blood on his face from red to pink, letting her see the pulse in his neck and at his temple.

*Should have died and saved me the trouble.*

Tasting bile she thrust her hand down into his uniform pants and found his big ring of keys. It took her a few moments to identify the handcuff key and then she had the shackle off, tossing it away into the mud. Still holding the keys she eased herself back into the cab. The big shotgun she'd seen was still locked to its custom bracket to the right of the transmission lever. She fumbled with the keys again, trying several before she unlocked the bracket and removed the short-barreled riot gun.

Shotgun in hand she levered herself out of the cab again and into the steadily pouring rain. She used the pump to push a shell into the chamber and stared down at the still unconscious form of the Police Chief. She felt a coldness grip her stomach and twist inside her guts. Rain coursed down her cheeks like tears and gathered in her eyelashes like jewels. She poked the muzzle of the shotgun under Skelton's chin, pushing until his head flopped to one side and the barrel of the gun pointed at one full side of his exposed neck. She pushed harder, feeling the metal move under his chin, felt her own finger put pressure on the trigger.

*Kill him.*

She hesitated and withdrew the barrel slightly. She knew if she waited too long she'd never be able to do anything like this again and thought of the hundred thousand wasted hours, the million minutes, the life she'd had torn from her. The child.

*Kill him.*

*Kill him because if he wakes up, he'll chase you and he'll find you and he won't hesitate for a second.*

*Sweetheart.*

*Kill him!*

*I can't.*

Rachel removed the muzzle of the gun, pulled Skelton's revolver from its holster on his hip and tossed it over the slanting top of the Land Rover and into the water-filled ditch. Then she dropped down from the side of the upended four by four, went around behind it, jumped the drainage ditch and headed into the forest.

Wren sat in Jerry Weems' studio and pushed the photograph across the table. The pudgy little photographer sat across the coffee table from him and nodded. Outside, the storm was in full cry, sheets of water gushing against the windows, thunder crashing like hammers on sheet metal.

'I found it when I searched her room,' said Wren. 'It's got your stamp on the back.'

'Yeah, she was here,' Jerry nodded.

'Who's the girl in the picture?'

'Sue Marsden. Anne McConnel's big sister.'

*Jesus. Anne McConnel, one of D'Arcy Quinn's witnesses.*

'Why was she so interested in this particular picture?'

'She kept on asking about Robin Skelton.' Jerry Weems pointed. 'That's his truck. Him and Sue were girlfriend-boyfriend.'

Wren flipped the picture, read the date on the back, then flipped it over again, peered closely, saw the quickly repaired taillight and knew why she'd been so interested.

'Christ!' he muttered under his breath. If this much of her story was true, why not all of it?'

'Hindsight's weird. I mean, I should have figured something,' said Weems.

'What do you mean?'

'The kid looking out through the cab window?'

'What about him?'

'Donald Hale.'

When Wren had questioned her she'd mentioned four names, two represented by the picture on the table, the third the woman prosecuting her in court. And the fourth?

'Was she interested in old pictures of Michael Parker?' asked the detective.

The photographer shook his head. 'Not that I remember.' He shrugged. 'Other than pictures of Skelton and Sue Marsden she seemed really taken by my *Life* cover.' He gestured toward the framed magazine cover on the wall. 'Like I said before, hindsight and all.'

Wren got up and walked over to the framed cover. Jerry Weems explained. 'See the guy in the tight leather pants? That's Paul Goodman; he kind of ran everything at Morningstar. A hippie Joe Stud, you know? Teaches psychology out at the college now.'

'Morningstar?' Rachel had talked about it; she'd been heading back to Morningstar when she supposedly ran into Skelton and the others. Morningstar was the place she'd torched her daughter.

'Yeah.'

'What about this Goodman guy?' asked Wren.

'Not him, the woman standing just behind him, kind of has her face half-turned away?'

'I see her.'

'Laura Talbot.'

Another piece fell into place. A telephone rang, the trilling sound barely audible over the crashing thunder outside. The photographer got up, disappeared into the rear of the loft and came back a few moments later holding a portable phone in his outstretched hand. 'It's for you,' he said, and handed the phone to Wren. It was Kenny Spearing.

'Yes?'

'Three things. One, the DA put the Kane woman's pre-liminary hearing on a waiver; she's been sent to Brockhurst for a psych evaluation.'

'Shit.' A psychiatric evaluation could take up to three or four weeks. If she really wasn't the killer the trail would be stone cold before he could get back to it. 'What else?'

'Guess who's transporting her up to the nuthouse as we speak?'

'I don't have time for twenty questions, Kenny.'

'The Chief.'

Wren's eyes widened. 'Skelton?'

'None other,' said the younger detective. 'Oh yeah, and number three, Anne McConnel just called the office. Her sister just got into town and she wants to talk to you. Urgently.'

Crashing through the trees she found the old trail almost immediately, an Indian path to the river a thousand years ago, widened to fit wagon wheels in the days when it was thought that gold could be found in Stoney Creek, finally narrowed to a skid road for logs back in the twenties, and now abandoned altogether. The trail down through the dripping forest was no wider than her outstretched arms, the center slumped and racing with churning muddy water. Stumbling, sliding forward, Rachel tried to keep to one side, away from the treacherous flow, the broad, slippery leaves of the ferns on the edges of the trail almost as dangerous.

*Run. Run faster.*

Heart pounding, she could almost see Robby turning, rising, groaning as he brought himself upright and slid down from the flank of the wounded Land Rover, then dragging himself across the ditch and beginning to track her through the woods.

*Faster.*

She plunged onward, almost blinded by the rain, sliding down a steep short hill that ran along a bouldered cliff of earth for a hundred yards or so, the foot of the hill strewn with pink calypso and wild violet that she barely saw. The trail was now a slick dark aisle between the buttresses of hemlock, fir and cedar, and in the distance Rachel thought she could hear the sound of a shouting voice.

*Wren, oh Christ, let it be Wren!*

She tumbled down through a tiny clearing edged with vine maple and more wildflowers that grew beside the old rotted stumps that marked the death spoor of loggers from half a century ago and then she was back on the trail, the shouting louder now. The trail lunged off to the right and Rachel suddenly lost her footing, grabbing at roots and clumps of grass as she fell forward, more roots slashing at her face and arms, the thin fabric of the jail jumpsuit tearing away in long shredding pennants. The shotgun spun out of her grip, disappeared into the rain and mud somewhere above her. She lost one, then both of her felt slippers and then she was at the bottom of the drop, barefoot, scrabbling herself upright, wiping the water from her eyes, streaking her face with mud, searching for the trail.

Finding it, she started to run again, limping now, only then realizing that she must have smashed her knee against something as she fell. Blood spattered down on to the green, turned to pink, then dissolved entirely in the sheeting downpour that was drowning everything. The path was swinging steadily downward, the trees on either side so close now that they brushed against her shoulders. Suddenly, on her left, a huge rock wall emerged out of the rain, moss covered, slippery green and then she saw the source of the shouting she had heard – the roaring fall of a rain-flooded stream, plunging down from the heights above, water smashing on to the algae-covered boulders below, trenching a new pathway down between the ferns and broken-rock scree, the sun-hot ground and the trees steaming through the curtain of drowning rain.

Ducking past the spraying water, Rachel slipped again and this time there was nothing to slow her fall. She slid headfirst toward the edge of the high earth bank above the swollen waters of Stoney Creek, slammed her forehead against the wet bark shoulder of a deadfall branch, then rolled, half-unconscious, overall the bank and into the thundering waters below.

# CHAPTER NINETEEN

Wren sat stiffly in Anne McConnel's perfect, just-so, Martha Stewart living room. Outside, the thunder and lightning had faded, leaving nothing but the abating rain. By evening the setting sun would be a firestorm of color on the mountainous horizon.

Anne McConnel sat across from him on the beige couch, hands folded demurely in her lap, knees together, lips pursed. Her sister sat beside her. Her hair was cut short now, shaggy and still dark, the soft curve of her mouth and cheek and jaw gone firmer with time, crows' feet cracking out from the corners of her eyes and strong caliper lines of laughter bracketing the thick, still sensuous lips. Different from the picture, and somehow better. The youthful beauty was fading but somewhere along the way it had been replaced by character and strength and humor. Wren felt a small urgent wrench in his belly, suddenly realizing that she reminded him of Rachel Kane.

Susan Marsden was wearing tight jeans over cowboy boots, a plaited leather belt set with oval silver beads, a blue chambray shirt with ragged cuffs and collar and a patchwork leather vest. She wore two

pieces of jewelry – a big turquoise ring on the middle
finger of her right hand and a plaited leather bracelet
set with tiny silver beads that made a match for the
belt around her waist. She sat with one leg crossed
over the other and she was smoking a cigarette. In
the kitchen, Wren could hear dishes slammed too
hard as they were unloaded from a dishwasher and
a scolding man's voice berating his children.

'Her husband doesn't like me much,' said the short-
haired woman, nodding toward the man's voice.

'That's not true!' Anne McConnel kept her voice
down to a harsh whisper. She glanced across at Wren,
her complexion reddening.

'Sure it is,' her sister answered, smiling easily. 'He
thinks I'm going to turn you into some kind of West
Coast biker dyke or something.' She laughed. 'Might
do you some good at that,' she added.

'Susie!' Color rose up to Anne McConnel's forehead.
She pasted on a desperate smile. 'She lives in
Hollywood,' the younger sister said, as though that
explained everything. She crossed her arms under
her breasts and squeezed her knees even more tightly
together.

'I just came back to visit the old haunts for a few
days,' said Marsden, looking across at Wren. 'I was
in New York anyway so I thought I'd come home for
a visit.' She tapped her cigarette into the ashtray
balanced on her boot. 'Annie here's been telling me
what's been going on; the conversation she had with
this woman.'

'Rachel Kane,' Wren supplied.

'Yes,' Sue Marsden nodded. 'It brought it all back.' She took a long drag on her cigarette then butted it. She put the ashtray on the coffee table and leaned back against the couch, turning to look briefly at her sister, then back at Wren. 'I remember the jacket most of all.'

'What jacket?'

'The Woodrow Wilson jacket Robby let me wear when we were dating.' She made a little snorting sound under her breath and her smile widened into a grimace. Teeth flashed. 'It was this big thing he and a few of the other BMOCs had going – they'd buy two letter jackets and give one to the girl; sort of like branding a cow.'

'It wasn't like that,' said Anne McConnel. She stared at the still-smoking butt in the ashtray as though she wanted to pick it up and smoke it.

'Yes it was,' said Sue Marsden. 'It was exactly like that. Robby Skelton and his asshole buddies were all pussy hounds and you know it.'

'The jacket,' Wren prompted.

'Right,' the older sister nodded. 'Annie and I were off on our big European jaunt when all of this stuff happened, but Robby and I had already split up by then and he'd taken back his stupid jacket and given it to the Quinn kid.'

'D'Arcy Quinn?' asked Wren. 'The District Attorney?'

'Everyone says cream rises to the top,' said Sue Marsden. She grinned. 'I'm beginning to think shit does the same thing.'

'Susie!'

*How many years has she been saying that when her sister does something outrageous?*

'All the boys used to call her D'Arcy Quim.'

'Susie! That's not true!'

'Of course it is. She thought she could fuck her way to the big time. From what I can tell she did just that.'

'The jacket,' Wren reminded her a second time.

'Robby gave it to D'Arcy; I knew he'd been going out with her on the side even before I left for Europe – that's one of the reasons we split up. But she was already out of the picture by the time we got back. End of September, early October.'

'October twelfth,' said Anne McConnel primly. From the kitchen there was the sound of pans and lids being put away. A garburetor growled.

'If you say so,' said Sue Marsden. She glanced at her sister and under all the sibling barbed wire Wren thought he could see true affection. 'Anyway, I wasn't back a week before Robby came sniffing around again. He gave me back the jacket. Told me we were going out again, as though I didn't have any say in the matter.'

'Presumably you didn't go along with that.'

'For about a day and a night,' the older woman answered. 'Just long enough for Robby to get that big fat tool of his up me one last time, which was all he really wanted in the first place.'

'Susie! For God's sake!'

'You're the only one blushing, Annie. Detective

Wren here isn't a virgin, after all.' She looked Wren straight in the face, grinned and winked broadly. 'You're not, are you?' she asked.

'Not for some time,' Wren answered, trying to keep a straight face. He found himself liking Susan Marsden immensely, even if she really was a 'West Coast biker dyke'.

'The point of all this is the jacket,' continued the Marsden woman. 'When Robby handed it back to me it stank of gasoline fumes and smoke; it was right down into the lining. The wooly stuff around the cuffs was all screwed up too . . . One side it was all black and sooty and actually burned. Even if I'd wanted to, I couldn't have worn it. It was like it had been in a fire or something.'

He remembered Rachel Kane's description of the fire that had immolated her little girl, and her description of it in the court transcripts of her preliminary hearing back in 1974. According to the record, her car had been parked with the trunk facing the entry road to the commune site. In his interview with Rachel she'd told him that she could see their faces reflected in the glow of the lighter, which meant that the woman with the lighter was looking back toward the rear of the car. That in turn meant that she must have used her left hand to set the gasoline soaked rag alight.

*And if I remember correctly, D'Arcy Quinn is left-handed.*

'Can you remember which one of the cuffs was burned?'

337

Sue Marsden frowned, then squeezed her eyes shut. She uncrossed her legs and half-turned on the couch, holding out her arms, trying to visualize. She turned back to Wren and opened her eyes. 'Yes,' she nodded emphatically. 'I'm sure it was the left.'

*She was telling me the truth. All of it.*

For a second he felt a wave of relief wash over him, but just as suddenly it was gone. He listened to the kitchen noises then turned his attention to Anne McConnel. 'According to the affidavit you swore out you told the police about the conversation you had with Ms Kane the following day, is that correct?'

'Yes.'

'Why?' Wren asked. Gossip was one thing, but going to the police with it was something else. He looked at the woman across from him but she wouldn't meet his eyes directly. Color blossomed in her cheeks again.

*Oh shit, don't tell me.*

He knew he was right. 'Who did you speak with?'

'Chief Skelton.'

'Robby?' asked Sue Marsden, turning to look at her sister.

'Yes.'

'You should have called Detective Division,' said Wren.

'I don't know anything about these things,' said Anne McConnel. 'I just asked to speak to Robby . . . to Chief Skelton.' She paused, blushing furiously now. 'I thought he should know.' Her whole face was turning strawberry.

'Because he was implicated in the death of Ms Kane's daughter?' asked Wren.

'You're fucking him!' whispered Sue Marsden, staring at her sister, eyes wide. 'It was pillow talk, wasn't it?'

'Susie!' The younger woman's eyes flickered toward the kitchen door. The clattering continued.

'I'll never tell,' Sue Marsden grinned. She reached out and punched her sister lightly on the shoulder. 'Way to go, kiddo, I didn't think you had it in you!'

'I want a cigarette,' said Anne McConnel. She turned toward the kitchen, scowling. 'Screw him.'

The doorbell rang and the prim woman jerked like a startled rabbit. 'Forget I said that,' she muttered, getting up. She went to the door and came back a moment later, a dripping Kenny Spearing in tow.

'Problem?' asked Wren.

'The Chief's ET went off.'

'ET?' asked Sue Marsden.

'Emergency Transponder,' explained Spearing. 'You know, ET, call home?'

'What happened?' Wren asked sharply. 'And where?'

'Stoney Creek Road, up by the Swiss Hill turnoff that leads to Route 52. The signal tripped when his airbag blew. Looks like they hit a deer and went off the road. The Chief's in pretty bad shape; they're bringing him back to the Medical Center now.'

'Dear God!' whispered Anne McConnel. 'Robby!' She sat down hard. Her sister lit another cigarette and handed it across to her without saying a word.

339

'The woman?' asked Wren.

'Gone,' Spearing answered. 'And she's got the riot gun.'

She rolled and turned and spun in the roiling silt-filled water, dreaming. Days of childhood and streets without sidewalks, spinning batons and soft dry lips, kissing boys. The faint ghost music of a marching band across the hot summer afternoon and the shivering tinsel sound of a soft wind in trees. Gentle fingertips across soft skin, eyes closed, willing the fingers to be someone else's other than her own, testing, hoping, shaking her head to feel the weight of her hair against her neck and wondering in the end what the point of the whole thing was.

*First time for everything, honeybunch.*

*He had such beautiful blue eyes and lips that felt like silk.*

And when he slipped between her parted thighs and entered her in that hard warm rush that took her from her belly to her cold soft tongue within his mouth and his hands beneath her shoulders holding her so, so softly that she thought she was about to . . .

*Die.*

Coughing and choking, the grit-filled water filling her mouth, she rose to the surface, arms flailing, trying to scream but only retching up more water. She felt herself going down again and then her fingers clawed, reached out and dug into cold wet earth. She pulled herself forward and up, saw in terrible detail the rotting bank of the overburdened river slipping down into the rushing stream, and handhold a split-second illusion.

Something tugged at her legs, winding around her ankles like bony fingers and she was torn away by the swirling floor, pulled under, and this time she knew with utter, perfect clarity, she wasn't coming up again. No marching bands or batons, no fingers tracing a lover's path across her skin.

Instead of seeing her life pass by, or hearing angels, she saw, in her mind, the framed print that had hung over the mantel in her grandmother's house. A red-haired woman, tresses spread across the water of a narrow creek, her face just submerged. Drowned, the Lady of Shalott, but there was no poetry to this death. This was choking mud and soiled filthy water.

*I don't have red hair anyway.*

The hand that reached down and grabbed the already tattered collar of the jumpsuit from the Prosper Jail was brown and strong, veins and sinews running back up into bulging forearms packed with solid muscle. A second hand snaked in under her arm and hooked around her chest above her breasts but without choking her. Steadily, the two hands and arms dragged her backwards and up until she found herself flat on her back, staring up into the scudding pewter sky, fat drops of rain washing the mud and blood away from her face and hair.

She gagged, and the hands and arms quickly turned her on her side. Her face was less than an inch away from the sodden grass above the creekbank as she retched again, vomiting out a bellyful of brown-blue water. The hands rolled her back again and she found herself staring into the face of a man she'd never seen before.

'Better now?' asked Allan Sloane.

# CHAPTER TWENTY

Rachel Kane sat in one of Sloane's two wooden armchairs, pulled close to the roaring fire, wrapped in a thick wool blanket, a big steaming mug of black sweet coffee cupped in her hands. Outside, the rain was beginning to slow and slashes of lowering sun cut through the clouds like a Sunday school religious landscape; what Rachel used to call a Billy Graham sky.

'You got tangled up in the chains I use to anchor my floating dock,' said Allan Sloane, seated across from her. 'They were coming loose; that's why I was out there in the storm.' He smiled. 'Good thing too. If I hadn't been out there you might have drowned.'

*Maybe that would have been better for all concerned.*

'You know who I am?' Rachel asked.

Sloane nodded toward the black plastic cube of a boom box that stood on the kitchen counter. 'I heard they arrested you.'

'They were sending me back to Brockhurst.'

'Jesus.'

'Robin Skelton was taking me there himself. We had an accident. I escaped.'

'And Skelton?'

'Banged his head. Knocked out. I don't think it's any worse than that.' She smiled weakly and tightened her grip on the mug in her hands. 'You don't seem too upset having an escaped murderer in your living room.'

'I think I can defend myself.' He paused. 'You didn't kill those people, did you?'

'No. But the police think I did.'

'Then they'll be after you.'

'Soon,' she nodded. 'How many other places along the river?'

'Not many.' He paused, took a deep breath, then let it out. 'Do you know who I am?'

She smiled and took a swallow of coffee. 'The angel who rescued me. Clarence. If you didn't have your wings before, you've got them now.'

'*It's a Wonderful Life*,' said Sloane.

'I could give you an argument about that.' She took another sip of coffee.

'My name's not Clarence. It's Allan Sloane.'

There was a long silence. Rain dripped from the eaves outside and wood sparked and crackled in the fireplace. She stared at him without speaking, then bent down and put the coffee mug down on the slate hearth in front of the fire. She shifted in the chair and pulled the blanket away from her shoulders, bending her head to roughly dry her hair.

'You remember who I am?' Sloane asked.

She dropped the blanket and stared at him for a long moment. 'Sure,' she said finally. 'In 1974 you gave Robby Skelton the alibi that got him and his friends off. You gave him the alibi that had me sent to a mental institution for more than twenty years.'

'You don't sound very angry.'

'Angry?' Rachel shrugged. 'Why should I be angry? It was a long time ago and I'm sure you had your reasons.' She sighed and ran her fingers back through her damp hair. 'When you get right down to it, I'm too tired of it all to really care any more.'

'I didn't want to lie.'

'But you did,' said Rachel.

'Skelton's father . . . knew something about me.'

'Something personal?'

'Yes. It would have killed my parents. Destroyed them. Skelton's father knew that. I couldn't let it happen.'

'He blackmailed you?'

'Yes.'

'Threatened to expose you?'

'Yes.'

'And Robby?'

'He knew.' Sloane's face twisted. 'He knows too many things.'

'Somehow he found out I was back in town. He must have thought I had some plan to expose him,' said Rachel. 'He killed Alberoni and Donald Hale to set me up. Clean up loose ends. Killing Laura Talbot was icing on the cake.' She picked up her coffee mug and sipped. 'It worked. No one's going to believe me now. They'll hunt me down with dogs and guns.'

'We have to get you out of here,' said Sloane. He got up and tossed another log on the fire from the wooden box beside his chair. He stood in front of the fire, staring down into the flames, then turned to Rachel. 'I owe you that much.'

'How?'

'I could drive you. Up to Canada. Somewhere.' He shrugged unhappily. 'If you stay here they'll find you.'

'You've already been an angel, Clarence, forget about being a hero.' She shook her head. 'Maybe I should just give myself up.'

'If you do that, then nothing will change.'

'So, what else is new?' said Rachel, smiling gently. 'People like Robin Skelton are made of stone; they don't change. Ever.'

'They got away with murder. Skelton will get away with it again unless we stop him.'

'I told you, no one is going to believe me; they didn't before, why would they now? I was the perfect fall guy twenty years ago and nothing has changed.'

'What about your lawyer?'

'Tucker?' She shook her head. 'He's got too many friends, his palm's been greased once too often.'

'There has to be somebody,' said Sloane.

She stared into the fire and thought, then nodded to herself. 'Maybe there is,' she said.

Kenny Spearing drove the big unmarked Caprice while Wren stared through the windshield. The storm had come and gone, leaving the houses on the outskirts of town gleaming in the lurid light of the setting sun. Neither man had spoken since leaving Anne McConnel and her sister. Spearing finally broke the silence.

'Maybe we should put a guard on the Chief's room at the hospital.'

'This isn't *The Godfather*,' said Wren. 'If she'd wanted to kill him she could have done it after the Land Rover went into the ditch.'

'She probably didn't even stop to check. Just ran,' said Spearing.

'She stopped long enough to get his keys and unlock the riot gun from the dash.'

'We've got the trackers and the dogs on their way. We'll find her,' said Spearing.

'Maybe.'

'You don't really think she'll come back, do you?'

'I don't know,' said Wren. He'd been thinking about it long and hard. 'From what I can tell so far everything she told me was true; she was unjustly accused of a crime she didn't commit. She watched her daughter being murdered and spent the next twenty years in an insane asylum. She comes back here looking for some kind of justice, closure, call it what you want, and she's set up to take another fall.' He glanced at his partner. 'If I was in her shoes right now I'd be seriously pissed off, wouldn't you?'

'What are we talking about, some kind of female Sly Stallone, a Rambette thing?' asked Spearing skeptically. 'She comes back into town wrapped up in ammo belts, looking for revenge?'

'I was thinking more along the lines of Stephen King myself,' said Wren. 'Sissy Spacek in *Carrie*.' He looked through the windshield; the storm clouds had turned to rags, shredded on the shaggy forested peaks along the horizon. The western sky was colored like a spilled box of children's crayons. He knew the colors wouldn't last; another hour and the night shadows would swallow everything. Wren found himself wishing he was anywhere other than where he was.

They fell into a longer silence. When they reached the Beechwood turnoff, Kenny Spearing turned right, heading for the Oneida College campus. 'You sure they're both going to be here?' asked the younger man.

Wren nodded. They turned again and drove between the ornamental gateposts. 'Parker is throwing a big cocktail party and dinner announcing D'Arcy Quinn's decision to run for Governor in the fall. Both of them were mentioned by Hale on that tape.'

Kenny Spearing cleared his throat. Every mover and shaker in Prosper County would be at a function like that. He glanced at Wren, slowing for the turn on to College Way. 'You think our fugitive with the riot gun might take a run at them?'

'It's possible,' Wren answered. He prayed that Rachel Kane had done the smart thing and disappeared, at least until things could sort themselves out; but maybe she'd waited long enough to see justice done.

Spearing pulled into the parking lot beside the

modern cedar and stone building housing the Oneida College Faculty Building. Every spot was taken so he parked in a striped fire lane, then flipped down the visor, showing off the 'Police – On Duty' sign. He turned to Wren. 'Are we here to warn them or confront them?' the young man asked.

Wren cracked his door open. Muffled, in the distance, he could hear the sound of big band music. Artie Shaw. The DA's campaign party was already in full swing. 'I haven't decided yet,' he said and climbed wearily out of the car.

It was almost dark by the time they reached the telephone booth at the edge of the clearing by the road where Miggs once had his store. The door to the booth was half-open when they arrived in Sloane's old truck and the low watt bulb inside was on. It was the only light; the Wallyburger truck was dark and empty, plywood shutters up over the glass, securely padlocked. Standing in the phone booth a hundred feet away, Rachel could still smell the almost overpowering reek of French fry grease. She made her call, hung up and crunched back across the gravel, her borrowed blue jeans loose around her hips and thighs, the T-shirt smelling ever so slightly of male sweat. The strangest feeling of all was Sloane's leather jacket. Rachel touched the entwined Ws of the crest – Woodrow Wilson High.

She climbed back into the truck. Sloane looked across at her from behind the wheel. 'Well?' he asked. 'Can he help, or do I drive you up to Canada?'

'He said he'd help,' said Rachel. 'He wants to meet with us.'

'When?' asked Sloane. 'They'll have figured out you wound up at my place by now. If they're using dogs the way you figure they'll find the jail clothes I buried.'

'Half an hour,' said Rachel. 'He said it would take him that long to get there. I think he was at a party or something. I could hear music in the background.

'Where does he want to meet you?' Sloane asked.

'Morningstar.'

He started the truck and drove away from the dark little clearing. 'Do you trust him?' Sloane asked.

'No,' she said quietly. 'I don't trust anyone any more, but he's the best chance I've got right at the moment.'

Sloane found the turnoff for the old mountain road that led up to the commune, headlights sweeping across the dark trees as they swung off the paved highway and on to the gravel. Sloane turned to Rachel finally, his face lit in sharp planes by the faint illumination of the dashboard lights. 'I'm sorry.'

Rachel looked away from the windshield. She nodded and put one hand gently on his shoulder, leaving it there for only a moment. 'I know,' she said softly. 'So am I.' She paused and then she laughed, easing the moment. 'Jesus, I wish I had a cigarette.'

In contrast to the stark modern exterior of the building, the interior of the private Faculty Reading Room looked like the library from an Edwardian men's club, complete with oversized leather armchairs, and scattered oriental rugs, dark-varnished coffered beams criss-crossing the high, thickly plastered ceiling, and a huge fieldstone fireplace that looked like something out of the final scenes of *Citizen Kane*. The decorator's obvious intent had been to give the room an overall feeling of calm, pipe-smoking, academic solidity, the rugs, chairs and fireplace backed up by walls of floor-to-ceiling solid oak bookcases with rolling ladders, the shelves crammed solidly with thousands of hardcover volumes; there wasn't a paperback or magazine to be seen anywhere.

The Prosper County District Attorney and the Chancellor of Oneida College sat in two of the big upholstered chairs, a stained glass reading lamp, a small Arts and Crafts side table and a cut glass ashtray between them. D'Arcy Quinn was smoking and Michael Parker looked more and more annoyed with each passing moment. Wren stood a few feet away from them, his back to the tall, honey-colored bookcases. Kenny Spearing stood in front of the tall, closed double doors that led out into the main lounge area. From the other side of the door Wren could hear the boozy laugh-chatter of the invited guests that was all but drowning out the music. A few minutes ago they'd been playing Artie Shaw on the PA system, an eerie, big band rendition of 'St James Infirmary Blues', but now they'd switched, fittingly, to Eddie Duchin doing his version of 'After Sunset'.

Parker was tapping his fingers on the overstuffed

arm of the chair. 'I don't really know why you're telling us all of this, Wren.' He paused, letting his mouth turn down into an appropriate frown. 'I'm sorry to hear about Skelton, but we have guests out there.'

'And I've got a fugitive on the loose with a loaded shotgun.'

'Then why don't you go out and find her, Detective,' said D'Arcy Quinn. 'Instead of crashing parties you weren't invited to.'

'The fugitive in question made some allegations concerning you and Mr Parker,' Wren answered. 'Since that time I've had some of those allegations corroborated.'

'I beg your pardon?' said Parker. 'Exactly what are you getting at?'

'Renee Lucas was sentenced to an indeterminate term in a state mental facility for the wrongful death of her child,' Wren said calmly. 'That doesn't mean someone else can't be charged with the same crime.'

'You're on thin ice here, Detective,' warned D'Arcy Quinn.

'On the tape recorded by Ms Lucas, Donald Hale clearly admits to his own involvement and implicates both you and Chancellor Parker.'

'I heard the tape,' said the District Attorney. 'It was obtained under duress. It has no weight in a court of law.'

'Perhaps not in a court of law,' said Wren. 'But I doubt whether it would do you much good in the court of public opinion.'

'Another threat,' said Parker.

'Not a threat,' Wren shrugged. 'Just a harsh reality. Unless this whole question is dealt with now it's bound to surface eventually.' He smiled coldly. 'It's not the sort of thing a spin doctor could do very much with.'

'Get to the point,' said D'Arcy Quinn.

'Forget about the past for a minute; let's talk about the here and now.' He paused and looked from Parker to Quinn and back again. 'Renee Lucas didn't kill Alberoni, Donald Hale or Laura Talbot; someone set her up and finished it off by salting her car with the murder weapon.' He paused again. 'I don't think it was Robin Skelton, but I think he knows who it was.'

'So ask him,' said D'Arcy Quinn.

'I can't,' said Wren. 'He's in a coma and I don't have time to wait for him to come out of it.'

'You think we know who it was?' asked Parker. 'You must be out of your mind!' He glanced at the District Attorney. 'Can't you fire this asshole or something?'

'Not after I've arrested the two of you,' said Wren, smiling pleasantly. 'Which I'll be happy to do unless you're willing to cooperate.'

'Why do you think we know anything?' D'Arcy Quinn asked slowly.

'Because I think the killings now are tied in to the Renee Lucas case back in 1974. I think it might all go back even farther than that, in fact.'

'Why?' asked Quinn.

'Richard Nixon and the White House couldn't keep

353

the lid on Watergate, but your fathers managed to keep this coverup sealed up like a tomb for more than twenty years.'

'That's assuming there was anything to cover up,' said Quinn.

'Let's not play coy,' Wren answered. 'Skelton's father forced Allan Sloane to act as an alibi that covered all of you. According to Renee Lucas, Parker Snr pensioned off old Chester Miggs and a Farmers' Union Bank trust still pays his upkeep at the Beechwood Home. Judge Quinn lets an obviously inadequate defense by Winston Tucker slide right by him, and I've got Donald Hale's father, the City Clerk, fudging birth records.' Wren paused. 'I don't think they were just doting parents protecting their children. I think there was something else they were covering up. Something that involved them directly.'

Michael Parker glanced at his cousin then looked toward Wren. He hesitated, then spoke. 'Are we off the record here?'

'For the time being,' said Wren, shrugging his shoulders. Parker squirmed in his chair and glanced at D'Arcy Quinn. 'D'Arce?'

'If I was you I wouldn't say another word,' said the District Attorney. She stood up and smoothed the front of her skirt. She smiled at Wren, then brushed past him on her way to the main doors out of the room. Spearing gave Wren a quick look and the older detective nodded. Spearing opened one of the doors and let the woman out of the room. Wren turned back to the seated figure of Michael Parker.

'You were going to say something,' Wren prompted.

'You think that woman is going to come after us?' Parker asked.

'I really don't know,' Wren answered honestly. 'It's a possibility.'

'I want protection.'

'We can arrange something,' Wren nodded. He waited.

Parker ran his hands nervously through his hair then sat forward in the big armchair. 'It was weird,' he said slowly. Wren waited again, watching as the man searched back in his memory. His hands were together on his lap now, clasping and unclasping. 'Robby's old man used to wear this perfectly fitted uniform, you know? The ultimate cop. I can remember him asking all of us questions, trying to get a picture in his head of exactly what had happened.' There was a long pause and Parker's tongue flicked out and licked his dry lips. 'He kept on asking us exactly where the woman had come from.'

'I don't understand,' Wren said quietly. 'What do you mean, where the woman had come from?'

'The direction,' Parker answered. 'When she came out of the woods, old Man Skelton wanted to know the direction she'd been coming from.'

*The commune.*

*Morningstar. It's all centered there.*

'What direction was she coming from?'

Parker thought for a moment. 'From the bottom of the meadow. The west.'

Wren frowned. 'In her testimony she said she'd gone to the pool, which was on the eastern side of the clearing. Why had she returned to her car from the opposite direction? Something nagged at the edge of his consciousness and he knew that he was very close now.

'What connection did Skelton's father have with the Morningstar commune?' Wren asked.

'None that I know of,' said Parker. He looked confused, then lifted his shoulders. 'Except for the fact that the place never got busted.'

'For drugs you mean?'

'For anything.' Parker shrugged again. 'It was like Paul led a charmed life or something back then.'

'Paul?'

'Goodman,' Parker nodded. He let out a little hollow laugh. 'Every pothead at W W used to buy weed from him back then and now he teaches here. Still leads a charmed life if you ask me, considering his class schedule.' He shook his head. 'Smooth son-of-a-bitch is probably out there pinching the asses off all the hired help at the party.'

'He's here?' asked Wren.

'He was a few minutes ago,' said Parker.

Wren turned to Spearing. 'Find him,' he said. The younger man nodded and left the room. There was a brief surge of party noises and then the door closed behind him. Wren remembered the framed *Life Magazine* cover in Jerry Weems' studio, saw the smiling, self-assured face of Paul Goodman back in 1969. Invulnerable. A high profile commune like

Morningstar survives unscathed and unbusted with a hard-nosed bull cop like Skelton's father only a few miles away.

*Charmed life.*

*Protected.*

*Why?*

'Did your father ever talk to you about that night?'

'Once,' Parker nodded. 'Two or three days after it happened. He told me never to mention it, or ask questions about it, just to go along with the flow.'

'And you did.'

'Sometimes it all seems like a bad dream,' Parker answered. 'Sometimes I can convince myself that none of it ever happened.'

*Dreams.*

After her arrest, Wren had gone through Rachel's original psychiatric evaluation, done by Amos Alberoni, wondering if it would offer any clues to why she'd killed him. One section of it jumped back into memory, almost verbatim.

*'Matthew was stillborn?'*

*'Yes.'*

*'You went to visit his grave?'*

*'Yes.'*

*'At Morningstar.'*

*'Yes.'*

*'You found it?'*

*'Yes. Saw the place, all the little flowers.'*

'Christ!' Wren whispered. 'All the little flowers!'

*The photographs?*

'What?' Parker asked.

Spearing came back into the room. 'Goodman's gone. He got a call on his cell phone and went out of here on the double.'

'Probably some girl,' muttered Parker from the chair. 'He uses his office like a clearing house.'

'Do you know his cell number?' asked Wren.

'You can get it from the switchboard,' Parker said. Wren turned to Spearing. 'Find the number and find out where the call came from.' He turned back to Parker as Spearing left the room again. 'What kind of car does Goodman drive?'

'A Jeep,' said Parker. 'A real antique. You can't miss it.'

Sloane's truck bounced and splashed along the muddy, rutted path that led up to the old commune, Rachel seated beside him, her hands braced against the dashboard.

'I never came up here much when I was a teenager,' said Sloane. 'Once or twice, just to see what it was like.' He turned and smiled at Rachel. 'I thought all of you hippie types were crazy.'

'A lot of us were,' said Rachel. Realizing what he'd said, Sloane began to apologize, but Rachel held up one hand and stopped him, smiling. 'Don't worry,' she said. 'Just because I spent the last twenty-odd years in an insane asylum doesn't really mean I was nuts.'

'Sorry.'

'It's okay. And it's true, a lot of us were pretty

loopy back then. I was all mixed up about love and sex and men and drugs.'

'Me too,' Sloane answered, fighting with the wheel as they jumped and jerked over a particularly bad patch.

Rachel turned to him. 'I take it that means you're gay?'

He nodded. 'That's what old man Skelton had on me back then. He caught me and Randy Piper fooling around in the boiler room of the church. I was fourteen.'

'Why would he want to blackmail a fourteen-year-old kid?' Rachel asked.

Sloane shrugged. 'Who knows? My father was the Purchasing Agent for the City Clerk's office. Maybe he thought he could get free snow tires or something. It didn't matter with Robby's old man. I think he collected other people's secrets; he liked to have something on everyone.' Sloane shook his head. 'It seems so stupid now.' He laughed. 'I mean, we've got gays in Congress for Christ sake.' He let out a long breath. 'All the time I wasted. All the stupid lies.'

'It was different back then,' said Rachel. 'Things change.'

'People don't,' Sloane answered.

They reached the edge of the sloping clearing that had once been home to Morningstar and Sloane pulled to a stop, dousing his headlights. A faint moon crescent was rising in the ragged sky and the old commune site was bathed in a cold, almost purple light. Rachel and Sloane both climbed down from the truck and stood silently for a moment.

'Too many memories.'

*She felt the slapping hand of the explosion rocking her back on her heels, saw the fireball rise into the air and the terrible look on the young girl's eyes as she flicked the rasping wheel of the lighter and ended her child's life.*

*They murdered Lauren.*

*They killed my little girl.*

'Did he tell you what he was going to do?' asked Sloane.

Rachel turned to him and shook her head absently. 'No. He just said to meet him here. To wait. He asked me if I was alone. I told him no, that you were with me.'

'What did he say to that?' asked Sloane.

'He said he was glad that I was safe.' Rachel walked away from the truck, following the narrow track that had once led down the steeply sloping meadow to the big hexagonal Alamo, the commune's center, or Hearthstone as Paul liked to call it. She closed her eyes for a moment and heard old voices riding on the gentle evening breeze. Someone was tuning a guitar and some of the kids were playing a naked game of tag in the last light of a summer's day. Off in the distance there was the steady biting sound of an ax splitting logs, and from inside the Alamo she could hear the laughing voices of her friends as everyone got together to make the communal supper.

Rachel lifted her hand to her cheek and felt the flow of tears across her face and then a terrible, deep wrench of sadness and longing that seemed to reach down to the bottom of her soul. It all seemed to begin and end right here, a gigantic wheel just like the song said, spinning and turning and bringing everything to an end where it had once begun so long ago.

*High Plains Drifter.*

*All these years I've been dead and buried, and I was the only person who didn't know it. I should have been dust by now.*

*Together with my children.*

'Somebody's been driving through here,' said Sloane. He was behind her in the gloom, bending down to examine a pair of narrow-wheeled tracks that led straight across the meadow to the far tree line. He stood up and looked around. 'I wonder what they were doing?'

Both Sloane and Rachel heard the vehicle approaching, growling and roaring as it came down the narrow trail that led from the old logging road. They turned just as the Jeep bounced into the clearing, headlights momentarily blinding both of them. Sloane put an arm up to shade his eyes and took a step forward. Suddenly, almost as though he'd peen punched by some enormous, invisible fist, he jerked backwards, twisting and groaning as he dropped to the ground. A split second later Rachel heard the sound of the deer rifle ringing echoes off the dark encircling hills.

The lights went out.

*Dear Christ! It's not him, it's that bastard Skelton.*

361

She felt a terrible rush of utterly savage anger
race through her veins. This was what writers meant
in books when they said 'hot blood'.

*I should have killed the filthy cocksucker when I
had the chance.*

Rachel ran, keeping low, slipping on the wet grass
as she headed for the protection of the trees fifty yards
away. She felt, rather than saw a thump and lift of
earth just in front of her and then the sound of a
second shot rang out. She jerked herself to one side,
lurching away, then fell to her knees. A third shot
crashed into the darkness as she climbed to her feet
and sprinted the last few yards to the trees. Once
into them she paused for a second to get her breath
and bearings, then headed west, away from the
direction the shots were coming from, branches
slashing across her face and arms as she stumbled
blindly forward in the darkness. If she could circle
around the edge of the meadow without being seen
there was a chance she could get back to Sloane's
truck.

'I'm going to get you, Renee.' His voice was calm,
pitched to carry across the distance separating them.
'And when I do, I'm going to blow your fucking brains
out, just like your faggot friend.'

She stopped, frozen to the spot, hot blood gone cold.
The voice wasn't Skelton's.

Betrayed. One more time.

'Come on out, Renee. No more of your little Hobbit
games. Believe me, I'll make it quick . . . just for old
time's sake.' He paused. 'What do you say my Luthien,

daughter of Thingol, most beautiful of the children of Illuvatar?' He fired again, the bullet buzzing like an angry wasp through the undergrowth only feet away from where she stood.

'You bastard,' she whispered. 'Oh you bastard.'

*Earandel.*

*Paul Goodman.*

'I won't let this happen again,' she said aloud. 'Enough.'

Barely breathing, she eased back, deeper into the trees, away from the edge of the clearing. She could see him out there, a vague silhouette against the pewter moon and the darkening sky. He was turning slowly, listening, the deer rifle held in the crook of his arm. If she'd had the massive handgun she'd used to scare Donald Hale she could have picked him off like a target in a shooting gallery, but she had nothing, and there was nothing close at hand, not even a branch or stick to use as a club if she got close enough to use it.

She turned away, slipping down between the bony trunks of the birch trees until she was below the ridge line that led back up to the road. For a moment she thought of continuing that way, but in the end she kept moving west; there'd be no traffic on the road at this time of night and eventually he'd come that way looking for her. Her only chance was the truck.

She kept moving, crouching low, eventually reaching the old swimming hole. Skirting it, she continued around the commune clearing, trying to judge the placement of Sloane's truck relative to her own position. The rain had turned the leaf-strewn forest floor into a skating rink and Rachel had to pick her way forward with excruciating care to keep from falling. Any sound now would bring him down on her neck in an instant. Another hundred feet or so and she could start making her way back up the ridge to see how close she was to her objective.

The ground slid out from under her feet and she stifled a yell as she slipped down the muddy slope into the hidden place that sometimes still haunted her dreams, the saucer-shaped depression in the forest floor where they'd buried Matthew, stillborn, so long ago. Covered in mud, Rachel rose to her knees and stared at the scene before her, the ravaged beds of wildflowers, the ferns, the moss-shrouded fallen logs and stumps that had made this place so special to her memory.

Empty, bleeding sockets in a great, dark, toothless jaw. Torn away, scooped out, instead of flowers and ferns there were dozens, scores, perhaps a hundred holes gouged out of the soil, most half-filled with water, others still only half-dug, the place where she'd buried Matthew vanished in the scattering of what looked at first glance to be postholes placed for some ghastly fence that would never be built.

She used the back of her hand to push the mud and ooze off her face and saw an empty, overturned paint can on the ground beside the hole, its label rotted off and beside it, a plastic garbage bag, its contents spilled out on to the wet earth.

Bones.

Tiny and delicate, like the skeleton of a bird, or of an angel, clean and white and pure against the deep, rich soil of the little dell in the woods.

Not an angel or a bird. Tumbled off to one side like something abandoned was a skull no bigger than Rachel's clenched fist, the sinews of the mandible long turned to the rich earth it had been committed to, the lower jaw vanished in the jumble of other bones Rachel could now see as the clouds fell away and the rising moon spread faint light across the pocked depression in the ground.

Bones everywhere. Children's bones scattered like ancient clicking runes around a hundred empty graves.

Lifting herself to her knees, Rachel put one hand against her throat as bile rose and she forced herself not to scream, tried to understand just what it was that she was seeing, and failed. Death and madness had intertwined for half her life, she had never known what was real and what was nightmare. Almost without conscious thought she dragged herself to her feet, climbed back up the ridge and stepped out into the clearing once again.

Goodman was a hundred yards away, still listening for her, head slightly cocked to one side, the deer rifle now held at port arms in his hands, ready to aim and fire at a moment's notice. Sloane's truck was on his left, too far away to reach without attracting his attention, but the Jeep was only a few yards ahead of her, squarely between her position and Goodman's.

*The Vorpal Blade.*

Rachel came out into the open, crouching low, trying to avoid the ruts of the open track, keeping the square, black shape of the Jeep between her and Goodman. Finally, creeping on all fours, she came up on the driver's side, then grabbed the edge of the old-fashioned doorless entry cutout in the side of the vehicle, boosting herself up until she was half-sitting and half-lying across the driver's seat. Working blindly, she jammed her arm back into the narrow space behind the passenger seat and pushed her hand under the springs, praying that the hidden machete was still in its old hiding place.

It wasn't.

'Looking for this?' asked Paul Goodman. She could see his strong, white teeth gleaming in the moonlight as he smiled, the light also catching the long, curved blade he held in his hand, the grip wrapped in criss-crossed leather strips. He was standing four feet in front of the Jeep, the deer rifle in the crook of his other arm.

Rachel froze. No machete, but something else, tubular. A can of something, caught under the seat. She pulled it out, saw what it was, kept it low, beneath the simple sheet-metal dashboard.

*Must belong to Beth, the girl I saw him with at the college.*

With studied casualness, Goodman set the deer rifle down on the squared-off fender of the old scout car. Still gripping the machete he boosted himself up on to the hood, half-crouched in front of the windshield, weaving the monstrous knife in front of himself in a long, sinuous movement, the handsome prince of hippies now a squatting demon, his face a gargoyle's mask. For a fleeting, hallucinating second Rachel was swept back a lifetime and saw Paul as he'd once been, naked and magnificent, his face and body painted as he stood at the huge hearth in the Alamo and handed out the ritual hits of blotter acid that invariably heralded one of the long hazed nights of orgiastic sex that Morningstar was famous for. Madman as Noble Savage. Reading *The Lord of the Flies* aloud, as though it was some kind of bible.

He was crazy, even then.

'One two, one two and through and through, the Vorpal Blade went snicker-snack,' he quoted. His words were lifeless and empty, cold as stone. 'I'm going to slice you up, Renee, just like the others.' He lunged forward, bringing the horrible blade around in a long curving arc toward her neck in an attempt to behead her with a single blow.

Rachel ducked beneath the sweeping blade and brought up the can, squeezing the nozzle with her fingertip. The hissing, reeking cloud of vapor from Beth's forgotten hairspray caught Goodman squarely in the eyes and, screaming, he toppled backward off the Jeep, dropping the machete, both hands up to his face. He staggered away, still screaming at the blinding pain, then turned and, roaring with fury, lurched back toward the Jeep, hands outstretched and groping, searching for the deer rifle.

*If he gets the rifle you're going to die.*

She squeezed her eyes shut, ran back into her

memory to summer days and midnight jaunts and to the hundred times she'd sat beside Paul Goodman as he started up the Jeep, then turned and smiled that smile of his and crashed it into gear.

*Think!*

*No key. Just a switch on the wheel and a starter button on the dash.*

She found the switch on the steering post, turned it, then pushed her foot down on the clutch and hit the fat black button on the dashboard. The Jeep started instantly. She popped the clutch, then stomped down on the gas pedal as hard as she could. Ahead of her, the blinded man slipped on the wet grass and fell to his knees. The fifty-year-old vehicle surged ahead down the slope, slipping almost sideways on the sodden turf. The sharp edge of the strip of cold rolled steel that served as a bumper caught Goodman's forehead with a glancing blow, slicing back to its temple, cutting into flesh and bone, smacking him backwards on to the ground. The Jeep continued down the sloping meadow, the springs, front axle and armor-plated belly pan beneath the engine crushing the last of his life away, ribs crunching like rock candy, splintered ribs slicing through his chest like broken knives, piercing his lungs and heart. The vehicle dragged what was left of its owner almost a hundred yards before the engine finally stalled. The Jeep smelled of fresh blood and hairspray.

Sobbing, Rachel sagged forward in the seat, her forehead touching the wheel. For a moment the night was utterly silent except for her breathing and the slowing sound of her beating heart. All the voices, all the ghosts were quiet at last and she knew they'd stay that way for ever now. Then, faintly in the distance, she heard the sound of approaching sirens.

*They killed my Lauren.*
*They killed my little girl.*
*They killed them all.*

# CHAPTER TWENTY-ONE

Wren and Rachel stood by the car outside the House of Wax. Her bags were packed, stuffed into the rear of the Golf and she'd already said her goodbyes to Eileen and to Allan Sloane, still in the hospital, slowly recovering from the nearly fatal shooting at Morningstar. Since the events at the old commune the week before, a great many secrets had finally been resolved, and even more uncovered. Robby Skelton, Police Chief of Prosper had died on the operating table three hours after the accident in the rain. Michael Parker had resigned his position at Oneida College and Winston Tucker was negotiating his *nolo contendere* plea for his part in the wrongful death of Lauren Lucas back in 1974. D'Arcy Quinn had resigned as District Attorney and was preparing her own defense on the same charge. As well as resigning her position D'Arcy Quinn had also withdrawn from the gubernatorial race; her political career was effectively over.

'So are they going to make you Chief?' Rachel asked Wren, one hip braced against the fender of the Golf.

'Just rumors so far,' the detective answered.

'I figure you're the best choice they've got,' smiled Rachel. 'A veritable Sherlock Holmes. You closed the books on a lot of bad things in this town.'

Wren shrugged. 'You know what they say about the guy who brings the bad news,' he said. By now both the State Police and the FBI were involved in the secret of the tiny graves up at the commune. So far more than a hundred individual burials had been identified, some dating back to the late twenties and early thirties. More than half of the infant skeletons had been wrapped up in plastic and stuffed into empty five gallon paint cans and the first tabloid TV shows who'd already picked up on it were all referring to the buried children as 'The Paint Can Babies'.

'Maybe I never should have come back,' said Rachel. The thought still haunted her as it had for the last week. 'If I hadn't gone to see Paul I don't think any of this would have happened.'

'You're not responsible for any of it,' Wren answered, frowning. 'When you went to see him he saw an opportunity to clean house and lay the blame on somebody else. From what I can figure out, Alberoni was getting ready to spill the beans about his connection with the whole phoney adoption thing that had been going on at the Model Maternity Home. Skelton's old man had been blackmailing Alberoni about it for half a lifetime and after the old Chief died, Robby just picked up where he left off. The same goes for Hale, Parker and Quinn; their fathers were all part of it. Rich girls from New York and a lot of other places came to Prosper to have their babies or to lose them. Quinn did all the legal work adopting the babies out, through the old Maryhill Orphanage, Hale, the City Clerk, fudged the registrations when it was necessary and forged the adoption papers. Parker's bank sanitized the money.' Wren shook his head, still numbed by the extent of the terrible, interlocking crimes that had spanned more than half a century, ruining lives like a deadly, spreading cancer. 'One of the forensic accountants from the FBI just did a rough total. The old records from the home suggest a minimum of a hundred and fifty to two hundred babies a year were born at the home from 1937 to 1947. That's two thousand babies. In those days a healthy white baby was selling on the black market for between three and six thousand dollars. At a $4,000 median price that's eight million dollars – very big money back then.'

'And the non-white, non-healthy babies got buried out at Morningstar.'

'Something like that,' Wren nodded. 'In the thirties the land was owned by Goodman's father. I don't think we have the real story yet, but I think Goodman's father and the others had half a dozen things going, not just the babies. I think Eileen knows a few things she's still not telling. Anyway, the Model Maternity Home had closed down in the late fifties simply because there wasn't enough business. Ten years later the market for illegal adoptions had opened up again. Skelton's old man caught Goodman with enough dope up at the commune to get the entire country stoned and he did a deal. If Goodman provided the occasional perfect white baby here and there, he wouldn't get busted. Everybody went along with it, including Laura Talbot; she was a trained nurse and a midwife.'

Rachel let out a long, weary sigh. 'I still don't really understand what any of this had to do with me.'

'Nothing,' said Wren. 'You were just in the wrong place at the wrong time.'

Rachel frowned. 'You said something before about little flowers.'

Wren nodded. 'That's what *you* said to Alberoni the night Robby and D'Arcy and the others killed your daughter. In the transcripts of his mental evaluation you said that you'd just come back from where they'd buried your stillborn child, Matthew. You said you'd seen "all the little flowers".'

*Matthew*.

'Oh God!' Rachel whispered. 'He thought I'd seen all the graves. He thought I'd stumbled on to their secret.'

Wren nodded. 'I think so. He panicked and told the others. They railroaded you into Brockhurst and made sure you stayed there. It was easy, especially since under the eyes of the law you'd actually kidnapped your daughter and stolen your husband's car. They thought they'd sewn up everything, kept all the secrets safe.'

'They were right,' said Rachel. 'And it almost worked again.'

'Nah.' Wren grinned. 'Not with old Sherlock here on the case. It was already starting to unravel when you were arrested. The Buck knife with the little identifying nick was too pat, not to mention finding the murder weapon in your car and the fact that Hale's body had obviously been killed somewhere else, then moved. The whole thing smelled to high heaven.' He reached out tentatively and put his hand over Rachel's where it lay on the sun-warm fender. 'I would have figured it out eventually and come to your rescue.'

*Except Robby boy was going to kill me. You would have been too late. I never told you that.*

*And never would.*

'My hero.' Rachel smiled. She let her fingers entwine with his, enjoying the touch of his warm, strong hand. She turned to him. 'Why did Paul kill Laura Talbot?'

'She knew too much. She'd already started to panic. According to Parker she came and asked him for money so that she could skip town. Threatened to tell his family and everybody else what had been going on – and by then he really had gone crazy – living inside his own nightmare.'

Rachel smiled softly. 'You really would have figured it out and come to rescue me.'

'Damn right,' he answered.

She stretched up and kissed him gently on the lips, then unclasped her hand from his. She pulled open the car door and Wren moved to stand on the other side of it, his hands on the sill. 'I'm going to miss you.'

'Sure you won't stay for a while longer?' he asked.

'Believe it or not, this can be a pretty nice place.' He paused. 'Especially if you've got a friend to talk to.'

Rachel smiled and shook her head. 'I don't think so, Wren.' She paused. 'It wouldn't work. Not here.' She slipped down and got behind the wheel.

Wren pushed the door closed, then bent down at the open window. 'I might need to get in touch with you,' he said.

She grinned, started the car, then pulled a pair of sunglasses off the visor and slipped them on. 'You're the detective, Wren,' she said, laughing. 'Come and find me.' She dropped the car into drive and Wren stood back.

'I may just do that little thing,' he said, and then she drove away, leaving Prosper at last.

## A selection of bestsellers from Headline

| | | | |
|---|---|---|---|
| STRAIT | Kit Craig | £5.99 | ☐ |
| DON'T TALK TO STRANGERS | Bethany Campbell | £5.99 | ☐ |
| HARVEST | Tess Gerritsen | £5.99 | ☐ |
| SORTED | Jeff Gulvin | £5.99 | ☐ |
| INHERITANCE | Keith Baker | £5.99 | ☐ |
| PRAYERS FOR THE DEAD | Faye Kellerman | £5.99 | ☐ |
| UNDONE | Michael Kimball | £5.99 | ☐ |
| THE VIG | John Lescroart | £5.99 | ☐ |
| ACQUIRED MOTIVE | Sarah Lovett | £5.99 | ☐ |
| THE JUDGE | Steve Martini | £5.99 | ☐ |
| BODY BLOW | Dianne Pugh | £5.99 | ☐ |
| BLOOD RELATIONS | Barbara Parker | £5.99 | ☐ |

*All Headline books are available at your local bookshop or newsagent, or can be ordered direct from the publisher. Just tick the titles you want and fill in the form below. Prices and availability subject to change without notice.*

Headline Book Publishing, Cash Sales Department, Bookpoint, 39 Milton Park, Abingdon, OXON, OX14 4TD, UK. If you have a credit card you may order by telephone – 01235 400400.

Please enclose a cheque or postal order made payable to Bookpoint Ltd to the value of the cover price and allow the following for postage and packing:

UK & BFPO: £1.00 for the first book, 50p for the second book and 30p for each additional book ordered up to a maximum charge of £3.00.
OVERSEAS & EIRE: £2.00 for the first book, £1.00 for the second book and 50p for each additional book.

Name ................................................................................................

Address ............................................................................................

........................................................................................................

........................................................................................................

If you would prefer to pay by credit card, please complete:
Please debit my Visa/Access/Diner's Card/American Express (delete as applicable) card no:

| | | | | | | | | | | | | | | | | | | |
|--|--|--|--|--|--|--|--|--|--|--|--|--|--|--|--|--|--|--|

Signature .................................................... Expiry Date ..............